It was the following afternoon when Hix encountered, albeit briefly, his first real vampire.

Hix told Inza, "As I recall, I dropped by to ask you about the vampire cult you were telling me about yesterday."

She nodded, closing his fingers around the card and keeping hold of his hand. "What I suspect, Hix, is that somebody at the restaurant overheard something of what I was confiding in you and came here to shut me up."

"Surely not Buck the stuntman? He's too obtuse to be involved in a cult of any kind."

"There were at least a dozen other people in the place while you were there."

"I only had eyes for you," he said. "Now tell me exactly what happened here."

"Okay, well, Nancy told me a lot about the workings of the vampire cult, though she wasn't supposed to." Inza's grip on his hand tightened. "They must suspect that, so they sent somebody to . . . to get rid of me. They sent a vampire to attack me."

"That's sure a possibility, yeah. Any idea who he was?"

"It wasn't a man." She shook her head, frowning. "It was a woman. And don't laugh, Hix, but from the quick glimpse I got of her . . . well, she looked a heck of a lot like Greta Garbo."

Hix didn't laugh.

—from "Garbo Quits" by Ron Goulart

Also Available from DAW Books:

***Hags, Harpies, and Other Bad Girls of Fantasy,* edited by Denise Little**
From hags and harpies to sorceresses and sirens, this volume features twenty all-new tales that prove women are far from the weaker sex—in all their alluring, magical, and monstrous roles. With stories by C.S. Friedman, Rosemary Edghill, Lisa Silverthorne, Jean Rabe, and Laura Resnick.

***If I Were an Evil Overlord,* edited by Martin H. Greenberg and Russell Davis**
Isn't it always more fun to be the "bad guy"? Some of fantasy's finest, such as Esther Friesner, Tanya Huff, Donald J. Bingle, David Bischoff, Fiona Patton and Dean Wesley Smith, have risen to the editors' evil challenge with stories ranging from a man given ultimate power by fortune cookie fortunes, to a tyrant's daughter bent on avenging her father's untimely demise—and, by the way, rising to power herself—to a fellow who takes his cutthroat business savvy and turns his expertise to the creation of a new career as an Evil Overlord, to a youth forced to play through game level after game level to fulfill someone else's schemes of conquest. . . .

***Under Cover of Darkness,* edited by Julie E. Czerneda and Jana Paniccia**
In our modern-day world, where rumors of conspiracies and covert organizations can spread with the speed of the Internet, it's often hard to separate truth from fiction. Down through the centuries there have been groups sworn to protect important artifacts and secrets, perhaps even exercising their power, both wordly and mystical, to guide the world's future. In this daring volume, authors such as Larry Niven, Janny Wurtz, Esther Friesner, Tanya Huff, and Russell Davis offer up fourteen stories of those unseen powers operating for their own purposes. From an unexpected ally who aids Lawrence of Arabia, to an assassin hired to target the one person he'd never want to kill, to a young woman who stumbles into an elfin war in the heart of London, to a man who steals time itself . . .

SECRET HISTORY OF VAMPIRES

EDITED BY DARRELL SCHWEITZER
AND MARTIN H. GREENBERG

DAW BOOKS, INC.
DONALD A. WOLLHEIM, FOUNDER
375 Hudson Street, New York, NY 10014
ELIZABETH R. WOLLHEIM
SHEILA E. GILBERT
PUBLISHERS
http://www.dawbooks.com

DAW Book Collectors No. 1398.

DAW Books is distributed by Penguin Group (USA).

First Printing, April 2007
1 2 3 4 5 6 7 8 9

DAW TRADEMARK REGISTERED
U.S. PAT. OFF. AND FOREIGN COUNTRIES
—MARCA REGISTRADA
HECHO EN U.S.A.

PRINTED IN THE U.S.A.

ACKNOWLEDGMENTS

CONTENTS

INTRODUCTION

by Darrell Schweitzer

As vampires down through the ages
ensanguine history's pages . . .

For all the time I have been working on this anthology, I've puzzled over the rest of that limerick. One envies the late Isaac Asimov's ability to compose them off the cuff, as easily as he made conversation. Nevertheless, for all my spontaneous wit may take long and hard practice, serious things may be spoken or written in jest, and the theme of an anthology may be summed up in two lines of an unfinished limerick.

Vampires. History. *Secret* history. That's what this book is about. The *history* in these stories is real, but the explanations behind the history, well, make more sense with a few undead denizens of the night wandering through them. "Secret history" as a genre, quite distinct from the more familiar form, alternate history, is the fiction of "what really happened." Think of that marvelous episode of *Red Dwarf* that provides its own twisted explanation of the JFK assassination and the identity of the gunman on the grassy knoll. Or, more seriously, consider any number of excellent Tim Powers novels, such as *Declare*, which is an occult, secret history of the Cold War.

We are familiar enough with the outward trappings, how the battles ended, who reigned when and for how long, et cetera, but as is also well-known, not everything gets into the history books. Why *did* Teddy Roosevelt carry a big stick and what precisely did he do with it? Mike Resnick, in this volume, has an answer. Harry Turtledove's secret historical speculation is so outrageous that I won't spoil it for you by even dropping a hint. Just go read it. Carrie Vaughn provides a plausible enough explanation for the sickliness of Prince Arthur, the older brother of the future Henry VIII. When Arthur died, Henry married his brother's widow, Catherine of Aragon, with momentous consequences for England and all of Christendom. But what *really* happened?

I also bring to your particular attention the Keith Taylor story, in which the author works out the sinister implications of the very peculiar architectural features of the Great Pyramid of Cheops. The conclusion is magnificent and ghastly.

The belief in vampires has been with us for a long time. Most cultures fear some sort of ravenous revenant, a hungry ghost or corpse returned from the grave to prey on the living. In Japan, according to Lafcadio Hearn, there are vampires whose heads detach from their bodies and fly around at night. The folklore of Thailand, S. P. Somtow tells us, includes vampires consisting of just the head and dangling entrails. This creature either floats through the air or wriggles along the ground. The ancient Romans feared the *strix,* a bloodthirsty female apparition/witch. Phlegon, a freedman of Hadrian (early second century), wrote an account of a corpse-bride bearing no resemblance to the subject of the recent Tim Burton film. This one seduced a handsome young man and would have dragged him into the grave had it not been stopped. The German poet Goethe wrote a play based on Phlegon, *The Bride of Corinth.*

More immediately to the point, there was an actual vampire "flap" in the Austro-Hungarian Empire in the middle of the eighteenth century. As the Turks were pushed back, and parts of eastern Europe, such as Transylvania, became accessible to westerners again, reports began filtering to Vienna of corpses attacking the living and of peasants digging up and mutilating the dead. Imperial agents were sent to investigate. The results were mixed. Some though that genuinely inexplicable events were taking place. Others only saw ignorant, frightened country folk doing something extraordinarily disgusting. (For details, see Paul Barber's excellent *Vampires, Burial, and Death,* Yale University Press, 1988.)

The result was that well before any vampire *stories* were written in English, the European public knew what a vampire was. I have a volume of *The New Monthly Magazine* (London, 1823) containing an article about the dire effects (particularly on sensitive young ladies) of too much vampire literature. One gets the impression that the presses were churning the stuff out. But John Polidori's "The Vampire: A

Tale" had only appeared in 1819 and Sheridan Le Fanu's "Carmilla" was not to come out until 1872, so we can only conclude that what so perturbed the young ladies was vampiric nonfiction, based originally on those reports to the Habsburg emperor and translated largely into French. These were apparently as familiar to the public as flying saucer books are today.

The original, folkloristic vampire of the Balkans did not look at all like Frank Langella's rendition of what a female friend of mine once referred to as "cuddly Dracula." He was an unruly peasant corpse, who didn't raise a creaking lid and emerge from his coffin, but often rested comfortably in his grave while projecting himself spiritually—astrally, we might call it—into the homes of his victims, who then wasted away and died. The vampire might be discovered, if his grave were opened, undecayed, ruddy-lipped, and *plump.* A stake went through his heart, and he expired with a hideous cry and a burst of stagnant, foul-smelling blood.

As Paul Barber explains, there was considerable *truth* to those reports the government investigators brought back. There *are* conditions under which a corpse bloats up but does not decay. Then, if you drive a stake through it, there is a "cry" as gases escape. No such corpse, after being staked and decapitated, has ever been seen to rise again.

The literary development of the vampire, then, is largely a product of the nineteenth century. It begins with Polidori, then Le Fanu, but the winner and still champion is Bram Stoker's *Dracula* (1897). It is from

Dracula and films based on *Dracula* that most modern vampire fiction derives. While I did not enforce any standard "rules" on the contributors to this volume, I tend to be a bit of a vampire fundamentalist myself. I prefer my vampires to be predatory and evil and damned, however alluring they may be, though of course I have to admit that Chelsea Quinn Yarbro has done splendid work in her Comte Saint-Germain series, which has now run many volumes, in which the vampire is not evil at all, and is in fact the hero. The only rule an editor needs to insist on is good fiction.

Yarbro's Saint-Germain series is a perfect example of vampire secret history. Her character has often been near the center of important occurrences in the past two thousand years, in Rome, Byzantium, medieval Europe, Renaissance Italy, and so on.

If, unlike those bloated Balkan corpses and more like Count Dracula—who is at his most human when bragging to Jonathan Harker about his family history and his centuries-old battles with the Turks—vampires take an interest in something more than where their next meal is coming from, these immortal, immensely powerful haunters of the night are ideal manipulators of world events. They could even be the chief force behind history as we know it, a notion suggested, for instance, in Michael Talbot's splendid (and now, alas, out of print and quite rare) novel *A Delicate Dependency* (1982). If the vampire lives on and on, and his mind keeps on growing, he could develop into a post-human supercreature. Stoker suggests this, that Dracula, over four hundred years old, is infinitely wise in a fiendish way, and superhumanly clever. Mortals are as children to him. There is also a great scene in the Michael Talbot novel in which a character gets to browse through the bookshelves and bric-a-brac of an intellectual, artistic, two-thousand-year-old vampire, with much implied about the owner, who has been able to explore where the rest of us cannot.

It's a fascinating idea. If immortal vampires lurk among us, what do they *want?* If they wanted to take over the planet, they probably would have by now. If, like Stoker's Dracula, they still have an interest in the affairs of nations, what might be their *secret agenda*?

That's what this book is about.

Oh, by the way, inspiration has finally struck. Here is the rest of the limerick:

a stake through the heart,
is barely a start,
to cope with their gory outrages.

UNDER ST. PETER'S

by Harry Turtledove

Incense in the air, even down here behind the doors. Frankincense and myrrh, the scents he remembered from days gone by, days when he could face the sun. Somber Latin chants. He recognized them even now, though the chanters didn't pronounce Latin the way the legionaries had back in those bright days.

And the hunger. Always the hunger.

Would he finally feed? It had been a long time, such a very long time. He could hardly remember the last time he'd had to wait so long.

He wouldn't die of starvation. He couldn't die of starvation. His laughter sent wild echoes chasing one another around his chamber. No, he couldn't very well die, not when he was already dead. But he could wish himself extinguished. He could, and he did, every waking moment—and every moment, from now to forever or the sun's next kiss, *was* a waking moment.

Much good wishing did him.

He waited, and he remembered. What else did he have to do? Nothing. *They* made sure of it. His memory since his death and resurrection was perfect. He could bring back any day, any instant, with absolute clarity, absolute accuracy.

Much good that did him, too.

He preferred recalling the days before, the days when he was only a man. (Was he ever *only* a man? He knew how many would say no. Maybe they were right, but he remembered himself as man and man alone. But his memories of those days blurred and shifted—as a man's would—so he might have been wrong. Maybe he was something else, something different, right from the start.)

He'd packed a lot into thirty-odd years. Refugee, carpenter, reformer, rebel . . . convict. He could still hear the thud of the hammer that drove in the spikes. He could still hear his own screams as those spikes pierced him. He'd never thought, down deep in his heart, that it would come to that—which only just went to show how much he knew.

He'd never thought, down deep in his heart, that it would come to *this*, either. Which, again, just went to show how much he knew.

If he were everything people said he was, would he have let it come to this? He could examine that portion of his—not of his life, no, but of his existence, with the perfect recall so very distant from mortality. He could examine it, and he had, time and again. Try as he would, he couldn't see anything he might have done differently.

And even if he did see something like that, it was much too late to matter now.

* * *

"Habemus papam!"

When you heard the Latin acclamation, when you knew it was for you . . . Was there any feeling to match that, any in all the world? People said a new Orthodox Patriarch once fell over dead with joy at learning he was chosen. That had never happened on this trunk of the tree that split in 1054, but seeing how it might wasn't hard. A lifetime of hopes, of dreams, of work, of prayer, of patience . . . and then, at last, you had to try to fill the Fisherman's sandals.

They will remember me forever, was the first thought that went through his mind. For a man who, by the nature of his office, had better not have children, it was the only kind of immortality he would ever get. A cardinal could run things behind the scenes for years, could be the greatest power in the oldest continually functioning institution in the world—and, five minutes after he was dead, even the scholars in the Curia would have trouble coming up with his name.

But once you heard *"Habemus papam!"* . . .

He would have to deal with Italians for the rest of his life. He would have to smell garlic for the rest of his life. Part of him had wanted to retire when his friend, his patron, passed at last: to go back north of the Alps, to rusticate.

That was only part of him, though. The rest . . . he *had* been running things behind the scenes for years. Getting his chance to come out and do it in the open, to be noted for it, to be noticed for it, was sweet. And his fellow cardinals hadn't waited long before they chose him, either. What greater honor was there than the approval of your own? More than anyone else, they understood what this meant. Some of them wanted it, too. Most of them wanted it, no doubt, but most of the ones who did also understood they had no chance of gaining it.

Coming out of the shadows, becoming the public face of the Church, wasn't easy for a man who'd spent so long in the background. But he'd shown what he could do when he was chosen to eulogize his predecessor. He wrote the farewell in his own tongue, then translated it into Italian. That wasn't the churchly *lingua franca* Latin had been, but still, no one who wasn't fluent in it could reasonably hope to occupy Peter's seat.

If he spoke slowly, if he showed Italian wasn't his native tongue—well, so what? It gave translators around the world the chance to stay with him. And delivering the eulogy meant people around the world saw him and learned who he was. When the College of Cardinals convened to deliberate, that had to be in the back of some minds.

He wouldn't have a reign to match the one that had gone before, not unless he lived well past the century mark. But Achilles said glory mattered more than length of days. And John XXIII showed you didn't need a long reign to make your mark.

Vatican II cleared away centuries of deadwood from the Church. Even the Latin of the Mass went. Well, there was reason behind that. Who spoke Latin nowadays? This wasn't the Roman Empire anymore, even if the cardinals' vestments came straight out of Byzantine court regalia.

But change always spawned a cry for more change. Female priests? Married priests? Homosexuality? Contraception? Abortion? When? Ever? The world shouted for all those things. The world, though, was a weather vane, turning now this way, now that, changeable as the breeze. The Church was supposed to stand for what was *right* . . . whatever that turned out to be.

If changes come, they'll come because of me. If they don't, that will also be because of me, the new Holy Father thought. *Which way more than a billion people go depends on me.*

Why anyone would *want* a job like this made him scratch his head. That he wanted it himself, or that most of him did, was true, no matter how strange it seemed. So much to decide, to do. So little time.

A tavern in the late afternoon. They were all worried. Even the publican was worried; he hadn't looked for such a big crowd so late in the day. They were all eating and drinking and talking. They showed no signs of getting up and leaving. If they kept hanging around, he would have to light the lamps, and olive oil wasn't cheap.

But they kept digging their right hands into the bowl of chickpeas and mashed garlic he'd set out, and eating more bread, and calling for wine. One of them had already drunk himself into quite a state.

Looking back from down here, understanding why was easy. Hindsight was always easy. Foresight? They'd called it prophecy in those days. Had he had the gift? His human memory wasn't sure. But then, his human memory wasn't sure about a lot of things. That was what made trying to trace the different threads twisting through the fabric so eternally fascinating.

He wished he hadn't used that word, even to himself. He kept hoping it wasn't so. He'd been down here a long, long, *long* time, but not forever. He wouldn't stay down here forever, either. He couldn't.

Could he?

He was *so* hungry.

The tavern. He'd been looking back at the tavern again. He wasn't hungry then. He'd eaten his fill, and he'd drunk plenty of wine, wine red as blood.

What did wine taste like? He remembered it was sweet, and he remembered it could mount to your head . . . almost the way any food did these days. But the taste? The taste, now, was a memory of a memory of a memory—and thus blurred, it was no memory at all. He'd lost the taste of wine, just as he'd lost the tastes of bread and chickpeas. Garlic, though, garlic he still knew.

He remembered the sensation of chewing, of reducing the resistive mass in his mouth—whatever it tasted like—to something that easily went down the throat. He almost smiled, there in the darkness. He hadn't needed to worry about *that* in a while.

Where was he? So easy to let thoughts wander down here. What else did they have to do? Oh, yes. The tavern. The wine. The feel of the cup in his hands. The smell of the stuff wafting upward, nearly as intoxicating as . . . but if his thoughts wandered there, they wouldn't come back. He was *so* hungry.

The tavern, then. The wine. The cup. The last cup. He remembered saying, "And I tell you, I won't drink from the fruit of the vine any more till that day when I drink it anew with you in my father's kingdom."

They'd nodded. He wasn't sure how much attention they paid, or whether they even took him seriously. How long could anybody go without drinking wine? What would you use instead? Water? Milk? You were asking for a flux of the bowels if you did.

But he'd kept that promise. He'd kept it longer than he dreamed he would, longer than he dreamed he could. He was still keeping it now, after all these years.

Soon, though, soon, he would have something else to drink.

If you paid attention to the television, you would think he was the first pope ever installed. His predecessor had had a long reign, so long that none of the reporters remembered the last succession. For them, it was as if nothing that came before this moment really happened. One innocent—an American, of course—even remarked, "The new pope is named after a previous one."

He was not a mirthful man, but he had to laugh at that. What did the fool *think* the Roman numeral after his name stood for? He wasn't named after just one previous pope. He was named after fifteen!

One of these days, he would have to try to figure out what to do about the United Sates. So many people there thought they could stay good Catholics while turning their backs on any teachings they didn't happen to like. If they did that, how were they any different from Protestants? How could he tell them they couldn't do that without turning them into Protestants? Well, he didn't have to decide right away, *Deo gratias*.

So much had happened, this first day of his new reign. If this wasn't enough to overwhelm a man, nothing ever would be. Pretty soon, he thought, he would get around to actually *being* pope. Pretty soon, yes, but not quite yet.

As if to prove as much, a tubby little Italian—not even a priest but a deacon—came up to him and waited to be noticed. The new pope had seen the fellow around for as long as he could remember. Actually, he didn't really remember *seeing* him around—the deacon was about as nondescript as any man ever born. But the odor of strong, garlicky sausages always clung to him.

When it became obvious the man wouldn't go away, the pope sighed a small, discreet sigh. "What is it, Giuseppe?"

"Please to excuse me, Holy Father, but there's one more thing each new Keeper of the Keys has to do," the deacon said.

"Ah?" Now the pope made a small, interested noise. "I thought I knew all the rituals." He was, in fact, sure he knew all the rituals—or he had been sure, till this moment.

But Deacon Giuseppe shook his head. He seemed most certain, and most self-assured. "No, Your Holiness. Only the popes know—the popes and the men of the Order of the Pipistrelle."

"The what?" The new pope had also been sure he was acquainted with all the orders, religious and honorary and commingled, in Vatican City.

"The Order of the Pipistrelle," Giuseppe repeated patiently. "We are small, and we are quiet, but we are the oldest order in this place. We go . . . back to the very beginning of things, close enough." Pride rang in his voice.

"Is that so?" The pope carefully held his tone neutral. Any order with a foundation date the least bit uncertain claimed to be much older than anyone outside its ranks would have wanted to believe. Even so, he'd never heard of an order with pretensions like that. Back to the beginning of things? "I suppose you came here with Peter?"

"That's right, your Holiness. We handled his baggage." Deacon Giuseppe spoke altogether without irony. He either believed what he was saying or could have gone on the stage with his acting.

"Did my friend, my predecessor, do . . . whatever this is?" the Pope asked.

"Yes, sir, he did. And all the others before him. If you don't do this, you aren't really the pope. You don't really understand what being the pope means."

Freemasonry. We have a freemasonry of our own. Who would have thought that? Freemasonry, of course, wasn't nearly so old as its members claimed, either. But that was—or might be—beside the point. "All right," the pope said. "This must be complete, whatever it is."

Deacon Giuseppe raised his right hand in what wasn't a formal salute but certainly suggested one. "*Grazie,* Holy Father. *Mille grazie,*" he said. "I knew you were a . . . thorough man." He nodded, seeming pleased he'd found the right word. And it *was* the right word; the pope also nodded, acknowledging its justice.

Deacon Giuseppe took his elbow and steered him down the long nave of St. Peter's, away from the papal altar and toward the main entrance. Past the haloed statue of St. Peter and the altar of St. Jerome they went, past the Chapel of the Sacrament and, on the pope's right, the tombs of Innocent VIII and Pius X.

Not far from the main entrance, a red porphyry disk was set into the floor, marking the spot where, in the Old St. Peter's that preceded Bernini's magnificent building, Charlemagne was crowned Holy Roman Emperor. Now, to the pope's surprise, crimson silk draperies surrounded the disk, discreetly walling it off from view.

Another surprise: "I've never seen these draperies before."

"They belong to the order," Deacon Giuseppe said, as if that explained everything. To him, it must have. But he had to see it didn't explain everything to his companion, for he added, "We don't use them very often. Will you step through with me?"

The pope did. Once inside the blood-red billowing silk, he was surprised yet again. "I didn't know that disk came up."

"You weren't supposed to, Holy Father," Deacon Giuseppe said. "You'd think we'd do this over in the Sacred Grotto. It would make more sense, what with the popes' tombs there—even Peter's, they say. Maybe it was like that years and years ago, but it hasn't been for a long, long time. Here we do it, and here it'll stay. Amen." He crossed himself.

"There's . . . a stairway going down," the Pope said. How many more amazements did the Vatican hold?

"Yes. That's where we're going. You first, Holy Father," Giuseppe said. "Be careful. It's narrow, and there's no bannister."

Air. Fresh air. Even through doors closed and locked and warded against him, he sensed it. His nostrils twitched. He knew what fresh air meant, sure as a hungry dog knew a bell meant it was time to salivate. When he was a man, he'd lived out in the fresh air. He'd taken it for granted. He'd lived in it. And, much too soon, he'd died in it.

Crucifixion was a Roman punishment, not a Jewish one. Jews killed even animals as mercifully as they could. When they had to kill men, the sword or the ax got it over with fast. The Romans wanted criminals to suffer, and be seen to suffer. They thought that resulted in fewer criminals. The number of men they crucified made the argument seem dubious, but they didn't care.

As for the suffering . . . they were right about that. The pain was the worst thing he'd ever known. It unmanned him so that he cried out on the cross. Then he swooned, swooned so deeply the watching soldiers and people thought he was dead.

He dimly remembered them taking him down from the cross—pulling out the spikes that nailed him to it was a fresh torment. And one more followed it, for one of the Roman soldiers bit him then, hard enough to tear his flesh open but not hard enough, evidently, to force a sound past his dry throat and parched lips.

How the rest of the Romans laughed! That was the

last purely human memory he had, of their mirth at their friend's savagery. When he woke to memory again, he was . . . changed.

No. There was one thing more. They'd called the biter Dacicus. At the time, it didn't mean anything to a man almost dead. But he never forgot it even though it was meaningless, so maybe—probably—the change in him had begun that soon. When he did think about it again, for a while he believed it was only a name.

Then he learned better. *Dacicus* meant *the Dacian,* the man from Dacia. Not one more human in ten thousand, these days, could tell you where Dacia lay—had lain. But its borders matched those of what they called Romania these days, or near enough. And people told stories about Romania. . . . He had no way to know how many of those stories were true. Some, like sliding under doors, surely weren't, or he would have. Considering what had happened to him, though, he had no reason to doubt others.

And now he smelled fresh air. Soon, very soon . . .

"How long has this been here?" the pope asked. "I never dreamed anything like this lay under St. Peter's!" The stone spiral stairway certainly seemed ancient. Deacon Giuseppe lit it, however, not with a flickering olive-oil lamp but with a large, powerful flashlight that he pulled from one of the large, deep pockets of his black vestments.

"Your Holiness, as far as I know, it's been here since Peter's day," Giuseppe answered seriously. "I told you before: the Order of the Pipistrelle is in charge of what Peter brought in his baggage."

"And that was?" the pope asked, a trifle impatiently.

"I don't want to talk about it now. You'll see soon enough. But I'm a keeper of the keys, too." Metal jingled as the deacon pulled a key ring from a pocket. The pope stopped and looked back over his shoulder. Giuseppe obligingly shone the flashlight beam on the keys. They were as ordinary, as modern, as boring, as the flashlight itself. The pope had hoped for massive, ancient keys, rusty or green with verdigris. No such luck.

At the bottom of the stairway, a short corridor led to a formidable steel door. The pope's slippers scuffed through the dust of ages. Motes he kicked up danced in the flashlight beam. "Who last came here?" he asked in a low voice.

"Why, your blessed predecessor, your Holiness," Deacon Giuseppe. "Oh, and mine, of course." He opened the door with the key, which worked smoothly. As he held it for the pope, he went on. "This used to be wood—well, naturally. That's what they had in the old days. They replaced it after the last war. Better safe than sorry, you know."

"Safe from what? Sorry because of what?" As the pope asked the question, the door swung shut behind them with what sounded like a most definitive and final click. A large and fancy crucifix was mounted on the inner surface. Another such door, seemingly identical, lay a short distance ahead.

"With Peter's baggage, of course," Giuseppe answered.

"Will you stop playing games with me?" The pope was a proud and touchy man.

"I'm not!" The deacon crossed himself again. "Before God, your Holiness, I'm not!" He seemed at least as touchy, and at least as proud, as the pope himself. And then, out of the same pocket from which he'd taken the flashlight, he produced a long, phallic chunk of sausage and bit off a good-sized chunk. The odors of pepper and garlic assailed the pope's nostrils.

And the incongruity assailed his strong sense of fitness even more. He knocked the sausage out of Giuseppe's hand and into the dust. "Stop that!" he cried.

To his amazement, the Italian picked up the sausage, brushed off most of whatever clung to it, and went on eating. The pope's gorge rose.

"Meaning no disrespect, Holy Father," Giuseppe mumbled with his mouth full, "but I need this. It's part of the ritual. God will strike me dead if I lie."

Not, *May God strike me dead if I lie.* The deacon said, *God will strike me dead.* The pope, relentlessly precise, noted the distinction. He pointed to the door ahead. "What is on the other side of that?" he asked, a sudden and startling quaver in his voice.

"An empty chamber," Deacon Giuseppe replied.

"And beyond that? Something, I hope."

"Think on the Last Supper, Holy Father," the deacon answered, which didn't help.

He thought of his last supper, which didn't help. Not now, not with his raging hunger. It was too long ago. They were out there. He could hear them out there, talking in that language that wasn't Latin but sounded a little like it. He could see the dancing light under the door. Any light at all stung his eyes, but he didn't mind. And he could smell them. Man's flesh was the most delicious odor in the world, but when he smelled it up close it was always mingled with the other smell, the hateful smell.

His keepers knew their business, all right. Even without garlic, the cross on the farthest door would have held him captive here—*had* held him captive here. He'd tasted the irony of that, times uncounted.

"This is my blood," he'd said. "This is my flesh." Irony there, too. Oh, yes. Now—soon—he hoped to taste something sweeter than irony.

Where would he have been without Dacicus? Not here—he was sure of that, anyhow. He supposed his body would have stayed in the tomb where they laid it, and his spirit would have soared up to the heavens where it belonged. Did he even have a spirit anymore? Or was he all body, all hunger, all appetite? He didn't know. He didn't much care, either. It had been too long.

Dacicus must have been new when he bit him, new or stubborn in believing he remained a man. After being bitten, rolling away the stone was easy. Going about with his friends was easy, too—for a little while. But then the sun began to pain him, and then the hunger began. Taking refuge in the daytime began to feel natural. So did slaking the hunger . . . when he could.

Soon now. Soon!

"Why the Last Supper?" the pope demanded.

"Because we reenact it—in a manner of speaking—down here," Deacon Giuseppe replied. "This is the mystery of the Order of the Pipistrelle. Even the Orthodox, even the Copts, would be jealous if they knew. They have relics of the Son. We have . . . the Son."

The pope stared at him. "Our Lord's body lies here?" he whispered hoarsely. "His body? He was not taken up as we preach? He was—a man?" Was *that* the mystery at—or rather, here below—the heart of the Church? The mystery being that there was no mystery, that since the days of the Roman Empire prelates had lived a lie?

His stern faith stumbled. No, his friend, his predecessor, would never have told him about this. It would have been too cruel.

But the little round sausage-munching deacon shook his head. "It's not so simple, your Holiness. I'll show you."

He had another key on the ring. He used it to unlock the last door, and he shone the flashlight into the chamber beyond.

Light! A spear of light! It stabbed into his eyes, stabbed straight through his eyes and into his brain! How long had he gone without? As long as he'd gone without food. But sustenance he cherished, he craved, he yearned for. Light was the pain that accompanied it, the pain he couldn't avoid or evade.

He got used to it, moment by agonizing moment. So long here in the silent dark, he had to remember how to see. Yes, there was the black-robed one, the untouchable, inedible one, the stinker, who carried his light-thrower like a sword. What had happened to torches and oil lamps? Like the last several of his predecessors, this black-robe had one of these unnatural things instead.

Well, I am an unnatural thing myself these days, he thought, and his lips skinned back from his teeth in a smile both wryly amused and hungry, so very hungry.

Now the pope crossed himself, violently. "Who is this?" he gasped. "*What* . . . is this?"

But even as he gasped, he found himself fearing he knew the answer. The short, scrawny young man impaled on the flashlight beam looked alarmingly like so many Byzantine images of the Second Person of the Trinity: shaggy dark brown hair and beard, long oval face, long nose. The wounds to his hands and feet, and the one in his side, looked fresh, even if they were bloodless. And there was another wound, a small one, on his neck. None of the art showed that one; none of the texts spoke of it. Seeing it made the pope think of films he'd watched as a boy. And when he did . . .

His hand shaped the sign of the cross once more. It had no effect on the young-looking man who stood there blinking. He hadn't thought it would, not really. "No!" he said. "It cannot be! It must not be!"

He noticed one thing more. Even when Deacon Giuseppe shone the flashlight full in the young-looking man's face, the pupils did not contract. Did not . . . or could not? With each passing second, the latter seemed more likely.

Deacon Giuseppe's somber nod told him it wasn't just likely—it was true. "Well, Holy Father, now you know," said the Deacon from the Order of the Pipistrelle. "Behold the Son of Man. Behold the Resurrection. Behold the greatest secret of the Church."

"But . . . why? How?" Not even the pope, as organized and coherent as any man now living, could speak clearly in the presence of—that.

"Once—that—happened to him, he couldn't stand the sun after a while." Deacon Giuseppe told the tale as if it had been told many times before. And so, no doubt, it had. "When Peter came to Rome, he came, too, in the saint's baggage—under the sign of the cross, of course, to make sure nothing . . . untoward happened. He's been here ever since. We keep him. We take care of him."

"Great God!" The pope tried to make sense of his whirling thoughts. "No wonder you told me to think of the Last Supper." He forced some iron into his spine. A long-dead *Feldwebel* who'd drilled him during the last round of global madness would have been proud of how well his lessons stuck. "All right. I've seen him. God help me, I have. Take me up to the light again."

"Not quite yet, your Holiness," the deacon replied. "We finish the ritual first."

"Eh?"

"We finish the ritual," Deacon Giuseppe repeated with sad patience. "Seeing him does not suffice. It is his first supper in a very long time, your predecessor being so young when he was chosen. Remember the text: your blood is his wine, your flesh his bread."

He said something else, in a language that wasn't Italian. The pope, a formidable scholar, recognized it as Aramaic. He even understood it: "Supper's ready!"

* * *

The last meal had been juicier. That was his first thought. But he wasn't complaining, not after so long. He drank and drank: his own communion with the world of the living. He would have drunk the life right out of him if not for the black-robed one.

"Be careful!" that one urged, still speaking the only language he really knew well. "Remember what happened time before last!"

He remembered. He'd got greedy. He'd drunk too much. The man died not long after coming down here to meet him. Then he'd fed again—twice in such a little while! They didn't let him do anything like that the next time, however much he wanted to. And that one lasted and lasted—lasted so long, he began to fear he'd made the man into one like himself.

He hadn't done that very often. He wondered whether Dacicus intended to do that with him—to him. He never had the chance to ask. Did Dacicus still wander the world, not alive any more but still quick? One of these centuries, if Dacicus did, they might meet again. You never could tell.

When he didn't let go fast enough, the black-robed one breathed full in his face. That horrible, poisonous stink made him back away in a hurry.

He hadn't got enough. It could never be enough, not if he drank the world dry. But it was ever so much better than nothing. Before he fed, he was *empty*. He couldn't end, barring stake, sunlight, or perhaps a surfeit of garlic, but he could wish he would. He could—and he had.

No more. Fresh vitality flowed through him. He wasn't happy—he didn't think he could be happy—but he felt as lively as a dead thing could.

* * *

"My God!" the new pope said, not in Aramaic, not in Latin, not even in Italian. His hand went to the wound on his neck. The bleeding had already stopped. He shuddered. He didn't know what he'd expected when Deacon Giuseppe took him down below St. Peter's, but not this. Never this.

"Are you all right, your Holiness?" Real concern rode the deacon's voice.

"I . . . think so." The pope had to think about it before he answered.

"Good." Deacon Giuseppe held out a hand. Automatically, the pope clasped it, and, in so doing, felt how cold his own flesh had gone. The round little nondescript Italian went on, "Can't let him have too much. We did that not so long ago, and it didn't work out well."

The new pope understood him altogether too well. Then he touched the wound again, a fresh horror filling him. Yes, he remembered the films too well. "Am I going to turn into . . . one of those?" He pointed toward the central figure of his faith, who was licking blood off his lips with a tongue that seemed longer and more prehensile than a mere man's had any business being.

"We don't think so," Giuseppe said matter-of-factly. "Just to be sure, though, the papal undertaker drives a thin ash spike through the heart after each passing. We don't talk about that to the press. One of the traditions of the Order of the Pipistrelle is that when the sixth ecumenical council anathematized Pope Honorius, back thirteen hundred years ago, it wasn't for his doctrine, but because . . ."

"Is . . . Honorius out there, too? Or under here somewhere?"

"No. He was dealt with a long time ago." Deacon Giuseppe made pounding motions.

"I see." The pope wondered if he could talk to . . . talk to the Son of God. *Or the son of someone, anyhow.* Did he have Aramaic enough for that? Or possibly Hebrew? *How the Rabbi of Rome would laugh—or cry—if he knew!* "Does every pope do this? Endure this?"

"Every single one," Giuseppe said proudly. "What better way to connect to the beginning of things? Here *is* the beginning of things. He *was* risen, you know, Holy Father. How much does *why* really matter?"

For a lot of the world, *why* would matter enormously. The Muslims . . . the Protestants . . . the Orthodox . . . his head began to hurt, although the wound didn't. Maybe talking with . . . Him wasn't such a good idea after all. *How much do I really want to know?*

"When we go back up, I have a lot of praying to do," the pope said. Would all the prayer in the world free him from the feel of teeth in his throat? And what could he tell his confessor? The truth? The priest would think he'd gone mad—or, worse, wouldn't think so and would start the scandal. A lie? But wasn't inadequate confession of sin a sin in and of itself? The headache got worse.

Deacon Giuseppe might have read his thoughts. "You have a dispensation against speaking of this, your Holiness. It dates from the fourth century, and it may be the oldest document in the Vatican Library.

It's not like the Donation of Constantine, either—there's no doubt it's genuine."

"*Deo gratias!*" the pope said again.

"Shall we go, then?" the deacon asked.

"One moment." The Pope flogged his memory and found enough Aramaic for the question he had to ask: "*Are* you the Son of God?"

The sharp-toothed mouth twisted in a—nostalgic?—smile. "You say it," came the reply.

Well, he told Pilate the same thing, even if the question was a bit different, the pope thought as he left the little chamber and Deacon Giuseppe meticulously closed and locked the doors behind them. And, when the pope was on the stairs going back up to the warmth and blessed light of St. Peter's, one more question occurred to him: How many popes had heard that same answer?

How many of them had asked that same question? He'd heard it in Aramaic, in Greek, in Latin, and in the language Latin had turned into. He always said the same thing, and he always said it in Aramaic.

"You say it," he murmured to himself, there alone in the comfortable darkness again. Was he really? How could he know? But if they thought he was, then he was—for them. Wasn't that the only thing that counted?

That Roman had washed his hands of finding absolute truth. He was a brute, but not a stupid brute.

And this new one was old, and likely wouldn't last long. Pretty soon, he would feed again. And if he had to try to answer that question one more time afterward . . . then he did, that was all.

Two Hunters in Manhattan

by Mike Resnick

Things had not been going well for New York's Commissioner of Police. He'd started like a house afire, cleaning up most of the more obvious crime within a year—but then he came to a stone wall. He'd never before met a problem that he couldn't overcome by the sheer force of his will, but although he had conquered the political world, the literary world, and what was left of the Wild West, Theodore Roosevelt had to admit that after making a good start, his efforts to conquer the criminal elements of his city had come to a dead halt.

He'd insisted that every policeman go armed. In their first three shoot-outs with wanted criminals, they'd killed two bystanders, wounded seven more, and totally missed their targets.

So he'd made target practice mandatory. When the city's budget couldn't accommodate the extra time required, almost a quarter of the force quit rather than practice for free.

He'd begun sleeping days and wandering the more dangerous areas by night—but everyone knew that Teddy Roosevelt wasn't a man to miss what he was aiming at, or to run away when confronted by superior numbers, so they just melted away when word went out (and it *always* went out) that he was on the prowl.

Eighteen ninety-six drew to a close, and he realized he wasn't much closer to achieving his goal than he'd been at the end of 1895. He seriously considered resigning. After all, he and Edith had four children now, he had two books on the bestseller list, he'd been offered a post as Chief Naturalist at the American Museum of Natural History, and he'd hardly been able to spend any time at his beloved Sagamore Hill since accepting the post as commissioner. But every time he thought about it, his chin jutted forward, he inadvertently bared his teeth in a cross between a humorless smile and a snarl, and he knew that he wasn't going anywhere until the job was done. Americans didn't quit when things got rough; that was when they showed the courage and sense of purpose that differentiated them from Europeans.

But if he was to stay, he couldn't continue to depend on his police force to do the job. Men were quitting every day, and many of the ones who stayed did so only because they knew a corrupt cop could make more money than an honest businessman.

There had to be a way to tame the city—and then one day it came to him. Who knew the criminal element better than anyone else? The criminals themselves. Who knew their haunts and their habits, their leaders and their hideouts? Same answer.

Then, on a Tuesday evening in June, he had two

members of the most notorious gang brought to his office. They glared at him with open hostility when they arrived.

"You got no right to pull us in here," said the taller of the two, a hard-looking man with a black eye patch. "We didn't do nothing."

"No one said you did," answered Roosevelt.

The shorter man, who had shaved his head bald—Roosevelt suspected it was to rid himself of lice or worse—looked around. "This ain't no jail. What are we doing here?"

"I thought we might get to know each other better," said Roosevelt.

"You gonna beat us and then put us in jail?" demanded Eye Patch.

"Why would I do something like that?" said Roosevelt. He turned to the officers who had brought them in. "You can leave us now."

"Are you sure, sir?" said one of them.

"Quite sure. Thank you for your efforts."

The officers looked at each other, shrugged, and walked out, closing the door behind them.

"You men look thirsty," said Roosevelt, producing a bottle and a pair of glasses from his desk drawer. "Why don't you help yourselves?"

"That's damned Christian of you, Mr. Roosevelt, sir," said Baldy. He poured himself a drink, lifted it to his lips, then froze.

"It's not poisoned," said Roosevelt.

"Then you drink it first," said Baldy.

"I don't like to imbibe," said Roosevelt, lifting the bottle to his lips and taking a swallow. "But I'll have enough to convince you that it's perfectly safe."

Baldy stood back, just in case Roosevelt was about to collapse, and when the commissioner remained standing and flashed him a toothy smile, he downed his drink, and Eye Patch followed suit a moment later.

"That's mighty good stuff, sir," said Baldy.

"I'm glad you like it," said Roosevelt.

"Maybe we was wrong about you," continued Baldy. "Maybe you ain't such a bad guy after all." He poured himself another drink.

"You still ain't told us what we're here for," said Eye Patch. "You got to want *something* from us."

"Just the pleasure of your company," said Roosevelt. "I figure men who get to know each other are less likely to be enemies."

"That suits me fine," said Baldy. "You mind if I sit down?"

"That's what chairs are for," said Roosevelt. He picked up the bottle, walked over to each of them, and refilled their glasses.

"They say you spent some time out West as a cowboy, sir," said Baldy. "Maybe you'd like to tell us about it. I ain't never been west of the Hudson River."

"I'd be happy to," said Roosevelt. "But I wasn't a cowboy. I was a rancher, and I hunted bear and elk and buffalo, and I spent some time as a lawman."

"You ever run into Doc Holliday or Billy the Kid?" asked Eye Patch.

Roosevelt shook his head. "No, I was in the Dakota Badlands and they were down in New Mexico and Arizona. But I did bring in three killers during the Winter of the Blue Snow."

He spent the next half hour telling them the story and making sure that their glasses stayed full. When he was done he walked to the door and opened it.

"This was most enjoyable, gentlemen," he said. "We must do it again very soon."

"Suits me fine," slurred Baldy. "You're an okay guy, Mr. Roosevelt, sir."

"That goes for me, too," said Eye Patch.

Roosevelt put an arm around each of them. "Anyone care for one last drink?"

Both men smiled happily at the mention of more liquor, and just then a man stepped into the doorway. There was a loud *pop!* and a blinding flash of light.

"What the hell was that?" asked Eye Patch, blinking his one functioning eye furiously.

"Oh, just a friend. Pay him no attention."

They had their final drink and staggered to the door.

"Boys," said Roosevelt, "you're in no condition to walk home, and I don't have a horse and buggy at my disposal. I suggest you spend the night right here. You won't be under arrest, your cell doors won't be locked or even closed, and you can leave first thing in the morning, or sooner if you feel up to it."

"And you won't lock us in or keep us if we want to leave?" said Eye Patch.

"You have my word on it."

"Well, they say you word is your bond . . ."

"I say we do it," said Baldy. "If we don't, I'm going to lay down and take a little nap right here."

"I'll summon a couple of men to take you to your

quarters," said Roosevelt. He stepped into the corridor outside his office, waved his hand, and a moment later the two men were led to a pair of cells. True to his word, Roosevelt insisted that the doors be kept open.

When they woke up, Roosevelt was standing just outside the cells, staring at them.

"Good morning, gentlemen," he said. "I trust you slept well?"

"God, my head feels like there's an army trying to get out," moaned Baldy.

"We're free to go, right?" said Eye Patch.

"Right," said Roosevelt. "But I thought we might have a little chat first."

"More stories about cowboy outlaws?"

"No, I thought we'd talk about New York City outlaws."

"Oh?" said Baldy, suddenly alert.

"The criminal element thinks it controls this city," answered Roosevelt. "And to be truthful, they are very close to being right. This is unacceptable. I will bring law and order to New York no matter what it takes." He paused, staring at each in turn through his spectacles. "I thought you two might like to help."

"I *knew* it!" said Baldy. He looked around. "Where's the rubber hoses?"

"Nobody's going to hurt you," said Roosevelt. "We're all friends, remember?"

"Sure we are."

"We *are*," insisted Roosevelt. "In fact, I have proof of it."

"What the hell are you talking about?" demanded Eye Patch.

"This," said Roosevelt. He handed each of them a photograph, taken the night before. There was Roosevelt, throwing his massive arms around the two happy criminals.

"I don't understand," said Baldy.

"You're going to become my spies," said Roosevelt. "I've rented a room under a false name in the worst section of the Bowery. I'll be there every Monday and Thursday night, and twice a week you're going to report to me and tell me everything that's being planned, who's behind it, who is responsible for crimes that have already been committed, and where I can find the perpetrators."

"You must be crazy!" said Baldy.

"Oh, I don't think so. There are more copies of that photo. If you *don't* agree to help me, the next time we capture a member from either of your gangs, that photo will be in every newspaper in the city, and the caption will say that it's a picture of me thanking you for informing on your friends."

"Oh, shit!" muttered Eye Patch. "You'd do it, too, wouldn't you?"

"Absolutely. One way or another, I'm going to bring law and order to New York. Do we have an agreement?"

"We ain't got no choice," said Baldy.

"No, you don't," agreed Roosevelt.

"How long are you going to hold that photo like a rope over our heads?" asked Eye Patch.

"As long as it takes to get some results."

"Are you open to a deal?"

"We just made one," said Roosevelt.

"A different one."

"Go ahead."

"We'll do what you want," said Eye Patch. "We ain't got any choice. But there's a guy who can get everything you need a lot quicker than we can, and maybe put a few of the biggest crooks out of action for you. You don't know him—nobody on your side of the fence does—but if I can put you together with him and he's what I say he is, will you burn the pictures?"

"He'll never go for it," said Baldy.

"I might," said Roosevelt.

"I don't mean you, sir," said Baldy. "I'm talking about Big D. There's no place he can't go, and he ain't scared of nothing."

"Big D," Roosevelt frowned. "I've never heard of him."

"That's not surprising," said Eye Patch. "He only comes around once a week or so, usually just before the bars close. But I've seen him talking and drinking with just about every man you want to nail. Yes, sir, if you'll go for my deal, we'll pass the word to Big D that you'd like to have a powwow with him."

Roosevelt pulled out a piece of paper and scribbled an address on it. "This is my room in the Bowery," he said, handing it to Eye Patch. "Beneath it is the name I will be using while there. Tell him there's money involved if he accepts my offer."

"Then we have a deal?"

"Not until I meet him and decide if he's the man I need."

"And if he's not?" persisted Eye Patch.

"Then you'll be no worse off than you are now," said Roosevelt.

"What happens to the photos if he kills you?" asked Baldy.

"You think he might?" asked Roosevelt.

"Anything's possible," said Baldy. "He's a strange one, that Big D." He paused uncomfortably. "So *if* he decides to kill you . . ." He let the sentence hang in the air.

"He'll find out what it's like to be up against a Harvard boxing champion," answered Roosevelt. "It's Wednesday morning. Can you get in touch with him in time for him to come to the room tomorrow night?"

"This town's got a pretty good grapevine," said Eye Patch.

"Bully! The sooner we get the crusade underway, the better. Gentlemen, you're free to go."

Eye Patch began walking toward the end of the cell block, but Baldy hung back for a moment.

"I don't figure I owe you nothing, the way you tricked us," he said to Roosevelt. He lowered his voice. "But watch yourself around him, sir." He made no attempt to hide the little shudder that ran through him. "I'm not kidding, sir. I ain't never been scared of nobody or nothing, but I'm scared of *him*."

Roosevelt went to his squalid Bowery room on Thursday night, laid his hand and a walking stick on a chair, and waited. He'd brought a book with him, in case this Big D character hadn't gotten the word or chose not to show up, and by midnight he was pretty sure he'd be reading straight through until dawn.

And then, at 2:30 A.M., there was a knock at the door.

"Come," said Roosevelt, who was sitting on an oft-repaired wooden chair. He closed the book and put it on the ugly table that held the room's only lamp.

The door opened and a tall, skeletally thin man entered. He had wild black hair that seemed to have resisted all efforts to brush or comb it, piercing blue eyes, and very pale skin. He wore an expensively tailored black suit that had seen better days.

"I understand you wish to speak to me," he said, articulating each word precisely.

"If you're Big D, I do," said Roosevelt.

A smile that Roosevelt thought seemed almost indistinguishable from a sneer briefly crossed the man's face. "I am the man you seek. But my name is not Big D."

"Oh?"

"They call me that because they are too uneducated to pronounce my real name. But you, Mr. Roosevelt, will have no difficulty with it."

"I didn't give my . . . ah . . . *representatives* permission to reveal my identity."

"They didn't," was the reply. "But you are a famous and easily recognized man, sir. I have read many of your books and seen your photograph in the newspapers."

"You still have the advantage of me," said Roosevelt. "If you are not to be called Big D . . ."

"You may call me Demosthenes."

"Like the ancient Greek?"

"Precisely," said Demosthenes.

"The Greeks are a swarthy race," said Roosevelt. "You don't look Mediterranean."

"I have been told that before."

"The hair seems right, though."

"Are we to discuss my looks or your proposition?" said Demosthenes.

"My proposition, by all means," said Roosevelt. He gestured toward a chair. "Have a seat."

"I prefer to stand."

"As you wish. But I must tell you that I am not intimidated by size."

Demosthenes smiled and sat down. "I like you already, Mr. Roosevelt. But from your books I knew I would. You take such pleasure in the slaughter of animals who want only to escape."

"I am a hunter and a sportsman, not a slaughterer," answered Roosevelt severely. "I shoot no animal that does not have a chance to escape."

"How inefficient," said Demosthenes. He cocked his head and read the spine of Roosevelt's book. "Jane Austen? I should have thought you were beyond a comedy of manners, Mr. Roosevelt."

"She has an exquisite felicity of expression which seems to have eluded you," said Roosevelt.

"Her felicity of expression is duly noted." Another cold smile. "It is manners that elude me."

"So I've noticed. Shall we get down to business?"

"Certainly," said Demosthenes. "Which particular criminal are you after?"

"What makes you think I'm after a criminal?" asked Roosevelt.

"Do not be obtuse, Mr. Roosevelt," said Demosthenes. "I move freely among the criminal element. Two lawbreakers have passed the word that you wished to meet with me. What other reason could you possibly have for this extravagant charade?"

"All right," said Roosevelt. "At present three men control seventy percent of the crime in Manhattan: William O'Brien, Antonio Pascale, and Israel Zuckerman. Thus far my men have been unable to ferret them out. I have been told that you have access to them, and the ability to adapt to dangerous situations. The City of New York will pay you a one-thousand-dollar bounty for each one you deliver to my office."

"And you think this will end crime in Manhattan?" asked Demosthenes, amused.

"No, but we have to start somewhere, and I prefer starting at the top. Each of them will implicate dozens of others if it will get them lighter sentences." Roosevelt paused and stared at the tall man. "Can you do it?"

"Of course."

"*Will* you do it?"

"Yes."

"I'll expect you to keep this agreement confidential," said Roosevelt. "Say one word of it to anyone else and I will feel no obligation to fulfill my end of it."

"I will say nothing of it," answered Demosthenes. "It is comforting to note that even the remarkable Theodore Roosevelt breaks the law when it suits his purposes."

"Only to apprehend greater lawbreakers. I don't question your morality or methodology; I'll thank you not to question mine."

"O'Brien, Pascale, Zuckerman," said Demosthenes. "Have the money ready, Mr. Roosevelt."

"I'll be in my office every afternoon."

"*I* won't." Before Roosevelt could object, he held up a hand. "These men hide by day and come out at night. It is at night that I shall apprehend them."

He turned and walked out of the room without another word.

Roosevelt went back to his Manhattan apartment and slept most of the day on Friday. He arose in late afternoon, had a hearty meal, and walked to his office just after sunset—

—and found the body of Antonio Pascale on the floor.

Damn! thought Roosevelt. *I told him I wanted this man alive for questioning!*

He inspected the body more closely. It seemed even more pale than Demosthenes. Pascale had a blue silk scarf wrapped around his neck. Roosevelt moved it and found that his throat had been ripped out.

Roosevelt wasn't sickened by the sight. He'd done too much taxidermy, spent too much time in the wilderness, to turn away in horror or disgust, but he *was* puzzled. Did Demosthenes keep a killer dog he hadn't mentioned? Roosevelt tried to reconstruct their meeting in his mind. Could Demosthenes possibly have misunderstood that Roosevelt wanted to get information from the gang leader?

Roosevelt summoned a team of policemen and had them take the body down to the morgue, then sat down heavily on his office chair. How could he get hold of Demosthenes before he killed another man who had information that Roosevelt needed?

He was still pondering the problem a few hours later when Demosthenes, his color a bit darker and richer than the previous evening, stepped through the doorway, lowering his head to avoid bumping it against the lintel. "You owe me a thousand dollars, Mr. Roosevelt."

"You owe *me* an explanation!" snapped Roosevelt. "You knew I wanted this man alive, that he had vital information!"

"He put up a fight," said Demosthenes calmly. "I killed him in self-defense."

"Did you tear out his throat in self-defense too?" demanded Roosevelt.

"No," answered Demosthenes. "I tore out his throat because I wanted to."

"Was there any doubt in your mind that I wanted him alive, that I was not paying you to kill him?"

"None whatsoever."

Roosevelt pulled a small pistol out of his pocket. "Then I am arresting you for murder."

"Put that toy away before I become annoyed with you, Mr. Roosevelt," said Demosthenes, unperturbed. "I will withdraw my request for the thousand dollars, and we'll call it even."

"You don't seem to understand," said Roosevelt. "You killed a man, and now you're going to stand trial for it."

"If you persist in threatening me, I may have to take that gun from you and destroy it."

"I wouldn't advise it."

"When I want your advice, Mr. Roosevelt," said Demosthenes, taking a step toward him, "you may rest assured I shall ask for it."

"That's close enough," said Roosevelt ominously.

"I'll be the judge of that," said Demosthenes.

Roosevelt fired his pistol point-blank at the tall man's chest. He could hear the *thunk!* of the bullet as it struck its target, but Demosthenes paid it no attention. He advanced another step and Roosevelt shot him right between the eyes, again to no effect. Finally the tall man reached out, grabbed the pistol, and bent the barrel in half.

"Who the hell *are* you?" demanded Roosevelt, as he tried to comprehend what had happened.

"I am the man who is going to clean up your city for you," answered Demosthenes calmly. "I have been doing so privately since I arrived here last year. Now I shall do so at the instigation of the Commissioner of Police. Keep your money. I will extract my own form of payment from those criminals whose presence we will no longer tolerate."

"Don't use the word 'we' as if we were partners," said Roosevelt. "You killed a man, and you're going to stand trial for it."

"I think not, Mr. Roosevelt," said Demosthenes. "I sincerely think not."

He turned and walked out of the office. Roosevelt raced to the doorway, spotted a trio of cops at the far end of the corridor, and yelled to them, "Stop that man! Use any force necessary!"

The three men charged Demosthenes, who knocked them flying like tenpins. Before they could gather themselves to resume the attack, he was gone.

"Who the hell was he, sir?" asked one of the cops, spitting out a bloody tooth.

"I wish I knew," answered Roosevelt, a troubled expression on his face.

All right, thought Roosevelt, sitting at his desk, where he had been for the two hours since Demosthenes had left. *He never saw my gun in the Bowery. Edith would have told me if we'd had a visitor at the apartment. The next time I saw him was right here, so he* couldn't *have disabled my weapon. He knew it worked, and he knew it wouldn't harm him.*

And what about the three officers who tried to stop him? He brushed them aside like they were insects buzzing around his face. Just what kind of a man am I dealing with here?

There's no precedent for this, and if any member of the force had seen him perform similar acts word would certainly have reached me. Yet he implied that he's been killing people for a year now. Probably the criminal element; those are the murders that no one bothers to report.

But what's going on here? It's easy to label him a madman, but he doesn't strike me as deranged.

Roosevelt stood up and began pacing his office. Suddenly he felt almost claustrophobic. It was time to breathe some fresh air, to walk off some of his nervous energy. Maybe just getting out and exercising, taking his mind off Demosthenes for a few minutes, might let him come back to the problem with fresh insights.

Suddenly he heard half a dozen gunshots and an agonized scream. He rushed down the stairs to the main entrance in time to see four of his policemen clustered together around a fifth, who lay motionless on the pavement. A few feet away was another body, as pale as Pascale had been.

"What's going on here?" he demanded, striding out into the open.

"I'll be damned if I know, Mr. Roosevelt, sir," said an officer. "Some tall guy, I mean *real* tall and skinny as a rail, came out of nowhere and dumped that body in front of the building. We confronted him and demanded that he come inside to be interrogated, and he refused. Jacobs walked up and grabbed him by the arm, and the guy threw him against that lamppost. Jacobs weighed about two hundred pounds, and the lamppost was twenty feet away." The officer paused. "I think he's dead, sir."

"The tall man?"

"Jacobs, sir. We drew our guns and demanded that the tall man surrender to us, and he just laughed and began walking away, so we opened fire. So help me, sir, we must have hit him four or five times, and he didn't even flinch."

"Let's take a look at the body he brought to us," said Roosevelt. He walked over to the corpse. "Do you recognize him?"

"It's Israel Zuckerman, the guy who runs the Jewish gang." The officer frowned. "At least I think it is."

"You're not sure?"

"I remember Zuckerman being darker, like he'd spent most of his life in the sun. Mediterranean, I think they call the type. This guy's so pale he looks like he's spent the last twenty years in jail."

"It's Zuckerman," said Roosevelt. "Leave that scarf around his neck until you move him inside."

"Whatever you say, sir."

Another officer approached them. "Jacobs is dead, sir."

"Do you have any explanation for what happened?" asked Roosevelt.

The officer shook his head. "It almost like something out of that crazy book everyone's reading."

"I don't know what you're talking about," said Roosevelt.

"It's some kind of thriller about, I don't know, this creature that kills people and drinks their blood."

"I don't read popular literature," said Roosevelt with an expression of distaste.

"Well, if you change your mind, sir," said the other officer, "it's called *Dracula.*"

"I think I heard someone mention it once or twice," said Roosevelt with no show of interest.

"It's about this guy who can't be hurt, at least at night. He drinks people's blood . . ."

"Enough!" said a third officer, who was examining Zuckerman's corpse. "I'd like to eat dinner again sometime before I die."

"Sorry," said the officer.

"All right," said Roosevelt. "Let's get these men inside before the sun comes up and we attract a crowd. Take them both down to the morgue, find out what killed Zuckerman—though I can hazard a pretty good guess right now—and have someone contact Officer Jacobs' widow."

"Shouldn't that be *your* job, sir?"

"It should be, but we've got a killer on the loose, a killer that bullets don't stop. I've got to find out what *will* stop him." He paused. "I suppose we should put a guard around O'Brien, but it wouldn't stop this man, and I'm not going to lose any more officers before I find out how to defeat him."

He went back into the building, climbed the stairs, and retrieved his hat and his walking stick from the corner of his office. Then he went back outside. A few minutes later he was walking up Park Avenue. After a mile he turned onto 34th Street, then turned left on Lexington. He wandered the city, considering the problem, discarding one approach after another, and suddenly realized that it was daylight.

He stopped by a newsstand to pick up a paper, was pleased to see that neither murder had been reported yet, and saw a full-page ad for the hot new bestseller *Dracula*—the same book his officers had been talking about. He waited until a bookseller's shop opened, walked inside, picked up a copy, and skimmed the first sixty or seventy pages.

It was a flight of fancy. Well-written, though the man couldn't hold a candle to Austen or the Brontës, or Americans such as Mark Twain or Walt Whitman. But the similarities between the fictional Dracula and the very real Demosthenes were striking, and finally he put the book back where he'd found it. He decided to head to the Astor Library to do some research. It wasn't easy. There were references to a Nosferatu, and to Wampyres, and to other creatures, but they were so far-fetched that he couldn't see them being of any use. Still, they were *something*, and that was more than he could find anywhere else.

He carried a dozen books to a table and began taking notes, researching the legend as meticulously as he researched ornithology or naval strategy. He created two columns. The first contained suppositions that three or more sources held in common. When he couldn't find at least three, or when they were contradicted by another source, they were moved to the second column.

By late afternoon he had only two items remaining in the first column. Sooner or later every other "fact," every supposition, had come into conflict with some other legend or the purported facts and suppositions.

It wasn't much to go on, but he decided he couldn't wait. Demosthenes wasn't going to stop killing, but once he delivered O'Brien, there was every chance that Roosevelt would never see him again.

It would take perhaps half an hour to prepare, but although the sun was low in the sky, he didn't really expect to see Demosthenes before midnight. His three previous appearances had been between midnight and dawn.

Roosevelt stopped by the apartment to have dinner with Edith. Then he finished his preparations, told Edith that he would probably be spending the night at the office, promised to find a cot and not sleep in his chair, and finally took his leave of her, after selecting a book to read, and stuffing a pile of personal correspondence that required responses into a leather case.

He reached the office at about 8:00 P.M., told the policemen on duty to pass the word that if Demosthenes showed up, even if he was carrying a corpse, not to try to stop him. They looked at him as if he'd been drinking, but he was the Commissioner of Police and finally they all agreed.

Roosevelt entered his office, sat down at his desk, and immediately destroyed all existing copies of the photo of himself with Baldy and Eye Patch. After all, he reasoned, they'd done their duty, even if no one had foreseen the consequences. An avid letter writer, he spent the next three hours catching up on his correspondence. Then he picked up a copy of F. C. Selous' latest African memoir and began reading it. He was soon so caught up in it that he didn't realize he was no longer alone until he heard the thud of a body being dropped to the floor.

"O'Brien," announced Demosthenes, gesturing toward the pale corpse.

"Why do you keep bringing them to me?" asked Roosevelt. "Our agreement has been abrogated."

"I am bound by a different moral code than you."

"Clearly," said Roosevelt, barely glancing at the body. "I'd like you to tell me something."

"If I can."

"Did you kill Pericles and Sophocles too, or is this a recent aberration?"

A cold smile crossed the tall man's face. "Ah! You know. But of course you would. You are not like the others, Mr. Roosevelt."

"I most certainly am," said Roosevelt. "I am a man. It is *you* who are not like the others, Demosthenes."

"They are sheep."

"Or cattle?" suggested Roosevelt. "You have relatives that live on cattle, do you not?"

Another smile. "You have done your homework, Mr. Roosevelt."

"Yes, I have. Enough that I find it difficult to believe you ever suggested that the warrior who runs away will live to fight another day."

"A misattribution," said Demosthenes with a shrug. "I do not retreat—ever."

"I don't doubt it."

"It nevertheless would have been good advice for you," said Demosthenes. "I intuit that you think you know enough to harm me. Do not believe everything you think you have learned. For example, it is said that a vampire may not cross over water, and yet I crossed the Atlantic Ocean to find fresh feeding grounds. They say the sunlight will kill me, yet I have walked down Fifth Avenue at high noon. They say I cannot enter a building without being invited, but you know that no one has invited me here."

"All that is true," agreed Roosevelt. "And it is all irrelevant."

"I admire you, Mr. Roosevelt. Do not do anything foolish that will force me to harm you."

"You are not going to harm me," said Roosevelt, getting to his feet.

"I warn you . . ." said Demosthenes.

"Save your warnings for those who are afraid of animals," said Roosevelt. "I told you before: I am a hunter."

"We are both hunters, each in our own way," said Demosthenes. "Do you think to slay me with your fabled Winchester rifle?" he added with a contemptuous smirk.

"No," answered Roosevelt, picking up his weapon and positioning himself between Demosthenes and the door. "We both know that bullets have no effect on you."

"Ah!" said Demosthenes with a smile. "You expect to beat me to death with your walking stick?"

"I have a motto," said Roosevelt. "Thus far I've shared it with very few people, but someday I think I shall make it public, for it has served me well in the past and will serve me even better tonight." He paused. "Speak softly and carry a big stick." He removed the metal tip from his wooden walking stick, revealing the sharp point that he had whittled earlier in the evening. "*This* is my big stick."

"So you've learned that much," said Demosthenes, unperturbed. "Has any of your research told you how to drive a wooden stake into the heart of a being with fifty times your strength?"

"Let's find out," said Roosevelt, advancing toward him.

Demosthenes reached out confidently and grabbed the walking stick with his right hand. An instant later he shrieked in agony and pulled his hand back as the flesh on it turned black and began bubbling.

"The wooden stake was not the only thing I learned this afternoon," said Roosevelt. "I took the liberty of rinsing my walking stick with holy water on the way here."

Demosthenes uttered a scream of rage and leaped forward. "If I die I will not die alone!" he snarled as the point of the stick plunged deep into his chest and his hands reached out for Roosevelt's throat.

"Alone and unmourned," promised Roosevelt, standing his ground.

A minute later the creature named Demosthenes was no more.

It didn't take long for new kingpins to move into the positions vacated by Pascale, Zuckerman, and O'Brien. Somehow, after Demosthenes, they didn't seem like the insurmountable problems they might have been a month earlier.

The Commissioner of Police looked forward to the challenge.

Smoke and Mirrors

by P. D. Cacek

There was more than just a hint of autumn in the night air; it was a brash statement that reddened noses and seeped beneath collar or cuff to conjured thoughts of warm fires and roasted chestnuts and winter coats that would soon have to be taken out of storage.

Another summer had come to an end and he was glad. Summer had always been her favorite time of year.

Hunching his shoulders under the black flannel overcoat that was a perfect match to both the approaching night and his mood, he sidestepped to avoid a headlong collision with two young ladies of fashion—faces rosy from the chill, giggling at trifles—and stumbled over a hidden crack in the sidewalk. Before he could catch himself, his shoulder glanced off a man in a sporty houndstooth jacket.

"Hey! Watch it, bub."

It was the standard response of the affluent Upper

West Side dweller, so he took no notice. New Yorkers, he'd come to understand, were proud of their boorish behavior and took delight in showing it off. As a New Yorker himself, residing as he did on 113th Street, he would have been well within his rights to counter the suggestion with a comparable reply, but an instant later, the man in the houndstooth recognized him with a great, and boisterous, outpouring of unmitigated respect.

"Oh, my God . . . Mr. Houdini, I'm . . . I apologize, sir. My fault entirely. Please forgive me."

Houdini nodded, mouthing words that never quite managed to reach his lips, and tried to move on—all too aware of the sudden silence as those who a moment before had been individuals, intent only on making their way home for the night, became a crowd.

"It's him!" A young feminine voice circled momentarily above the others like a bright bird. "It's really *him!*"

"Saw your show last year, sir. Wonderful, absolutely won—"

"Thought he was taller than that!"

"Do a trick!"

"Oh, yes. Give us a trick!"

And then the voices condensed into one. "Trick! Trick! Give us a trick!"

A trick . . . that's all they thought he could do. To them, he was just another stage magician, more well known, perhaps, but no different from any street corner sleight-of-hand hustler who'd mastered the skill of palming peas and moving walnut shells.

"Here, someone grab his hands!" Someone yelled and another someone did just that. Grabbed his hands and held one while shouting "There now. Used to row for Princeton and still have a fair grip, I warrant. Let see you get out of this!"

The crowd—*mob*—howled in delight and he heard, somehow, another voice bray that if the Great Houdini could get out of handcuffs "—a man's grip shouldn't be a problem."

Houdini took a deep breath and stared at the man holding him. It was Houndstooth, grinning, his eyes alight; his hand tightening until Houdini felt the bones of his wrists grind against one another.

"Go on," the man coaxed, "get free."

So he did.

Dislocating the bones of his hands and folding his flesh in upon itself, he slipped free and stepped back just as one of New York's finest began dispersing the crowd with less-than-gentle admonishments.

Houndstooth gaped, loose-jawed, at Houdini and raised hands that were still clenched, holding nothing but air.

"My God . . . he did it."

There was little of the crowd remaining, but the police officer waited until what applause there was had faded before apologizing for their behavior.

"Sorry, Mr. Houdini. Would you like me to accompany you, sir?"

Shaking his head, he pulled his hat's brim lower over his eyes. "That won't be necessary, officer. My destination is just up the street, but thank you. For everything."

"My pleasure, sir. And may I say that I took my family to see your last performance and, well, sir, it was marvelous. Good night, sir."

Houdini watched the officer fade into the dim autumn twilight before turning toward the elegant brownstone two doors away.

It had been almost a full year since the publication of his Margery pamphlet for *Scientific American* in which he exposed the famous Chicago medium for the cheat she was . . . and lost forever, he thought, a dear friend.

Almost a year. Another year.

Mameh. One more year, making eleven that she'd been gone.

Houdini took a deep breath and forced the thought from him. He couldn't allow himself to appear vulnerable tonight . . . especially not tonight. And especially not in front of the man who had requested his presence.

The note had come on thick vellum edged in gold, the envelope addressed in a masculine hand. The words were kept to a minimum.

Houdini,

Have proof even you cannot refute.

Will expect you this evening. Seven o'clock.

—ACD

ACD: Arthur Conan Doyle. Sir Arthur—the man whose friendship he'd thought lost forever. The man, though brilliant and practical, apparently still believed it was possible for the dead to commune with the living.

"As if a thing were possible," he whispered to remind himself that it wasn't. For *if* the dead could pierce the veil, *she* would have already done so.

The wind shifted and tugged at his coat. Straightening his shoulders, he took the envelope from his pocket and checked the address against the polished brass numerals of the brownstone he now stood before. Lights shone in the front windows, the lace curtains casting golden spiderwebs across the twin stone lions that guarded the stoop. Houdini patted one as he ascended. The cut-glass porch lamp illuminated the small, thin gold ring on his little finger as he reached for the ram's head doorknocker. It had been his mother's and was the only thing he had left of her.

The only thing he would ever have, despite the Englishman's supposed *proof.*

The butler who answered the door nodded a greeting as he took Houdini's hat and coat, then immediately led the way to the dark-paneled drawing room where his one-time friend sat staring into the coals of a dying fire. Only the firelight moved in the room; the man himself could have been carved from marble. The butler, well-trained, cleared his throat before announcing, "Mr. Houdini, my lord."

My lord. Houdini brushed a finger across his lips to hide the smile. How like the man to preserve aristocratic ceremony in a rented brownstone.

"Harry. I'm glad you're here." Houdini watched an elderly man in maroon brocade push himself to his feet with the use of a silver tipped cane. It had been only been a few years, but in that time age seemed to have crept up on the man like a strangling vine.

And how old do I seem to him? he asked himself as their hands met in a firm clasp.

Sir Arthur's smile faded a moment later when his gaze fell on the torn breast pocket of Houdini's suit coat. "Still in mourning, I see."

It wasn't a condemnation, merely a fact. Houdini nodded and was the first to break the clasp.

"Always, Sir Arthur. You're looking well." Small talk—safe and polite, just the sort of thing to test the water. "The newspapers made no mention that you were in town. Doing research for a new book?"

The Englishman smiled, but shook his head and motioned toward a chair opposite the one he'd just left. "Research, yes, but not for a book of fiction. No, this time I'm here for you, Harry, to give you immutable and inexorable proof of the spirit realm."

"So your note stated." Houdini tried to keep his emotions in check as he sat, but could already feel the rush of blood pulsing beneath his collar. "Immutable? Inexorable? You mean, of course, indisputable, don't you, Sir Arthur? I would have thought, after all that has happened, this particular subject was dead between us."

"Marvelous pun," Sir Arthur chuckled over his shoulder. He was bending over a small round table, pouring sherry into two fluted glasses. "You should have been a writer, Harry."

"I am."

Sir Arthur handed Houdini a glass, finishing his

own before he returned to his chair. "Ah, yes, those . . . articles for *Scientific American*. I understand your reasons behind it, but still maintain my original position that the poor lady was nervous and so wanted to impress you, that she . . ."

Houdini took a sip to keep from offering *his* position. Again.

". . . made a mistake in judgment. I am still convinced of her ability, but Margery is not the reason I sent that note."

Houdini lowered his glass. "If the proof you've mentioned in any way relates to this lady, you will forgive me if I—"

Sir Arthur waved him back into his chair. "No, Harry, it's not about Margery, though perhaps, one day, we may discuss her again. The proof I have will convince even a skeptic such as yourself . . . *Ehrich*."

The glass slipped from Houdini's fingers, bleeding its last drop into the thick Persian rug at his feet. *Ehrich* was her pet name for him; no one else called him that, not even Bess.

Mameh.

"How?"

But again the Englishman waved. "Do you confirm the name, Harry?"

Houdini sat back in the chair, folding his hands into his lap to conceal their trembling. "Yes. But that's an easy thing to find out, Sir Arthur."

"I didn't think it would be that easy, Harry. So—"

Leaning forward, Sir Arthur reached into the breast pocket of his brocade smoking jacket and pulled from it, as slowly and carefully as any theatrical illusionist, an embroidered silken handkerchief.

Houdini closed his eyes, but could still see the tiny blue forget-me-nots that decorated one corner above the lavender-hued initials: *C. W.*

Cecelia Weiss.

"Did this belong to your mother?"

The room swam momentarily when he opened his eyes, and he watched his hand, a pale and shaking thing, take the handkerchief and carry it to his face. The scent of Arlequinade, his mother's favorite perfume, filled his head. It was her hankerchief, the same one she had embroidered a year before her death; the same one he himself had placed beneath her hands as she lay in her coffin. It was the last thing he'd done before they closed the lid.

How could anyone have taken it?

"It is hers, isn't it, Harry?"

"It is." Houdini caressed the gossamer material between his fingers. "*Where* did you get it?"

A wide smile bristled Sir Arthur's silver walrus mustache as he rapped the tip of the cane into the rug's thick nap. The sound was as hollow as a dying heartbeat.

"Then it's true . . . it's true! It *is* your mother's!"

Houdini vaulted to his feet, the delicate cloth now crushed beneath the fist he shook before the Englishman's still smiling face. "I asked you where you got it!"

"From a man, Harry. A spiritualist."

"A grave robber, you mean!"

"Harry, please, sit down and listen."

When it was obvious that Sir Arthur wouldn't continue until he did, Houdini took a deep breath and forced himself to comply. Sir Arthur nodded.

"A month ago in London, at the home of Lord and Lady Bancroft, I watched the man I have just mentioned pull that handkerchief from thin air. He was sitting in a chair surrounded by a dozen people, myself included. No one was near enough to touch him or be touched in return. It was—"

"Magic," Houdini said and, before Sir Arthur's eyes, made the handkerchief disappear and then, a moment later, reappear. "Sleight-of-hand is the first trick every magician learns, Sir Arthur. And if that is the basis of your *proof*—"

"It's not, and do give me some credit, if you please. I have watched you and others perform enough to know the difference. And this *was* different, Harry. A moment after the handkerchief appeared there was a voice—disembodied, floating in the very air around us—a woman's voice. A voice that sounded very much as I remember your mother's to be."

"Good God." Houdini didn't even attempt to stop the laughter that came from his lips. Or minimize its sarcastic tone. "Hand magic and a recorded woman's voice which may or may *not* have been—"

"Your mother—the voice gave us a message for you, by name, *Ehrich*. I apologize for the pronunciation." Sir Arthur cleared his throat and, finally, had the good grace to appear contrite. "The message is, '*Nit azoy gich, mine zun.*' I'm afraid I don't know what it means."

Houdini looked down and gently opened his hand. "It means, 'Not so fast, my son.' It was the last thing my mother said to me before I got on the boat for Europe. I'd run down the gangplank, you see, to give her one last kiss and almost slipped. She scolded me for it."

"She'd whispered to me, Sir Arthur. No one, I thought, had heard it. Who is this man?"

"His name is Yeildgrave."

"As ludicrous a stage name as ever I've heard, but an appropriate one for a grave robber." Chuckling low in his throat, Houdini folded the handkerchief and tucked it into his vest pocket. "I'm sorry, Sir Arthur, but if that's your proof, it can be easily explained. A stolen keepsake, an overheard conversation between mother and son and a willing actress to record the supposed spirit's voice. My well publicized crusade against such counterfeit mediums has, I assure you, brought many similar challenges, but I am surprised that you were taken in by such a pitiful display, Sir Arthur. The man only did his homework, that's all."

But the Englishman only shook his head after each point Houdini had made. "No. It was more than that, Harry. I was there, I saw the handkerchief simply appear as if by—"

Houdini extended his seemingly empty hand, twisted his wrist to one side and, a moment later, held the fluted wineglass that had fallen to the rug between his fingers.

"As if by magic, Sir Arthur." Handing the Englishman the glass, he stood up and dipped his head in a modified bow. "That's exactly what it was, stage magic, nothing else; and no more evidence of the spirit world than was Margery's nimble foot tapping upon the 'spirit box' beneath my chair. You were taken in, Sir Arthur, as easily as a barefoot boy at his first carnival. This Yeildgrave is nothing more than a drawing-room charlatan preying on the earnest gullibility of his betters. He's a fraud."

A sudden chill whispered against the back of Houdini's neck.

"I find that word . . . offensive. *Sir.*"

The voice was deep and mellow, the accent educated and cultured, a nearly perfect imitation of a native-born Englishman; and one that had undoubtedly convinced Sir Arthur that he was a kinsman. Houdini, however, caught a faint but familiar inflection beneath the genteel veneer, and answered as he turned.

"Meu a-şi cere iertare, domnule."

The man was standing just beyond the room's threshold, his features shadowed from both the firelight and room's shaded incandescent lamps, but Houdini saw the pale, long-fingered hands clench momentarily.

"Apology accepted," the cultured voice replied.

"You—" Sir Arthur was on his feet, moving past Houdini toward the newcomer, the sherry glass still in his hand. "You speak—"

"Romanian," the man answered and stepped forward. "I have an ear for languages, Mr. Doyle, and speak many."

A response—clever, witty, and caustic—died on Houdini's lips as Yieldgrave stepped into the light. The man was a walking corpse. He was gaunt to the point of emaciation, his flesh was the color of curdled cream; the deep blue of his velvet dressing gown only serving to deepen the hollows that engulfed his coal-black eyes. Only his lips showed color. Red as fresh as raw meat.

Houdini involuntarily leaned back when the man offered his hand. He'd seen this before, both in his homeland and then in the slums his family first called home in America. The man was dying of consumption.

Houdini's flesh crawled when the long, cold fingers closed around his own.

"I am Lord Yieldgrave, and I'm honored to meet you, Mr. *Houdini.*" The man, obviously having overhead Houdini's comment about his name, smiled as he bowed. "I have watched your career for many years and am familiar with your latest . . . talent, that of spiritual investigator. It will therefore be an indescribable pleasure to become the single flame that enlightens you."

Houdini broke the grasp and moved quickly toward the fireplace to keep from knocking the man down. His anger more than made up for the fire's lack of warmth.

"By robbing more graves?"

A tiny touch of color bloomed above the man's cavernous cheeks. "I have never robbed graves, Houdini. While in communication with your mother, she gave me that memento, the same way she whispered those wor—"

"FRAUD!"

Houdini had no memory of moving from the fireplace or of striking the man, but a moment later he stood—legs braced, fists clenched—and looked down at Yeildgrave's smiling face. A small, bloodless slit at the left corner enlarged the man's already wide mouth by a fraction of an inch.

"Harry! What have you done?" Muttering apologies, Sir Arthur helped Yieldgrave to his feet and, after noticing the sherry glass still in his hand, offered to get the man something much stronger.

"Thank you, no, Sir Arthur. I do not communicate with those particular spirits." With a courteous nod, Yieldgrave brushed aside the older man's attempts at solace and again turned his full attention to Houdini. "I underestimated you, Houdini, but be assured that will never happen again."

Houdini's fists trembled with the desire to strike again. "You will never have the opportunity. I've seen enough to know what you are, Yieldgrave."

"No," the man chuckled, "I don't think you do."

"Oh, I think—"

"Enough!" The sherry glass snapped in Sir Arthur's hand as he took a step forward. "This man is my guest and you will treat him with the respect or—"

"Hush."

It was but one word, softly spoken, but Sir Arthur stumbled back as if struck.

"I can fight my own battles," Yieldgrave said, but to Houdini, not his host. "As I've said, I have watched your career with something less than the usual boredom I feel when viewing . . . the population at large. You are an excellent performer, Houdini, but you've let that one talent grow into arrogance and conceit. And now you've donned the mantle of defender to protect men and women against—how did you put it? Ah yes, against their own 'earnest gullibility.' Generally, I would never have bother myself with such a petty matter—or man—but I've decided to make this city my home . . . and even the tiniest of thorns will, after a while, become an irritation."

Yieldgrave leaned forward until Houdini could see himself reflected in the man's black eyes.

"And you, magician, could very well become such an irritation. Therefore—" Yieldgrave stepped back and walked with a graceful stride to the fireplace. "It is my . . . *obligation* to convince you not only of the communication between the living and dead, but of my own remarkable talents in that respect. And I have no doubt that once you've witnessed it, you will become my greatest supporter."

Houdini tried to speak, but a sudden constriction of the throat made it all but impossible. The only sound he could produce was a thin, weak murmur of disgust.

"Think of it, Houdini, after you write another pamphlet, expounding upon the wonders I alone can show you, it will be an endorsement that shall welcome me into every drawing room and parlor, private club and salon in New York.

"You wish to say something?"

Yieldgrave smiled as he blinked those empty, black, hollow eyes and Houdini felt his throat open with a gasping sob.

"Then prove it. Now!"

Yieldgrave laughed, hands clapping in delight as Sir Arthur, blinking as though he'd just woken from a deep sleep, cleared his throat.

"No, Harry. Not now . . . not here."

Houdini nodded, with a smirk. "Yes, of course. How insensitive of me. You undoubtedly haven't had time to set up your illusions."

A flush came to Sir Arthur's cheeks, but Yieldgrave still laughed. "There are no illusions, Houdini, no tricks. That is your realm, not mine."

"Then why don't you convince me now?"

"Because, Harry," the Englishman said, glancing from Houdini to Yieldgrave and back again, "you would think exactly as you do now, that I had planned this evening in retribution for your attack on Margery. No, Harry, Lord Yieldgrave and I want no doubts whatsoever in your mind, so, with your permission, we would like to hold the séance at your home. On the day and time of your choosing."

"My home?"

Sir Arthur nodded. "It's the only way you will be convinced. Invite as many or as few people as you like and pick the room to be used. That way you can be sure that nothing has been tampered with. Lord Yieldgrave and I shall appear at the appointed time and not a moment before. Are you agreeable to that, Harry?"

Houdini though a moment before nodding. "Yes, Sir Arthur, I am *most* agreeable. Shall we say tomorrow night, then? Eight o'clock."

Yieldgrave bowed. "Tomorrow it will be . . . and I promise you, Houdini, an evening you will long remember."

The first message had arrived at dawn, the second an hour later and the third only moments before Houdini, still tying the sash of his dressing gown, walked into the morning parlor for breakfast. Bess waited until he'd finished his cup of coffee before handing him the notes. They were written in the same hand and on the same stationery as the one he'd received the previous night.

"From Sir Arthur," he said in response to his wife's silent, but obvious, curiosity.

"Oh."

He tried not to smile as he set the cards down next to his plate and reached for a slice of toasted bread. But he did count—slowly—and managed to reach six before Bess cleared her throat.

"Well aren't you going to look at them? I mean, the first *did* wake cook."

Which explained the toast's charred surface.

Using a butter knife against the sealed flaps, he opened all three before reading the notes in order of arrival.

Imperative I speak with you. Please contact me at earliest. Do not telephone.
—ACD

Houdini—must speak with you. Utmost urgency.
—ACD

Harry,
For God's sake, if not your own, cancel tonight's engagement. Do NOT allow Yieldgrave into your home. This is beyond all madness or reason, I know, but there is no proof here of anything you need know. Forgive me, Harry.
—ACD

Houdini carefully slid the last note back into its envelope before placing all three into the pocket of his dressing gown with a chuckle.

Bess, still in the role of indifferent observer, casually glanced at him over the rim of her teacup. "Sir Arthur sent a joke?"

"More along the lines of a hook, dear one," Houdini said and began scooping eggs onto his plate. He had no intention of taking so obvious a bait. "He's attempting to play on my sense of the theatrical. Oh, by the way, I'm going to be hosting a small gathering here tonight after supper. Will that be all right?"

Her smile then, at the table, and later while she helped him clear the dining room after the meal, gave him his answer.

She didn't even raise an eyebrow after he confessed the nature of the "gathering," but continued to place chairs as he directed—against the walls facing the single lattice-backed armchair he'd placed beneath the crystal chandelier at the room's center.

"There'll be no tricks tonight," he told her, winking as the first of his guests arrived. "None."

He'd originally thought to view the performance alone, but, since he'd already anticipated publishing another pamphlet which exposed *Lord* Yieldgrave as the fraud he was, Houdini thought more collaborative observers would be best. Impeachable witnesses, better still, so he chose carefully from among their many friends. The final list included his personal doctor and his wife, their rabbi, the police commissioner, the deputy mayor, and a very prominent newspaper reporter who was, among other things, one of his greatest admirers.

Houdini didn't attempt to conceal his smile. As

Yieldgrave himself noted, it most certainly would be an evening to remember.

At half-past the hour only three dining chairs—the ones reserved for Bess, Houdini, and Sir Arthur—and the seat of honor remained empty.

When the doorbell rang a few minutes later, Houdini waved Bess away. "Seat yourself, my dear, I'll attend to this myself."

As well rehearsed as any performance line, Houdini had begun his welcome speech as he opened the door, bowing courteously to the two figures standing beneath the glow of the porch lamp. It was only after he looked up that his smile faded.

Normally robust and ruddy of cheek, the Englishman leaned heavily on his cane and seemed to breathe with great difficulty. Pale and trembling he appeared . . . withered. Stricken. Yieldgrave, on the other hand, had blossomed into full health. His face had filled out and glowed with vitality. His lips remained their unnaturally bright coloration.

"Sir Arthur, you look . . . Are you all right?"

Houdini stepped aside as the Englishman limped forward, ashamed that he hadn't made the effort to reply to the morning's messages. It hadn't been a ploy or theatrics—the man was clearly ill.

"What? Oh, yes, yes . . . just a . . . Just caught a chill, is all. Nothing serious, I assure you."

It was an unconvincing performance, made even more so by the man's refusal to give up the white silken scarf he'd wrapped around his neck.

"No," he said, bringing his hand to his throat when Houdini reached for it. "Best keep it on."

But it was the look in the man's eyes that spoke of something beyond mere illness.

"Of course. We're in the dining room, Sir Arthur. Please go right in. And ask Bess for a glass of port—for the chill."

He nodded, mechanically, then nodded again and mumbled something that sounded like appreciation, but continued to lean heavily on his cane and look back toward the doorway.

It was then that Houdini realized Yieldgrave was still on the porch.

"I am rather old-fashioned," he said. "Will you invite me in, Houdini?"

Sir Arthur made a small noise in his throat as Houdini opened the door farther. "Yes, of course. Please come in."

"Harry . . ." Houdini's eyes met those of the Englishman as Yieldgrave swept into the brightly lit foyer. "I . . ."

"Ah," Yieldgrave said, placing a hand on the Englishman's shoulder, "I hear voices. The more the merrier, isn't that the saying? Why don't you go in to them, Sir Arthur? We shall be along in a moment."

It hadn't been a command, but Houdini saw the older man tremble as if struck, then hurry away.

"I shouldn't worry about him," Yieldgrave said, drawing Houdini's attention. "I believe he spent a bad night. Now, shall we go in?"

Houdini took the man's coat and top hat and set it on the sideboard beside Sir Arthur's before motioning the man toward the dining room. "You'll find all in order, I suspect," he said when they reached the near-sterile room. "But do tell me if you require anything else . . . draperies, mirrors . . . darkness."

Yieldgrave took the empty chair in the middle of the room and casually crossed his legs.

"No smoke or mirrors, Houdini. You're the illusionist, not I. As for darkness . . ." He glanced up at the sparkling crystals above his head. "The more light the better. I want none here to think me . . . a fraud." Seemingly satisfied, he nodded. "Would you be so good, Sir Arthur?"

Voice trembling, Sir Arthur stood and formally introduced Lord Yieldgrave to Houdini's guests, giving a slightly lengthier version of the tale he'd told the night before.

". . . will have absolute proof, not only of the world which exists beyond the shroud of death, but that Lord Yieldgrave is, without question or doubt, the . . . greatest spiritualist in the world."

Houdini almost applauded the performance, but Yieldgrave took it as his due.

"Thank you, Sir Arthur," he began. "Now, were this a 'normal' séance, I would ask that the lights be lowered and all of us clasp hands so that we might form a mystical circle to better 'commune' with the spirits. That, my friends, is trickery, as I'm sure you're all aware, due to Mr. Houdini's relentless . . . investigations in this area. Also, were this a mere deception, I would, upon its conclusion, ask for gratuities."

Yieldgrave sought Houdini's eyes and nodded. "But that again is the mark of . . . charlatans. There is a saying older than almost time itself, '*exigo infidus, verum exsisto solvo*'—'sell lies, but truth must be free.' I will not accept payment for what I do here tonight."

"Then what are you after?" Houdini's friend, the reporter asked.

"Only the privilege of being invited into your homes. Now then . . ." Yieldgrave looked around the room. "Can I take it there is no servant lurking nearby who will suddenly burst forth through a concealed door to act as a ghostly intruder? No strings attached to gramophone recordings of howling winds and blaring trumpets? No hidden pockets or flash powder?"

Houdini's answer came as a low growl. "None."

"I thought not, but considering your profession, I wanted to make certain your guests knew that nothing that happens here tonight was anything less than real. Let us begin."

A heartbeat later, the faint scent of Arlequinade perfume filled the room. Bess gasped from behind cupped hands.

"Harry!"

"Hush, Bess, it's nothing. It's—"

Yieldgrave lifted one hand and for an instant the lights seemed to dim slightly.

"Ehrich?"

The voice came from nowhere and everywhere, and then the air next to Yieldgrave's chair began to shimmer. Soft whispers and gasps followed as a form—small and pale—began to materialize.

"Ehrich? Mein zun . . . is it you?"

The whispering stopped as Houdini pushed himself forward, clutching the upholstered armrests of the chair to keep himself from running toward the tiny, white-haired figure.

She was exactly as he last remembered seeing her,

dressed in the high-collared, long-sleeved gray moiré gown that had been her favorite from the moment he had given it to her. The one she had been buried in.

"Oh God, Harry . . ." Bess's voice was so low that for a moment Houdini thought he'd thought the words himself. "It's Mama."

"No . . . It's not possible."

"*Ehrich? Mein zun* . . . is it you?"

Houdini felt the floor shift beneath his feet as he turned. Smiling, her hands reaching out to him, she took a step forward. His mother.

"I've missed you so much, my son. Why did you leave me? I was so alone."

Houdini's eyes burned as she began moving toward him, the soft rustle of her dress filling the stillness as her perfume filled his head.

But there was something else . . . something beneath the sweet scent . . . something dark and rank and decayed.

"It's not real."

"*Ehrich, vos zogt ir?* It's me, Mama. Come here. Come my little boy and let me hold you. It's been so long. Give Mama a kiss."

As had happened the night before, Houdini didn't realize he'd moved until he felt her in his arms, the mingled scents—perfume, decay, face powder, grave dirt—filling his head as she—*his mother*—brushed his cheek with her cold lips.

"My dear little boy," she whispered. "My sweet angel. I've missed you. Let Mama kiss you . . . let me . . . just give my boy . . . a kiss . . ."

A cloud of stinking mist enveloped him as she pulled him close.

"NO!"

A hand gripped his shoulder and hauled him back at the same moment his mother . . . the *image* of his mother changed . . . reshaped itself into the visage of a feral beast . . . a monster. Blackened lips curled back to reveal elongated fangs as sounds filled the room. Shouts and prayers and the scrape of chair legs against the floor and . . .

"Harry! Harry, for God's sake! Help me!"

Staggering, his hand going to his throat to find his collar ripped away, Houdini watched Sir Arthur struggle to drive the silver tip of his cane into Yieldgrave's chest. Or what had been Yieldgrave a moment before. As with his mother, or whatever it had been, Yieldgrave's face transformed from man to beast, feline—no, batlike in aspect—the inch-long fangs yellow and dripping a viscous saliva that glistened against the Englishman's hand.

"FOOL! YOU DARE CHALLENGE ME?" The face a monster's, the voice a man's.

"Not possible," Houdini whispered.

"Harry!" Sir Arthur yelled. "This is our only chance! HELP ME!"

Without thinking, for rational thought would have stopped him, Houdini rushed forward and added his strength to the older man's. Black viscous fluid overflowed the gaping jaws, as the cane, awash with gore, pierced Yieldgrave's chest. Houdini gagged and backed away as the tip exited through the chair's lattice back.

Behind and around him, hoarse cries and groans of horror filled the very air of the room as those who had been invited to partake in the unmasking of a charlatan witnessed something that went beyond all understanding. The sounds in the room changed as the man, the *creature*, slumped forward over the shaft of the cane, a decomposed corpse.

Houdini stared at the nightmare and prayed he'd wake up. "My God. What *was* it?"

"I tried to tell you." Sir Arthur grabbed Houdini's arms for support. "My . . . my messages this morning. Last night . . . last night Louise came to me and . . ."

Sobbing, the older man slowly removed the scarf from around his neck. The swollen wounds looked like the bite of a giant snake.

"Vampire, Harry. He'd turned her . . . years ago and only now . . . only . . . He was waiting, you see, for his chance. And he found it. Through me."

Sir Arthur collapsed to the floor, taking Houdini with him.

"Forgive me, Harry . . . please, forgive me."

Houdini held the older man as he would a child, rocking him slowly back and forth. "Hush, it's all right. We . . . killed it. It's over."

"No," the whisper came, "it's not. You—your mother is still out there. Don't you understand what he meant? Harry . . . *Ehrich,* she's still out there."

GARBO QUITS

by Ron Goulart

He was one of the few people who knew the real reason Greta Garbo left the movies in the early 1940s while still a major star. But Hix, the short, feisty, opportunistic and aggressively second-rate writer of numerous B movies, was forced to keep his mouth shut. He came that close to proving it and then everything went flooey.

He first got wind of the vampire cult on an overcast afternoon in the early spring of 1941. He was partaking of a nutburger in a health-conscious greasy spoon in Gower Gulch in Hollywood. The joint, shaped like a giant tomato, was across the street from Pentagram Studios, the outfit that was filming Hix's latest script, *The Invisible Vampire Returns.* A big budget film, by Pentagram standards: they were devoting seven days to shooting.

"God created the world, according to reliable sources, in six days," Hix was explaining to the very pretty, slim blonde waitress who was lingering beside his booth. "So my film will be one day better, Inza."

Inza Cramer nodded down at his plate. "What do you think of your nutburger?"

Narrowing one eye, he ran his fingers through his crinkly hair and grew thoughtful. "It has," he informed her, "a nutlike flavor."

"Seriously. The chef's trying out a new recipe and he asked me to query the customers."

"You have a *chef* here?"

"You know, Freddy."

Hix inquired, "Well, what did the other patrons say?"

"So far, you're the only one who's ordered a nutburger this week."

"It's an honor to consume Freddy's maiden effort." He took another bite of the burger. "Tell him that I further said, 'Yum yum.' "

The Inza Cramer leaned closer. "Can you be serious for a minute, Hix?"

"I can do that, sure. Why, kid?"

She lowered her voice. "You heard about Nancy Decker?"

"Starlet over at MGM," he answered. "They found her dead in Griffith Park couple nights ago. Cause was a bad case of pernicious anemia."

"You're, aren't you, sort of an expert on . . . well, spooky stuff?" She leaned against the edge of his booth, lowering her voice even further.

"As the man who single-handedly scripted not only *The Invisible Vampire Returns,* but *The Bride of the Werewolf* and *Zombies on Parade,* I certainly qualify as an expert on spooky stuff, yep," he admitted, frazzled hair fluttering as he nodded his head very positively. "Fact is, UCLA is contemplating awarding me an honorary degree in occultism. Any day now."

"Nancy was murdered, Hix."

He sat up. "Oh, so?"

Her voice was a whisper now. "It was vampires did Nancy in."

"What the hell makes you say that, Inza?"

"I was a friend of hers. We did extra work together before she got picked up by MGM," said the blonde. "But she got involved with this funny cult and—"

"Coffee," requested the suntanned stuntman two booths over. "If you're through flirting with that undersized hack, honey."

Hix rose up from his bench. "Five foot six is not undersized, Buck," he announced and sat down again. "Besides, Mickey Rooney isn't even that tall and he's the idol of millions."

"You also deny the hack part?" asked the stuntman.

"I'll accept that appellation," replied the scriptwriter, "if you add much-beloved to modify hack."

"Done. So can I get a refill now, Inza honey?"

"Excuse me, Hix." The slim waitress went hurrying off toward the kitchen.

"Vampire cult," murmured Hix. "Vampire cult. Maybe I can do something with that."

It was the following afternoon that Hix encountered, albeit briefly, his first real vampire.

He'd been sitting in his cubicle at Pentagram in the former stable that had been converted, with the aid of considerable plywood, into the Writers' Building. Hix leaned back from his venerable Underwood typewriter and tapped the fingers of his right hand on the cover of one of the copies of *Whiz Comics* strewn atop his small, slightly lopsided desk. He had hit a snag in outlining his proposed sequel to *The Invisible Vampire Returns.* It was going to be a more socially conscious film that he was, tentatively, calling *The Invisible Vampire Joins the Army.*

"Inza," he said aloud. "I ought to talk to her about that vampire cult she alluded to yesterday. Right, Inza Cramer could be a definite source of inspiration in these troubled times. Besides she's got a very provocative backside."

He trotted down the hall to the pay phone that the studio provided for its writers and called the tomato-shaped restaurant where the pretty blonde worked.

Turned out it was her day off, but by exercising his considerable powers of cajolery, complementing him on his nutburgers, and promising to slip him two bucks the next time he popped in, Hix obtained the aspiring actress' address from Freddy the chef. She apparently didn't have a telephone.

After scribbling "Out to research" on a cocktail napkin he happened to have in the pocket of his tweed sport coat and affixing it to the moderately warped plywood door, Hix headed for the small coastal town of Santa Rita Beach.

The closer his sporadically rattling old Plymouth coupe got to the late afternoon Pacific Ocean, the thicker the chilly gray fog grew. Tired of talking to himself, the fuzzy-haired writer clicked on the radio.

Johnny Whistler, the piping-voiced Hollywood gossip columnist, was in mid-broadcast.

". . . about time the great Greta Garbo lensed another flicker? I thought the dour Swede was a knock-out in *Ninotchka* and proved she sure can do comedy. But insiders here in Tinseltown are saying that was two years ago and maybe the Great Sphinx of the movies is afraid to try again. Or is Louis B. Mayer, the mighty mogul of MGM, afraid that his once favorite star ain't got another comedy in her? I'll be back in a minute with an open letter to Randolph Scott. Right now here's a message of hope for those of you, who like me, are bothered by occasional irregularity, from Weber's Delicious Painless Laxative. And—"

"Even though I occasionally suffer like Johnny Whistler, I think I'll skip the commercial." He changed stations.

The rest of the foggy journey he listened to a cooking show where a kindly maternal lady told him exactly how to make a jelly roll that would serve six.

Inza lived in a small shingle cottage on a wooded hillside a few hundred yards above a strip of beach that stretched away from the choppy gray Pacific.

Hix parked his coupe on the twisty lane that ran in front of the waitress' cottage and the scatter of other small houses dotting this wooded section of hillside. His car went through the usual rattling shudders it evidenced whenever the motor was turned off.

The fog hung heavy around the cottage and the lighted front window was a hazy rectangle. "Mist enshrouded the humble dwelling in a blanket of chilling grayness," Hix said to himself, trying to come up with an apt phrase to describe the setup.

Just about ten seconds after he noticed that the weathered redwood door of the young woman's cottage was hanging half open, he heard a scream from inside.

"Hey!" he shouted and went running along the flagstone path to push into the house.

From the rear came the sound of something, probably a lamp, falling over and smacking the floor.

Hix, crinkly hair flickering, sprinted in that direction.

At the far side of the kitchen a slim figure in tan trousers, a dark ski sweater, and a knit cap was bending over, back turned, the sprawled body of Inza.

"Hey!" repeated Hix, hesitating on the threshold of the white and yellow room.

Without turning, the crouching figure dived for the rear door of the kitchen, yanked it open, and ran out into the deep fog.

Hix reached the door in time to see the slender figure being swallowed up by the thick gray fog.

He decided, no doubt influenced by numerous B-movies he'd scripted, to give chase.

He'd covered only a few feet of the surrounding woodlands when something whacked him on the side of the head.

Hix staggered, started to turn to see who was attacking him, and was sapped again across the temple. Harder.

He took two wobbly steps, gray fog engulfed him, and he tumbled down into it.

"You saved my life, Hix. If you hadn't showed up just when you did, gosh, I don't know what would've happened. Well, no actually, I do know. I'd have met the same fate as poor Nancy Decker."

Hix found himself reclining on an intricate crazy quilt of many colors. He and the quilt were spread over an imitation antique spool bed. The odors of a pungent potpourri and recently applied iodine mingled in the air.

Sitting on the edge of the bed, a white bandage on the left side of her throat, was Inza. There was an expression of gratitude on her pale face.

Although Hix blinked a few times, the blonde didn't immediately come into focus. "Here's a line I've found useful in many a brilliant script of mine," he said, noticing that his voice was sounding moderately froggy. "Where am I?"

"My bedroom. And I bandaged your poor head."

He lifted a hand and managed, after two tries, to touch the injured side of his head. "Ouch, ow, damn," he observed. "How'd you manage to drag me in from the woods, kiddo?"

"Oh, I had help." From the pocket of her pink striped blouse Inza extracted an embossed business card. "A very nice girl. Her name is Sara Hampton and her profession is—this is right up your alley, Hix—occult investigator."

He abandoned his attempt to sit up as soon as he experienced the throbbing head, aching bones, and displays of Stuart Davis–style flashing of colored lights it caused. "An occult investigator just happened to be passing this joint when there was some heavy lifting to be done?"

"No, she was trailing somebody. When she found you sprawled out cold at the edge of my backyard and then noticed me gradually recovering from a vampire attack in my dinky kitchen, she took the time to lend a hand. How's your noggin feeling?"

"Both my coco and the rest of me are still feeling relatively lousy, thank you. Where is this mystical Samaritan now?"

"She had something else to take care of, but she'll be back shortly. She'd appreciate it if you wait around."

"Good. I don't intend to move from this supine position for quite some time," decided Hix as the light display he'd been enjoying started to dim and fade. "I look forward to meeting her."

"Here, keep her card." Inza pressed it into his hand.

Hix told her, "As I recall, I dropped by to ask you about the vampire cult you were telling me about yesterday."

She nodded, closing his fingers around the card and keeping hold of his hand. "What I suspect, Hix, is that somebody at the restaurant overheard something of what I was confiding in you and came here to shut me up."

"Surely not Buck the stuntman? He's too obtuse to be involved in a cult of any kind."

"There were at least a dozen other people in the place while you were there."

"I only had eyes for you. And my nutburger," he said. "Now tell me exactly what happened here."

"Okay, well, Nancy told me a lot about the workings of the vampire cult, though she wasn't supposed to." Inza's grip on his hand tightened. "They must suspect that, so they sent somebody to . . . to get rid of me. They sent a vampire to attack me."

"That's sure a possibility, yeah. Any idea who he was?"

"It wasn't a man." She shook her head, frowning. "It was a woman. And don't laugh, Hix, but from the quick glimpse I got of her . . . well, she looked a heck of a lot like Greta Garbo."

Hix didn't laugh.

"Much of the folklore about vampirism does contain a considerable amount of truth," explained Sara Hampton while tacking a garlic chain to the front door frame of Inza's cottage. "Garlic really is a surefire protection against vampires."

"I never much liked the smell of the stuff." Inza was standing on the threshold watching the occult investigator. "Freddy, though, loves garlic and uses tons of it at the restaurant."

Sara was a small, slightly plump woman of about thirty, dressed in a tweed skirt, thick cardigan, and fairly sensible shoes. "This'll keep them out." Taking a step back, she studied the doorway and then glanced toward the windows. "All right, Miss Cramer, I've got garlands attached to all your windows and doors." She made a let's-go-back-inside gesture.

Some of the night fog followed the two women into the parlor.

Hix, a small green ice bag adorning his injured head and flattening his frazzled hair, was slumped in a sturdy armchair. The light from a floor lamp with a glazed shade depicting red sailboats in the sunset was shining down on him. "Okay, she's protected while she's at home," he said. "What happens when she ventures into the outside world?"

"This will take care of that." From her large black purse the occult specialist drew a small silver cross on a silver chain. "Wear this all the time, dear. *All the time.*"

Nodding, Inza accepted the silver cross and hung it around her neck. "You're sure I'll be safe now?"

"You'll be okay, yes."

"Shouldn't she lay in a supply of silver bullets and a couple of wooden stakes?" Hix readjusted his ice bag. "Aren't those essential tools for dispatching vampires? In my script for *The Invisible Vampire Returns* I—"

"Yes, a wooden stake in the heart never fails." Sara seated herself on the sofa near the pale waitress. "Silver bullets, though, I've found, work best on werewolves. I've known a well-placed silver bullet to stop a vampire, but you can't always count on that."

Hix frowned. "In all of my near-award-winning scripts I've stated that vampires only come out after the sun goes down," he said. "But Inza's vampire jumped her in broad daylight."

"That part of folk belief is strictly flapdoodle," Sara told him. "Vampires can strike at any hour, all around the clock. And, by the way, except for the ones with an especialy morbid streak, they seldom sleep in coffins."

"How about being immortal?" Hix removed his ice bag, set it on his knee, decided it was too cold for that, and dropped it to the flowered rug. "In *Count Drago Returns*, one of the big Poverty Row hits of 1938, my vampire was way along in years. Some of my less successful and overly mean-minded colleagues accused me of swiping that notion from *Count Dracula Returns*, but I actually did nearly two hours of research at the West Hollywood branch of the public library."

"The immorality business is true in some cases, isn't it, Miss Hampton?" asked Inza. "That's one of the things that appealed to Nancy Decker, the notion that if she was accepted into the vampire cult she'd eventually attain immortality."

"Dumb idea for an actress," observed Hix, reaching down to retrieve the icebag. "Most actresses only stay on top for ten or twenty years. If you're immortal you're going to be out of work for a hell of a long time. Though you could sure collect a lot of unemployment insurance *and* Social Security."

"Let's be serious again, Hix." Sara, hands clasped on her lap, leaned forward. "Despite the fact that you're just an average B-movie writer, you do seem to have a knack for occult detective work. You handled that werewolf case last year very well and the business with the demon was—"

"I'm an *above* average hack," he corrected. "And how'd you hear about the werewolf? The studio involved hushed that up."

She smiled faintly. "I'm an above average investigator," she answered. "I'd like you to cooperate with me on this vampire case."

When Hix scratched at his frizzy hair, it made

crackling noises. "Sure, kiddo, I can do that," he decided. "But, first, tell us how you happened to be in the vicinity this afternoon?"

"I was following someone."

"The vampire who bears a striking resemblance to Greta Garbo?"

"No," Sara said. "One of the operatives MGM hired to keep an eye on Garbo."

It was raining in Beverly Hills. The sharp night wind drove the rain smack into the windshield of Hix's Plymouth coupe as he drove through the open iron gates of the sprawling mansion that was his destination. His windshield wipers creaked on every backstroke.

The big house at the end of the long white-graveled drive looked as though its architect had been inspired both by the California missions and some French Foreign Legion movies. The slanting roofs were of red tile, the many narrow windows guarded by considerable ornamental iron.

When his headlights swept the wide oak door, Hix saw that two chains of garlic were hanging from it.

He parked the coupe, as instructed, near the five-car garage. Clamping the wide-brimmed fedora he borrowed from the studio costume department—well, swiped actually—he hopped free of the car to run for the house.

Sara Hampton, a flashlight in her hand, opened the door. "You're over half an hour late, Hix," she said, shining the beam of the light on him and the redbrick porch.

"Decided to take a roundabout route," he explained

as he entered. "I had the impression, when I left my palatial homestead, that I was being tailed. Using several of the cunning evasive driving techniques that I first devised for my epic screen mystery *Mr. Woo in Rio* I eluded all pursuit. Far as I can tell."

She invited him into the mansion. "They'll probably pick you up when you leave here."

"Until I met you last night, ma'am, my life was a serene idyll." Hix followed her into the large, beam-ceiling living room. "Marred only by the fact that my salary isn't what an obvious Oscar contender like me should be dragging down."

Sara nodded at a leather-and-redwood chair near the deep, empty fireplace. "I'm afraid you truly walked into something when you decided to visit Inza Cramer yesterday."

He settled into the chair, depositing his damp fedora on a Navajo rug. "I trust I'm here so you can fill me in on what exactly I've stepped in."

The occult investigator sat in a chair matching his and facing it. "Yes, that's why I asked you over."

He gestured at the big, lofty room. "Impressive digs you've got."

"I'm only borrowing the place from a friend while he's back in New York doing a play on Broadway."

"Who?"

"Larz Nordstrom."

"Hey, it's a good thing he's got a job back East," observed Hix. "His movie career has been on the skids since 1933 or thereabouts. It's my theory that the public is only dumb enough to put up with an actor of Nordstrom's limited ability for, oh, five, six years tops."

"He's a very nice man."

"So's my dentist, but I wouldn't fork over two bits to see him in a movie," said Hix. "And he's not handicapped by a Swedish accent."

Sara said, "I telephoned Inza this afternoon and she seems to be faring well."

"Yeah, I dropped in at the restaurant for lunch and she looked only moderately terrified," he said. "I had another nutburger, even though I've decided I loathe the damn things." He exhaled slowly, making a sound that resembled a forlorn sigh. "I guess the vampires have transferred their affections to me."

Standing, Sara crossed to the walnut mantel above the dead fireplace. "It isn't only vampires you have to worry about."

"Don't tell me that collection agency in Santa Monica is after me again?"

She lifted a thick manila folder off the mantelpiece. "Actually, Hix dear, you are now in a position where two separate factions are down on you," Sara told him. "There's the vampire cult, of which Garbo is a member, and there's a very aggressive bunch of Metro Goldwyn Mayer troubleshooters, who take their orders straight from Louis B. Mayer. Let me explain."

"Yeah, kiddo, you'd better."

It was raining in Santa Monica. The heavy drops were falling straight down on the slanted shingle roof of the small stucco house that Hix rented on the outskirts of town, fairly close to the ocean.

Wearing a faded USC sweatshirt, another item on

extended loan from a studio wardrobe department, Levi's, and some strange blood-colored slippers he was pretty certain he'd purchased while on a weekend south of the border in Tijuana, Hix was pacing the threadbare Persian rug in his low-ceilinged, small living room.

As was usual when he was alone late at night, Hix was talking to himself. "There's got to be a socko movie in what Sara told me tonight," he was saying as he paced from his venerable Atwater Kent radio to the leaning tower of back issues of *Variety* and *The Hollywood Reporter* against the peach-colored far wall.

"Have to change the names, make Garbo something other than Swedish, come up with something else to call L. B. Mayer."

He remembered that the banana he'd started eating earlier was now residing on his coffee table. Retrieving it, taking a thoughtful bite, he continued pacing.

"Okay. According to the research Sara's done while working for a large, very clandestine outfit devoted to eliminating vampires, this vampire cult that started at MGM years ago now has about two dozen active members. Apparently Garbo's the only big star involved. I can't sell this story to MGM, but I bet Warner would go for it. Maybe Fox."

He finished the banana, carried the peel out to the kitchen, tossed it in the sink.

"Garbo first got mixed up with this stuff back home in Sweden in the twenties when she was just plain Greta Gustafson. The guy who discovered her, Mauritz Stiller, was more than a director. Turns out, says Sara, he was a cross between Svengali and Dracula. Now, some directors sleep with the girls they discover, but Stiller initiated her into a small, dedicated group of Scandinavian vampires."

Hix returned to the living room, slumped down on the sofa. "Stiller, in my script, I'll make a Hollywood mogul. Garbo I'll change into a virginal dame from Kansas or some place like that."

Bouncing to his feet, he resumed pacing. He frizzy hair swayed as he bounced back and forth. "According to Sara, Garbo was still a practicing vampire when Mayer brought her over here in the mid-twenties. When he got wind of it, he suggested that she cease and desist. Sex and drug scandals were bad enough, he sure didn't want a vampire scandal affecting the box office appeal of his big new star. Stiller he shipped back to Sweden. Could be L. B. had the guy rubbed out over there, but whatever happened, Stiller conked out. Garbo he sent to a very private sanitarium for a spell and they claimed they cured her of her bloodlust."

The rain was hitting heavier and the wind that came up was rattling everything outside that could be rattled.

"Came the talkies and Garbo became bigger than ever, one of Mayer's top actresses. Hotter at the box office than Mickey Rooney is now. Then, a couple of years ago, she apparently got that old feeling and some of the MGM folks who were still tied in with the cult welcomed her back into the fold. Eventually Mayer found out and had a fatherly chat with her. She promised to swear off, but didn't really. To protect his investment, he put some of his best troubleshooting goons to following her. If they couldn't stop her from attacking somebody, they would at least cover up her trail. That guy who bopped me on the sconce at Inza's was making sure I didn't follow her."

He sat again, yawned. "Nancy Decker apparently was getting tired of the cult and immortality lost some of its appeal. She was planning to tell what she knew to folks like Hedda Hopper, Louella Parsons, and Johnny Whistler. The cult took care of her."

He listened to the night rain for a moment, watching the peach-colored ceiling and hoping his roof didn't develop any leaks. "Right now I'm not important enough to either side to get knocked off," he told himself. "So I can concentrate on turning out a treatment that'll sell the idea to a major studio. Been a long time since I've had an A movie. Actually I've never had one." Sitting up straight, he rubbed his hands together. "I'll call it *Vampires Go Hollywood.* Yeah, *Vampires Go Hollywood* with Tyrone Power as the Hix surrogate. I hear the guy's a bit swish, but he does look quite a lot like me. Alice Faye, playing against type, as the virgin from Kansas who becomes a killer vampire. And Betty Grable as whatever I decide to call Nancy Decker. This whole project cries out for Technicolor and the 20th-Century Fox touch. Sure, maybe I can cook up a few catchy tunes and it can be a musical, too. That way I'll earn—"

The phone on the coffee table rang.

"Hello?"

"Hix?"

"None other. And you are?"

"Forget about vampires, buddy," advised a gruff male voice. "They don't exist. And you won't either if you don't knock it off."

"Hey, wait a minute, pal. Nobody threatens Hix and gets away with it."

"I just did." He hung up.

When the full moon rose on Friday, Hix was sitting, very quietly, in a darkened saloon on the MGM backlot. Out above the swinging doors he could see the dark night sky and the advent of the moon.

He was wearing dark slacks and a navy blue pullover. Resting next to the thermos of coffee that sat on the round saloon table was the camera he'd borrowed from a *Los Angeles Times* photographer he knew. The camera was loaded with film that could take night shots without the aid of a flash.

He intended to wait here until about eleven thirty and then sneak over to the Andy Hardy house a quarter of a mile from here.

Absently, he touched at the silver crucifix hanging around his neck. Inza, who'd bought one for him, gave the cross to Hix when he dropped into the restaurant for lunch. For good measure, Hix had picked up several garlic bulbs at the Farmers' Market and was carrying them in his trouser pockets.

Something the blonde waitress had remembered was his reason for being on the MGM lot after hours.

"Nancy Decker told me there was going to be a meeting of the vampire cult tonight, the first night of the full moon," she'd told him.

Looking up from his nutburger, he asked, "Where and when, kid?"

"They meet once a month at different spots around Metro. Tonight at midnight they'll be getting together at the house that's used in those dippy Mickey Rooney movies," Inza told him. "You know where Lewis Stone is his sourpuss father who's always advising—"

"Why'd you just remember this now?"

"I remembered it right after Nancy died. But after being attacked by Garbo and then worrying about you, it slipped my mind until now."

Hix sat up straighter. "This will fit in with my plan."

"Which plan is that?"

"I was going to forget about investigating this bunch further and let Sara handle that end of things," he replied. "Contenting myself with turning what I already know, cleverly disguised, of course, into a socko screenplay with the working title of *Vampires Go Hollywood.* However—"

"Maybe that's what you ought to do."

"However, now that these vampires have threatened me, warned me off . . ." His right hand clenched into a fist. "I'm going to track them down and get absolute proof of what they're up to. Then I'll expose the whole bloodthirsty bunch."

"Gee, Hix, that could get you in a whole lot of trouble."

"What it'll get me, toots, is a whole lot of publicity. Followed by offers from the major studios."

Sighing, Inza reached into a pocket of her blue-and-white waitress uniform. "That reminds me, I bought this for you. The guy at the shop says it's been blessed by a bishop." She handed him a cross on a chain. "If you're planning to go anywhere near vampires, Hix, you really better take this along."

He'd taken off from his far-from-spacious office at Pentagram a little before four to drive over to the Metro Goldwyn Mayer lot in Culver City. He called on a fellow writer, Frank Denby, who was working at MGM on the second draft of a William Powell comedy. After leaving Denby's closer-to-spacious office, Hix cleverly eluded scrutiny and made his way to the backlot to await midnight.

Because the luminous dial on Hix's wristwatch had lost most of its glow, he had to hold it up very close to his face to read the time. When, squinting, he determined that 11:30 P.M. was nigh, he tucked the thermos into the small canvas suitcase he'd brought along, gathered up the borrowed camera, and ventured out of the Wild West saloon.

Easing near to soundlessly through the swinging doors, Hix made his way along the dusty night street. Keeping to the shadows as best he could, the frizzy-haired writer cut along a narrow Cairo street, then skulked past a Paris sidewalk café, annoying into motion a scruffy gray cat who'd been dozing atop one of the round outdoor tables.

Around the next corner stood the two-story house where Andy Hardy and his family resided through a long and successful series of movies.

Hix sneaked forward to station himself behind one of the elm trees that lined the typical small-town street. "Aha," he said quietly to himself after observing the house for a couple of minutes. "Nary a sign of life."

Very cautiously, Hix sprinted across the street, hurried over the lawn, and made his way to the rear of the Hardy home. Tiptoeing up the back stairs, he let himself into the kitchen. After standing in the dark, listening, Hix inhaled slowly and moved deeper into the house. He climbed upstairs and entered what looked to be the bedroom occupied by the teenage Andy.

Peering unobtrusively out the front window, Hix could see the front yard and anyone who approached the house. He crouched, stationing himself where he could use his borrowed camera to catch a photo of everyone who attended tonight's midnight vampire get-together.

Greta Garbo was the fifth to arrive at the midnight meeting. Hix was confident he got two excellent photographs of the actress cautiously approaching the Hardy household. She wore a dark head scarf, a deep blue coat over dark slacks, and a pair of dark glasses.

Of the four vampire cultists who preceded her, Hix recognized three. An assistant art director, a veteran gaffer, and a cute platinum blonde bit player he was pretty sure he'd spent some time with after a beach party at Malibu last summer.

"Her name's Trixie something," he recalled. "Although Trixie isn't a very appropriate name for a vampire. 'Hi, I'm Dracula's daughter. Just call me Trixie.' "

The other cult member, whom Hix didn't recognize, was a plump, very well-groomed fellow in his fifties. Front office type.

After Garbo's advent, no one else showed up. Hix

abandoned the window, tucked the camera into his small canvas suitcase, and extracted a glass tumbler. He'd used this gimmick in two of the Mr. Woo flickers he'd scripted for Star Spangled Studios and one of the Dr. Crimebusters over at Columbia. He'd tested it on his cubicle wall at Star Spangled and clearly overheard the washed-up Broadway playwright they'd hired to do the second rewrite on *The Return of the Man in the Iron Mask* talking to his bookie.

Of course, the walls of the writers' cubicles over there were nearly as thin as they were at Pentagram.

Stretching out on the floor of Andy Hardy's bedroom, Hix rolled up a portion of the rug and placed the upended glass on the bare floor. He put his ear to the base of the tumbler. "Eureka!" he exclaimed internally.

The glass worked for him as a listening device, same as it had for Mr. Woo and Dr. Crimebuster. He could hear what they were saying in the living room below.

". . . getting too dangerous to continue meeting on the lot," the assistant art director was saying.

"Hell of a lot safer than meeting at one of our homes," said somebody with a deep, slightly boozy voice. Must be the front office type. "Though I don't think the studio brass has any idea what's going on, I—"

"You are wrong there, my friend," said Garbo. "I am very much afraid that I have been under surveillance by Mr. Mayer's minions for several weeks now. Therefore, I would like to suggest that—"

"Hey, honey, they're naturally going to keep an

eye on you," put in Trixie in her slightly nasal voice. "Probably has nothing to do with our activities. It's just, you know, that you're one of the most valuable properties the old boy has and—"

"Wrong, sister," said a new voice, one that sounded familiar to Hix. "We know exactly what all you screwballs are up to. As of tonight, sweetheart, it's all over."

"Jesus!" exclaimed the assistant art director.

A chair fell over, Trixie screamed, several more people came heavily into the living room.

The front office guy protested. "What do you mean by intruding on a private—"

"Won't work," said the intruder. "I'm, as you damn well know, Healy, with the Metro security staff. We've had our eyes on you people for quite some time."

"How'd you know where we were going to meet tonight ?"

"Because we're a lot smarter than you."

Hix sat up. "Damn, that's the bozo who telephoned and warned me to lay off," he realized, frowning. "That means it wasn't the vampire gang who were threatening me. It was the MGM goons."

But why? To avoid bad publicity? Because they'd heard of Hix's capabilities as an amateur sleuth and didn't want him nosing around?

Yeah, but it didn't exactly make sense.

Returning his ear to the listening device, he heard, ". . . my boys will escort you to the Administration Building. Miss Garbo, I'm afraid Mr. Mayer is extremely upset by your conduct, by your betrayal of MGM's code of behavior, and he's returned to the studio tonight to have a very serious talk with you in his office and . . ."

Breathing very carefully, Hix again sat up. He concentrated on not making a sound.

"Maybe I ought to hide under Andy's bed until they haul all the vampires away. I don't want to get caught and tabbed a bloodsucker. It wouldn't do my reputation in this town any good."

Hix decided to eavesdrop once more. And this time he heard something even more perplexing.

Sara Hampton was wide awake and fully clothed. "I thought you might be dropping by, Hix," she said as she took two paces back and invited him into the Beverly Hills mansion where she was staying. "Watch out for the luggage."

"Has Larz returned from Broadway?"

The occult investigator shook her head, then gave a sideways nod toward the three matched dark-leather suitcases lined up on the mosaic tiles of the early morning hallway. "They're mine," she told him. "I'm leaving Los Angeles this morning, in a few hours."

His hair fluttered as he held up his hand in a stop-right-there gesture. "Whoa, Sara," he advised. "You'll want to stick around when you hear what I found out whilst snooping around at MGM tonight and—"

"Come on into the living room," she invited. "You were eavesdropping on the vampire gathering?"

"I was, yeah." His sat on one of the redwood-and-leather chairs but didn't exactly settle into it. "I brought a camera and got some great shots of all who attended."

"Have you developed the pictures yet?" She stood in front of the dead fireplace.

"Nope, they're still in the camera out in the car," he answered. "But that's not what I rushed over here in the middle of the night to tell you about, kiddo. First off, Mayer's troubleshooters got a tip and raided the joint. They rounded up four out of the five vampires. I thought Garbo was there, too, but—"

"But it wasn't actually Garbo."

He bounced once in his chair, edged farther forward, and his frizzy hair stood up straighter. "How the hell did you know that, Sara?" he inquired, frowning at her. "Yeah, after they took the others away to God knows where, Garbo and Mayer's head goon stayed behind and had a little chat. But she ain't Garbo. She looks like Garbo, she walks like Garbo, and, when there are people around, she sounds like Garbo. Talking with this guy, though, she has a definite New England accent. She asks him, 'How did I do?' and he shoots back with, 'For only your second outing, Sally, you were swell. You did a terrific job.' " Quite a few new frown lines formed on Hix's high forehead. "We've got to find out who this impersonator is and what's become of the real Garbo."

"Her name is Sally Brinkerhoff, she's thirty-one, and Louis B. Mayer has been grooming her for a possible takeover for close to a year."

Hix touched his fingertips to his cheek. "Plastic surgery, too?"

"Several operations, yes. And they broke one of her legs and reset it so they'd make a better match."

"You knew about this?"

"For the past few days," she said. "Mayer had tried something like this with Jean Harlow a few years back, but she died too soon for him to get a ringer in place."

Standing up, facing her, Hix asked, "Where's Greta Garbo?"

"Dead and buried," Sara told him. "Someplace where no one will ever find her body."

"But that was really Garbo who attacked Inza."

"It was. They took care of her later that same night, when it became evident she wasn't going to be able to stop."

Hix inhaled and exhaled, slowly, twice. Turning his back on the woman, he said, "In my movies it doesn't bother me when a couple of ham actors pretend to drive a stake into the heart of a blonde with a large bosom and a small talent. But, Jesus, to really kill Garbo."

"Nobody—well, very few—will ever know, Hix. They'll see Sally on the screen from now on and never be able to tell the difference."

He spun around, poking his thumb against his chest. "I'll know."

Sighing, Sara said, "There are times when you dispatch a vampire and it's someone you know or admire. That can be very difficult. But, Hix, I'm dedicated—as is the organization that employs me—to destroying these dreadful creatures. And that's what happening in this case."

"You," he realized, "had a hand in this."

"They wanted another expert to sit in, someone to

back up the vampire executioner Mayer hired some months ago."

"Hey, you told me you were opposed to these MGM heavies. You said—"

"A few days ago a representative from Metro Goldwyn Mayer contacted me," Sara explained. "We had a very useful meeting and I decided that we had similar goals. Therefore I agreed to cooperate. Five vampires have been destroyed and that is, to my way of thinking, Hix, a very successful—"

"Five? They killed those four poor saps they rounded up tonight?"

"Either they have or they will shortly. It may take a few days, since the deaths have to be made to look like accidents of one kind or another. These are vicious, unclean people, Hix, people who've killed in order to—"

"C'mon, you shouldn't be that dedicated to your work. You helped them kill Greta Garbo, one of the best damn actresses in this whole phony town. That's—"

"And what were you intending to do? What was the end result of your amateur detective work going to be?"

"For one thing, I wanted to make sure nobody tried to hurt Inza again," he told her. "Once I had the goods on them, I'd give them a chance to take the cure or have the public find out what they were up to."

"Except for Garbo, you don't really care if they are destroyed or not. What you really want is some publicity so you can sell one more B-movie script."

"A-movie, Sara. *Vampires Go Hollywood* is destined to be a big-budget opus. In Technicolor."

Sara said, after glancing at her watch, "Were I you, dear, I'd forget the whole thing," she advised. "Nobody's going to believe you if you try to make any of this public. And if you claim that Greta Garbo is dead, Mayer will just drag out his just about perfect simulacrum. Fact is, early next week MGM is going to announce that Garbo will be starring in a new comedy called *Two-Faced Woman*. So how can she be dead?"

"An apt title. But I've got pictures and, when I show them to some people I know at the *LA Times* and tell them what I know, they'll write it all up. This is front page news, guaranteed to get me a whole stewpot of publicity."

"Unwise." Sara started for the doorway. "But do what you feel you have to."

"Pick up a copy of tomorrow's *Times*," he suggested as he followed her into the hall.

Hix didn't get to the *Los Angeles Times*. Where he ended up about an hour after leaving Sara was the West Hollywood Emergency Hospital.

As he drove his venerable Plymouth down through the dark after-midnight streets of Beverly Hills toward his almost-oceanside place in Santa Monica, Hix was carrying on an intense conversation with himself.

"Even if she was a vampire, even though she took a bite out of Inza," he was saying while descending the winding roads and lanes, "they shouldn't have bumped off Garbo. She was a socko actress and, besides, I doubt this Sally whoever can do that good a job. Sometimes old Mayer does dumbbell stuff. Like this Garbo business, like never hiring me to knock out a script for MGM, like—yoicks!"

A car had snuck up behind his coupe, its high beams suddenly illuminating the interior.

Rolling down his window, Hix thrust out his left hand into the chill night air. Resisting an impulse to give this tailgater the finger, he repeated a pass-me-schmuck gesture several times. "Get off my backside, moron!"

After riding his rear bumper for another full minute or more, the car started to come around on the right of his. But it didn't pass, only stayed beside him on the narrow road. The car was big, long, and deep black.

Hix was unable to see the interior clearly, but the guy at the wheel was heavyset, wearing a dark suit and a wide-brim fedora pulled low.

When the bit black car started to nudge him, Hix yelled, "C'mon, you jerks. Don't you realize what a cliché this is? Husky guys in a black car, for Christ's sake. I used this in *two* Mr. Woos and also in *The Fargo Kid in Manhattan.* Go away."

He intended to say more, but the heavier car rammed into him with such force that he lost control. His coupe went jumping sideways, fishtailed, and then left the road entirely. Rattling vigorously, it went bucking down into the wooded hillside bordering the road, ignoring Hix's fierce struggle with his steering wheel.

The car slammed, hard, smack into a broad and sturdy oak. It knocked Hix out cold.

* * *

Inza set the small basket of fruit on his bedside table. "I hope you like persimmons and quinces, Hix," she said. "That's all they had left at that dinky little market across from the—"

"Makes no diff, kiddo. I'm not in the mood for food." He gestured at his suspended left leg and the heavy plaster cast encasing it. "How many cheesy comedies have you seen wherein some poor sap is trussed up like this? It's often Babe Hardy and he ends up dangling out the window upside—"

"It really is my fault," the blonde said apologetically, sitting somewhat timidly on the straight-backed white chair beside his hospital bed. "If you hadn't tried to help me—"

"No, no, kiddo. This happened because I was about to reveal a sensational story to the whole blinking world," he told her.

"About Greta Garbo being a vampire?"

"Among other things, yeah. And I had the pictures to prove it."

"Well then, Hix, when you're up and around again in a couple of weeks, you can take them to your buddies at the *Times* and—"

"The important word, sweetheart, is *had.* I ain't in possession no more," he said, sighing. "Whilst I was unconscious after my encounter with that tree, somebody swiped my camera and, for good measure, my notebook, from my mangled jalopy. Had I turned that stuff over to the *LA Times,* boy, what publicity I would've gotten. The name Hix would now be a household word in the mansion of every important Hollywood mogul."

"Well, you did get a mention in the trades. *Variety* had a cute little story about your accident in the back pages someplace. The headline was PRINCE OF POVERTY ROW HACKS BREAKS A LEG. Quite a few of my customers at the restaurant commented on it and—"

"And no doubt guffawed at my pain and suffering." As best he could, with the help of the pretty young woman, Hix sat up a bit higher in bed and folded his arms across his narrow chest.

"Speaking of the trades," Inza said, "they all had stories about Greta Garbo today. She's signed with MGM to do a new movie. *Two-Faced Woman* is the title and Melvyn Douglas is co-starring with her again. I don't like him as well as Cary Grant, but he's darn good. Don't you think so?"

"Melvyn Douglas is my dreamboy, yeah," he assured her.

Standing, Inza said, "Got to get back to work." She leaned to kiss him on the cheek, lowering her voice. "If she's making a movie, that may cut down on her other activities, huh?"

Hix said, "It's possible, Toots, that she'll never sink her choppers into another throat."

Even though he changed agents after a couple of months, Hix was unable to get a major studio to so much as look at his proposal for *Vampires Go Hollywood.* His new agent, whose office was several blocks nearer to the offices of the high-powered agencies, told him that Universal had evidenced enthusiasm about having him write it as an Abbott and Costello movie. But that was an out and out lie.

So he revised his pitch and sold the idea to Pentagram. The resultant movie, *The Invisible Vampire Goes Hollywood,* opened in selected fleapits around the nation the same week as the Garbo flicker *Two-Faced Woman.* The MGM film got considerably more attention in the press than his latest. Hell, the latest Ken Maynard cowboy quickie got more attention.

Nobody much liked the Garbo film or her performance therein. The picture was destined to do badly at the box office. One afternoon, still limping slightly, Hix was pacing his cubicle at Pentagram and thinking out loud about his latest B movie, *Mr. Woo Meets the Invisible Vampire,* when a Johnny Whistler fifteen-minute Hollywood gossip broadcast came on the radio.

After reading an open letter to Rita Hayworth and extolling the many virtues of his sponsor's laxative product, Whistler turned his attention to *Two-Faced Woman.* He concluded his critique with, "As you and you and especially you know, the Swedish Sphinx has no greater champion in Movieland than your humble servant. But as I sat in the darkened screening room watching this picture, I said sadly to myself, 'This isn't the Greta Garbo I know and love.' "

Hix clicked off the portable ratio atop his desk. "That's because, Johnny, it isn't Greta Garbo at all."

He wandered over to a spot near the far wall where there might have been a window if Pentagram went in for that sort of thing. Gazing at the blank wall, he said, "Sally Brinkerhoff fooled all those nitwit friends of Garbo's, people like Gaylord Hauser and Salka Viertel. Well, a guy like Gaylord Hauser, who eats yogurt and raw vegetables, it can't be too tough to con him. She fooled the reporters and the crews at MGM . . . but you can't fool the camera. This dame ain't the actress that Garbo was."

Limping back to his desk, he sat down. "If only they hadn't swiped those damn pictures. If only Sara Hampton hadn't sold out to MGM. If only I'd had the nerve to tell the story to the papers without any proof and . . ." Hix snapped his fingers. "Hey, I can use that Sara business in this new script. Sure, a double-crossing dame is always good."

The woman calling herself Greta Garbo never made another movie and eventually ended her association with MGM. There was considerable speculation over the years as to the reason why.

But Hix knew.

Blood of Dreams

by Sarah A. Hoyt

I met him at the base of Impotent Man's Dream—the local name for the soaring, silver rocket commemorating Soviet space exploration. It was a winter night, blind and white as only the Russian winter can be.

Sheets of snow blew past us, clinging to my hair and the scarf I had stylishly draped around my neck. Truth be told, to do this weather justice, I should have worn one of the huge overcoats favored by Russian babushkas. Something huge, shapeless and impermeable, under which I could layer enough clothing not to feel the sting of the cold and the snow.

But I didn't have that option. I was wearing what I'd been advised to wear. A knee-length skirt, tight to the knee and slit at the back. Nylons. A fitted blouse and jacket. I had at least managed to wear the scarf, even if it was fuzzy and multicolored, and a hat, even if it was little more than an amusing scrap of fabric perched on my head at an interesting angle. My chestnut curls I left hanging free down my back and they were slowly getting crusted with snowflakes. It was all I could do not to allow my teeth to chatter.

The man I'd come across the Atlantic to meet was similarly ill-attired for the weather, but it didn't seem to disturb him. He wore his customary charcoal gray suit, and he walked in the slow, measured step of someone who has all the time in the world, which I suppose he did.

As he got closer, he smiled at me, a smile that barely uncovered the very tip of his fangs. The rest of him looked exactly as it had in countless statues, in numerous paintings, and, of course, on the corpse beneath glass in the mausoleum on Red Square. A bald head surrounded by wispy dark hair slopped down to a neat, oval face with large, expressive eyes and a neat mustache crowning small lips. A little beard completed the whole.

He looked to be in his forties and no one who didn't know it would have guessed he was dead, much less that he was Vladimir Ilych Lenin, the founder of Russian communism.

He walked toward me, with the unnerving little smile, and I wondered if he would try to attack. To be sure, I didn't even know what to expect. What I'd learned about this particular man was only that he'd become a vampire early in his career and that he remained alive. The mausoleum and the preserved body were a ruse. The book by his embalmers was only the latest and most complete scrap of fraud.

Other than that, I knew practically nothing about

vampirism. Oh, I knew that it was caused by a virus in the saliva of the vampire. Which is why the only victims allowed to live changed into vampires themselves. And that, after a period in which the bearer became ever more charismatic, a period sometimes as long as twenty years, in which the vampire could gain control of a crowd or a society, it led to undying death. The vampire must avoid light, sleep during the day, and remain active only during nighttime.

This might seem like an awful lot of knowledge, but it wasn't. The most important piece was missing—how strong was the vampire? And how great his need for blood?

I steeled myself to his approach and did my best to return his smile with a small one of my own, endeavoring to look confident and prepared. He would be less likely to try to eliminate me if he thought I had a plan that would either prevent it or avenge me. Something I had learned as a journalist, working in the most troubled spots of the world from Rwanda to Sudan to the wastelands of Afghanistan, was that if you appeared to be in control the enemy was less likely to attack.

An expression of amusement crossed his gaze and I thought he must have seen a lot of people trying to bluff it. But it didn't matter. He didn't rush for me. Instead, he stopped in front of me and inspected me carefully, from the tip of my ridiculously high-heeled boots—at least I'd insisted on boots—to my snow-flecked hair and the little twist of red fabric perched on top of it.

He stretched his hand. "Call me Lenin," he said.

It would, of course, have been safer not to touch him at all. But then I might as well admit my fear.

So I stretched my hand and gave him my name, in a voice that came out unexpectedly fluted and high.

"You wished to speak to me?" he said.

I nodded. I'd left the little rolled up note beneath the edge of his glass sarcophagus, where he was likely to find it upon opening the lid and reaching out, early in the evening. It said I knew what he was and that I wished to speak to him. In a way it was a bit of blackmail, and in a way, like all blackmailers, I was scared. I didn't want to push my luck and wasn't sure where the boundary lay between safe pressure and the kind that would backfire. "Yes," I said. "But not here."

And I headed through the blinding snow to the side street where I'd parked my little rental car. Confident that he would follow me. Or at least wishing to appear so.

I did not hear his steps behind me, but when I opened the passenger door of my car, he was there, sliding in.

A small, confined space might seem a bad choice of place to be alone with a vampire. But I assumed he'd find it uncomfortable to attack me while I was driving and perhaps get ripped apart. My informer had told me that they didn't like getting severely wounded, that it could take them months to heal. And that Lenin, on display as he was, sleeping in his glass coffin all day, could not afford it.

I'd believe that. I'd believed so much already and risked so much on this quest. I drove through the snow in which my car headlights made no more than a faint web of light a few inches wide. But I remembered the streets—having learned them by heart—and the turns and presently fetched us up in front of the modest hotel I'd chosen.

We got out in front of reception, where light shone brightly through the plate glass window. The hotel was one of the few that had someone at the reception desk at all hours, as well as a valet to park the cars and a couple of burly guards to keep the workers safe through the night. Two were alert and paying attention, the others within reach of a frantic scream.

Lenin either acknowledged the futility of attacking me here, or his curiosity in knowing how I'd learned of him was greater than his need to obliterate the threat. He followed me up the stairs, three flights to my room. For obvious reasons I didn't care to take the elevator.

When we got into the room, he looked around and sniffed, as if detecting some sort of odor. Then he smiled fully at me, showing me his fangs. "There is no one in the rooms on either side or above," he said, with a sort of gleeful malice. "Even if you have the room bugged or if you are bugged, no one will get here in time to save your life."

The room, though opulent by old Russian standards, was spare by either Western standards or the standards of new Russian luxury. It had a single bed, a desk and straight-backed chair, and an armchair in the corner by the window, where the open curtains showed the unending panorama of swirling snow. A mirror on the back of the shutting door reflected the window and the snow.

It felt cold and lonely, as if I were the last woman alive at the end of the universe. I wondered if he was projecting that feeling. I knew vampires could influence people, but how? Could he reach into my feelings and make me feel things?

I smiled at him, feeling cold sweat trickle down the back of my neck. What he said wasn't true, not exactly, but could someone get to the room in time to save my life if he attacked? Somehow I doubted it. "How do you know there is no one nearby?" I asked instead, affably.

"We can feel the life nearby," he said. "We can hear the heartbeats. The nearest ones are downstairs." He grinned again. "This means you are at my mercy. How did you hear of me? How did you find out the truth about me?"

"Oh, don't be foolish," I said, and smiled in turn, with confidence I didn't feel. "If I told you that, what reason would you have for keeping me alive?"

"What reason do I have in any case?" he asked. "You're nothing but a mortal who somehow stumbled onto my true nature. Why would anyone believe you? And if I kill you, who would care?"

There was something to his features, a sharpness, as if wolf-hunger were shaping his thoughts and moving him toward a goal I would not like. He could smell my blood. It was a disquieting thought. It took all my well-practiced willpower to put a smile on my lips. "Reason enough. You're not as secure as you might think you are, in your glass coffin. There is talk of burying you."

"There was talk of burying me almost twenty years ago," Lenin said. "It hasn't happened yet. I still have loyal followers. People who would never allow the symbol of the revolution to be swept away or defiled."

"They let your statues be cut down," I reminded him.

He blinked, as if hearing of this for the first time, and took a deep breath and shrugged. "What does it matter?" he asked. "Statues are just statues. My body, they won't touch. For too many years worshiping me was the only religion allowed." He put his hands in the pockets of his suit pants, making them bulge in a way they weren't designed for, and bunching the coat above them. He took a step nearer me. "They worship me. They won't let me be buried."

I shrugged. "Well, perhaps not, but recently they have reburied Anton Dinikin with all honors, have they not? And did he not fight against the Red Army?"

He stopped and chewed on his mustache. Then, taking his hands from his pockets, he opened his arms in a show of helplessness, a show of willingness to listen. "Very well," he said, and backed up to sit on the armchair. He crossed his legs, one over the other, with the accustomed ease of the diplomat who has listened to every story and sat, smiling, through the longest speech. Not that he was a diplomat, of course. But he had pretended to be one at times, and clearly the training held. "Very well," he said again. "It is possible my nightly excursions through the city have missed something, if not of the state of the city, at least of the state of the world. So tell me, how do you propose to make me more secure?"

He came to the point too fast. I expected to have

more time to work on him with those womanly charms that, I'd been assured, worked on vampires as well as on living men.

I gained time, standing in front of my mirror shaking out my curls. "You need another life," I said. "if this one should come to an end. I could get you sequestered from your coffin and . . ."

He shook his head. I saw it in the mirror and realized that at least one myth had been wrong.

"If they should decide to bury me, I'm sure they would do the thing thoroughly, making sure that I was in the coffin first. Perhaps even making sure I was staked first. There are people in the hierarchy who know the truth. Some that have to, of course, like the people who pretend to be responsible for preserving my body. They are well compensated and some . . ." He grinned, fangs gleaming. "Are allowed to write books about it and profit by them. But there are other people who know, and some of them might still be alive and in power." He looked scared suddenly—or not scared so much as though he remembered something that scared him, making his eyes widen and his mouth open a little in an expression that was half shock and half fear. "They staked Stalin, you know? Staked him and buried him."

I remembered not to show surprise. Or rather, I remembered not to act as if this were old news, and I were surprised he knew it. Instead, I trembled a little and my eyes widened and I said, "Stalin? He was one of you?"

He chuckled, delighted, as if he were a child who had bested me in a game. "Oh, you don't know everything, Miss American reporter, do you now?"

I shrugged. "Stalin is not being discussed now. He seems like old history. Though he might have," I said, judging it the time to drive in a little wedge of jealousy, "had more influence on communism than you did."

Lenin didn't take the bait. He shrugged. "Not on communism," he said. "On the regime, on the government of the Soviet republic, but not on communism. Communism would never have existed anywhere, it would have died a ghost without me. I took the poor clay of the March revolution and issued my April Theses and I set everything in motion. Everything to make the dream of communism come true. The dream of a perfect state where there would be no inequality and no injustice." He paused and frowned. "Only it all seems to have been too much like a dream that lasts only a short time and from which you wake to find the real world intruding upon your thoughts." He rubbed the middle of his forehead with two fingers. "It wasn't supposed to be this way. I didn't count on the way people would refuse to cooperate, refuse to be perfected. Or perhaps it was Stalin. He never had any finesse. But at least . . . he died for his trouble. Truly died. Staked and buried in the Kremlin." He looked up and tilted his head at me.

Was it my imagination that his fangs were growing longer? Probably. Only the same little bit of them protruded beneath the lips as he smiled, a slow, lazy smile. "And now we come to you. You have somehow found my secret. And you want to help me."

"Why are you in the glass coffin at all?" I asked,

trying not to think that I'd come into this willingly. That I'd willingly set my neck within reach of his fangs. "And why did you make Stalin a vampire and your successor, if you did not truly wish it?"

His eyes flashed with anger. He showed his teeth in a snarl. For a moment I thought he'd spring at me. But instead he punched the arm of his chair, hard. "He tricked me. The Georgian swine tricked me. He came into my room, when I was . . . When I was dying and becoming . . . as I am now. He so maddened me. He told me that as soon as I was in his power he'd stake me. And he'd have Trotsky killed. I was . . ." He cleared his throat and seemed to recover a little self-control. "I was ill. I could not prevent my anger from rising. I sprang for his neck." He paused and took a deep breath and I felt he was controlling an anger that would have, otherwise, taken him over the edge and into the abyss. "But he'd calculated it and it was near dawn when, as my body changed, I'd started to fall into the sleep of death. Though not a full vampire yet, not yet shunning the sun, I was already controlled by the cycle of the day." Again the open arms and open hands, in a show of helplessness. "I didn't drain him, as I meant to. And when I came to, later, he was already on the way to becoming one like me. I couldn't drain him. And when I became fully dead, a full vampire, he had me placed in the mausoleum as a way of having me watched. Of knowing where I was. He didn't dare stake me then, not yet, as he was not sure whether this would mean I'd turn into ashes and people would wonder where my body had gone.

But he had me on display. Where I dare not move night or day, I dare not leave the mausoleum because of that damned honor guard."

He got up and went to the window and looked down at Moscow. "It all looks so different now. I really believed it was true, you know—Marxism. I believed that the rich and the poor would grow farther and farther apart in their modes of life and that a proletarian revolution would result. I was only trying to accelerate things, trying to bring about the brighter day. I thought it was inevitable and it would cause a bloodbath whenever it happened. I was only trying to make it happen faster. For Sasha, you know. My brother Alexander. He rebelled against the tsar and he was hanged." He sighed. "And now Sasha is dead, and I'm here, but other than that . . . Was everything I did no more than a passing diversion in the course of history? Is man never to live in a truly equal society?"

"You believed so much," I said, judging the time to be right. I could hear rustling in the room next door and I judged that the person waiting there was growing impatient. If I did not move fast, he would let Lenin know of his presence. He would reveal himself. Try to take things by force. As he had suggested at first. "That you found out about the vampire legend, in Siberia. You found that there were indeed vampires, creatures who lived forever and who fed on human blood. But they didn't die immediately. No. Vampirism was like an illness, and in the incubation period, leading up to the death, the vampire became . . . powerful. Capable of influencing individuals and groups. You were a man of thought, Vladimir Ilyich Ulianov. But you were not a leader. You were one of these men more comfortable in the realm of words and thoughts than in dealing with real people. You knew if you became a vampire—or a vampire larvae—you could do it. So you sought out an old woman, in the freezing vastness of Siberia, who gave you the ashes of a vampire, dissolved in blood, to drink."

He chuckled, more surprised than amused. "Blood. I purchased my dreams in blood, it's true. The blood I drank, the blood I had to spill. And my blood, the blood of my family. Because I am a vampire, I never had children. I would have liked to have had children with Nadezhda. Now Nadezhda is gone and my communist state is gone and you say they will soon bury me. Even if I remain alive beneath the dirt, or if I dig myself out, what good is there in it? What good will my life have been?"

I turned around and grinned at him. "You can make me into a vampire," I said. "Into one like you. And then I'll have the strength and the charisma to get into politics in America. To get to the top."

He grinned in turn. "Is that all this is?" he asked. "You want the power? You know better. I gave Stalin the power and look at what he did. He made an unsteady dream even shakier. I would never—"

"Listen, it's not just the power for power's sake," I said. "I too have a dream. We know more about how the world works now. About we know how to control things with money. You ignored human nature, but people will do a lot for money. We can manipulate international markets. We can equalize classes, distribute wealth and knowledge. We can make the world a better place. If I get to the top of the most powerful nation in the world, I can do all that."

For just a moment, he grinned at me, then he sighed. "All those dreams cost in blood."

"My blood," I said, tossing my head aside to reveal my pale neck. "And you can have it. Just not all of it."

"How did you find out?" he asked again. "About me?" Somehow he'd gotten out of his chair and he was right next to me.

I shrugged. "Old letters. Old papers. But I've told people. People would know."

He smiled, fangs gleaming. "No one would believe you."

Close up, he smelled of mothballs and old wool. His hands reached for my arms, gripped them with the strength of vises. "No one would believe you," he said.

The bite on my neck hurt very little. Like a pinprick or an injection. I wondered if vampires, like certain poisonous animals, had an anesthetic in their fangs that dulled the pain. And then the world grew dim. And I realized he was not going to stop. That he was going to drain me completely, not just infect me with the virus that caused vampirism. That I would die here.

The door shook, rattled, and opened. "Let her go," a voice with a strong Georgian accent said.

He dropped me. "You?" he said.

I thought at least it was true that vampires had good manners. They could not talk with their mouth full. I tried to giggle, but I couldn't even stand, and

I fell to the floor, in time to look up and see Joseph Stalin stepping between myself and Lenin.

Stalin was attired as I'd always seen him attired in the year and a half I'd known him—after he'd chosen me and tracked me down through a web of shared acquaintances and contacts. He wore Armani, well cut and better made. "Me," he said. "Me, the Georgian swine." His tone of voice implied there would be vengeance taken on the one that had uttered those words. "Me. Why would you think they staked me before they buried me in the Kremlin?"

"Krushchev," Lenin said, wiping away from the corner of his mouth a trickle of my blood. "He would never have dared to denounce you to reveal the stories of oppression under you, even to a limited number of people, unless he knew you could no longer get at him."

Stalin laughed. "Krushchev. Dear Nikita knew nothing of why I'd had you—or myself—'embalmed.' He put me in the mausoleum, beside you, because the crowd demanded it and not because he realized he needed to keep an eye on me. And he had me buried because he found me embarrassing." He smiled, displaying the pockmarks that disfigured him ever since he'd had smallpox as a child. "I wasn't as pretty a corpse as you. But I dug myself out, little by little. As long as it took, I dug myself out. And I spoke a word in Brezhnev's ear, when he became secretary general. And that was the end of the nonsense. It was only when I had found my way through the Russian . . . black market network, and when I found communism a hampering of my ability to make money and increase my power that I spoke words in the right ears and allowed Gorbachev and his glasnost to flourish." He waved his hands in a self-deprecating manner. "You have before you one of the most successful businessmen in Russia. Oh, no one you'd hear about in the papers. But all the ones you do hear about owe me money."

"I should kill you," Lenin said, somberly.

"You should," Stalin said. "You should have years ago. But you didn't. And now you can't kill me. Or her. Because I might not have as much charisma or strength as you have. But I have quite enough to ensure you don't kill her. You don't want to fight me, Lenin. Your corpse might be disfigured. People might find out."

For a moment, Lenin hesitated. But then he turned and made for the door.

As Stalin bent to offer me his hand, I could hear Lenin slapping frantically at the button.

I felt woozy and weak and too close to death for my taste. That death that I'd arranged to meet—through being infected with a powerful vampire's blood—much sooner than would otherwise have happened.

"It will all be worth it, you'll see," Stalin said. "The part of the virus that induces charisma seems to lose force with each generation. I've infected people—a young student on a tour of Russia once, for instance. And though it still can make someone president of America, it doesn't seem to be as intense. They don't seem to command the following they should. The following that made Lenin and I living gods. You'll be as powerful as I am, you'll see. You'll maneuver to lead the West. I'm very close to owning the East. Together, we will rule the world."

I nodded, but my neck hurt, and I felt very far from powerful as I leaned on his stocky body that smelled only of very expensive cologne. "And then I'll die."

He grinned at me, his fangs stubby amid his large, broad teeth. "Don't let that worry you, my dear. Our kind always rise."

A Princess of Spain

by Carrie Vaughn

November 14, 1501, Baynard's Castle

Catherine of Aragon, sixteen years old, danced a pavan in the Spanish style before the royal court of England. Lutes, horns, and tabors played a slow, stately tempo to which she stepped in time. The ladies of her court, who had traveled with her from Spain, danced with her, treading circles around one another—floating, graceful, without a wasted movement. Her body must have seemed like air, drifting with the heavy gown of velvet and gold. She did not even tip her head, framed within its gem-encrusted hood. She was a piece of artwork, a prize. A prize for the usurper of the English throne, so that his son's succession would not be questioned. King Henry had the backing of Spain now.

Henry VII watched with a quiet, smug smile on his creased face. Elizabeth of York, his wife, sat nearby, more demonstrative in her pride, smiling and laughing. At a nearby table sat their two sons and two daughters—an impressive household. All made legitimate by Catherine's presence here, for she had been sent by Spain to marry the eldest son: Arthur, Prince of Wales, heir to the throne, thin and pale at fifteen years old.

But all these English were pale, past the point of fair and well toward ill, for their skies were always laden with clouds. Arthur slouched in his chair and occasionally coughed into his sleeve. He had declined to dance with her, claiming that he preferred to gaze upon her beauty while he may, before he claimed it later that evening.

Catherine's heart ached, torn between anticipation and foreboding. But she must dance her best, as befitted an infanta of Spain. "You must show the English what we Spanish are—superior," her mother, Reina Isabella, told her before Catherine departed. She would most likely never see her parents again.

Arthur did not look at her. Catherine saw his gaze turn to the side of the hall, where one of the foreign envoys sat at table. There, a woman gazed back at the prince. She was fair-skinned, with dark eyes and a lock of dark, curling hair hanging outside her hood. Her high-necked gown was elegant without being ostentatious, both modest and fashionable, calculated to not upstage the prince and princess on their wedding day. But it was she who drew the prince's eye.

Catherine saw this; long practice kept her steps in time until the music finished at last.

The musicians struck up a livelier tune, and Prince Henry, the king's younger son, grabbed his sister Margaret's arm and pulled her to the middle of the hall, laughing. All of ten years old, he showed the promise of cutting a fine figure when he came of age—strong-limbed, lanky, with a head of unruly, ruddy hair. Already he was as tall as any of his siblings, including his elder brother Arthur. At this rate he would become a giant of a man. Word at court said he loved hunting, fighting, dancing, learning—all the pursuits worthy of any prince of Europe. But at this moment he was a boy.

He said something—Catherine had only a few words of English, and did not understand. A moment later he pulled off his fine court coat, leaving only his bare shirt. The room was hot with torches and bodies. He must have been stifling in the finely wrought garment. Because he was a boy the court thought the gesture amusing rather than immodest; everyone smiled indulgently.

Catherine took her seat again, the place of honor at the king's right hand. She gazed, though, at Arthur. She did not even know him. She did not know if she wanted to. Tonight would be better. Tonight, all would be well.

He continued staring at the foreign woman.

The evening drew on, and soon the momentous occasion would be upon them: Arthur and Catherine would be put to bed to consummate their marriage. To seal the alliance between England and Spain with their bodies. Her ladies fluttered, readying to spirit her off to her chambers to prepare her.

In the confusion, the lanky figure of a very tall boy slipped beside her. The young prince, Henry.

He smiled at her, like a child would, earnestly wanting to be friends.

"You've seen it too," he said in Latin. She could understand him. "My brother, staring at that woman."

"*Sí.* Yes. Do you know her?"

"She's from the Low Countries," he said. "Or so it's put out at court, though it's also well known that she speaks French with no accent. She's a lady-in-waiting to the daughter of the Dutch ambassador. But the daughter kept to her apartments tonight, and the lady isn't with her, which seems strange, doesn't it?"

"But she must have some reason to be here." And that reason might very well be the young groom who could not take his gaze from her.

"Certainly. Perhaps I'll order someone to spy on her." Henry's eyes gleamed.

Catherine pressed her lips together but didn't manage a smile. "It is no matter. A passing fancy. It will mean nothing tomorrow."

Arthur was *her* husband. Tonight would make that a fact and not simply a legality. With a sudden burning in her gut, she longed for that moment.

"*In nomine Patris, Filii, et Spiritus Sancti.*"

The bishop sprinkled holy water over the bed where Catherine and Arthur were tucked, dressed in costly nightclothes, put to bed in a most formal manner for their wedding night, so that all might know that the marriage was made complete. At last, the witnesses left them, and for the first time, Catherine was alone with her husband.

All she could do was stare at him, his white face and lank ruddy hair, as her heart raced in her chest.

He stared back until she felt she should say something, but her voice faltered. Words failed, when she couldn't decide whether to speak French, Latin, or attempt a phrase in her still halting English. *Why could he not understand Spanish?*

"You are quite pretty," he said in Latin, and leaned forward on shaking arms to kiss her on the lips.

She flushed with relief. Perhaps all would be well. He was her husband, she was his wife. She even *felt* married, lying here with him. Warm from her scalp to her toes—pleasant, illicit, yet sanctioned by God and Church. This was her wedding night, a most glorious night—

Before she could kiss him back, before she could hold him as her body told her to do, he pulled away. Unbidden, her arm rose to reach for him. Quickly, she drew it back and folded her hands on her lap. Must she maintain her princess' decorum, even here?

Arthur coughed. He bent double with coughing, putting his fist to his mouth. His thin body shook.

She left the bed and retrieved a goblet of wine from the table. Returning, she sat beside him and touched his hand, urging him to take a drink. His skin was cold, damp as the English winter she'd found herself in.

"Por Dios," she whispered. What had God brought her to? She said in Latin, "I'll send for a physician."

Arthur shook his head. "It is nothing. It will pass. It always does." He took a drink of wine, swallowing loudly, as if his throat were closing.

But he had been this pale and sickly every time she'd seen him. This would not pass.

If they could have a child, if he would live long enough for them to have a child, a son, a new heir, her place in this country would be assured.

The wine would revive him. She touched his cheek. He looked up. She hoped to see some fire in his eyes, some desire there to match her own. She hoped he would touch her back. But she only saw exhaustion from the day's activities. He was a child on the verge of sleep.

She was a princess of Spain, not made for seduction.

He gave the goblet back to her. With a sigh, he settled back against the pillows. By his next breath, he was asleep.

Catherine set the goblet on the table. The room was chilled. Every room in this country was chilled. Yet at this moment, while her skin burned, the cool tiles of the floor felt good against her bare feet.

She knelt by the bed, clasped her hands tightly together, and prayed.

December 15, 1501, Richmond

Another feast lay spread before her. King Henry displayed his wealth in calculated presentations of food, music, entertainment. However much the politics and finances of his realm were strained, he would give no appearance other than that of a successful, stable monarch.

Catherine did not dance, though the musicians played a pavan. She sat at the table, beside her husband, watching. Husband in name only. He had not once come to her chamber. He had not once summoned her to his. But appearances must be maintained.

He slouched in his chair, leaning on one carved wooden arm, clutching a goblet in both hands. He had grown even more wan, even more sickly, if possible. Did no one else see it?

She touched the arm of his chair. "My husband, have you eaten enough? Should I call for more food?"

He shook his head and waved her off. It was not natural, to treat one's wife so. He was in danger of failing his duty as a prince and as a Christian husband.

But what could she do? A princess was meant to serve her husband, not command or judge him.

"Your husband will take mistresses," her mother told her, in her final instructions before Catherine set sail. She told her that it was the way of things and she could not fight it. But Isabella also said that her husband would do his duty toward her, so that she might do *her* duty and bear him many children.

Her duty was turning to dust in her hands, through no fault of her own.

In the tiled space in the center of the hall, the young Prince Henry danced with the strange foreign woman. Catherine had no evidence that this woman was her husband's mistress except for the way Arthur watched her, desperately, with too-bright eyes.

The woman danced gracefully. She must have been a dozen years older than her partner, but she tolerated him with an air of amusement, wearing a thin and placid smile, as though sitting for a portrait.

Henry was a lively enough partner that he made every step a joy. His father was training him for the clergy, it was said. He might be the greatest bishop in England someday—the crown's voice in the Church.

Catherine begged leave to retire early, before the music and dancing had finished. She claimed fatigue and a sensitive stomach. People nodded knowingly at the information and offered each other winks. They thought she was with child, as any young bride ought to be.

But she wasn't. Never would be, if things kept on in this manner.

It was difficult to spy in the king's house unless one had command of the guards and could order them to stay, or leave, or watch. She did not have command of anything except her own household, which the English court treated as the foreigners they were. Really, though, her duenna and stewards commanded her household—Catherine was too young for it, they said. Her parents had sent able guardians to look after her.

Nevertheless, against all her instincts, after dark—well after the candles and lanterns had been snuffed—Catherine donned a black traveling cloak over her shift and set out, stepping quietly past her ladies-in-waiting who slept in the outer chamber. Very quietly she opened the heavy door, giving herself barely enough space to slip through. The iron hinges squeaked, but only once, softly, like a woman sighing in her sleep.

Two more chambers, sitting rooms, lay between her and Arthur. The rooms were dark, chill. Thick windows let in very little of the faint moonlight. Her slippered feet made no sound on the wood floors. She kept to the paneled walls and felt her way around, step by careful step.

Guards walked their rounds. They passed from room to room, pikes resting on their shoulders. England had finished its wars of succession relatively recently; for the royal family, there was always danger.

If she were very quiet, and moved very carefully, they would not see her. She hoped. If they found her, most likely nothing would happen to her, but she didn't want to have to explain herself. This was very improper for a woman of her rank. She should go back to her own room and pray to God to make this right.

Her knees were worn out with praying.

She listened for booted footsteps and the rattle of armor. Heard nothing.

She reached the chamber outside Arthur's bedroom. A light shone under the door, faint, buttery—candlelight. A step away from the door she paused, listening. What did she think she might hear? Conversation? Laughter? Deep sighs? She had no idea.

She touched the door. Surely it would be locked. It would be a relief to have to walk away, still ignorant. She touched the latch—

It wasn't locked.

Softly, she pushed open the door and looked in.

Looking like an ill child far younger than his years, Arthur lay propped up in bed, limp, his eyes half-closed, senseless. Beside him crouched the foreign woman, fully clothed, her hands on his shoulders, clutching his linen nightclothes. Her mouth was open, and her teeth shone dark with blood. A gash on Arthur's neck bled.

"You're killing him!" Catherine cried. She stood, too shocked to scream—she ought to scream, to call for the guards. Even if they could not understand her Spanish, they would come at the sound of panic.

In a moment, a scant heartbeat, the foreign woman appeared before Catherine. She might as well have flown; the princess didn't see her move. This was some dream, some vision. Some devil had crept into her mind.

The woman pressed her to the wall, closing Catherine's mouth with one hand. Catherine kicked and writhed, trying to break away, but the woman was strong. Fantastically strong. Catherine swatted at her, pulled at a strand of her dark hair which had come loose from her hood. She might as well have been a fly in the woman's grasp. With her free hand she grabbed Catherine's wrists and held her arms still.

Then she caught Catherine's gaze.

Her eyes were blue, the dark, clear blue of the twilight sky over Spain.

"I am not killing him. Be silent, say nothing of what you have seen, and you will keep your husband." Her voice was subdued, but clear. Later, Catherine could not recall what language she had spoken.

Catherine nearly laughed. What husband? She might as well have chosen the convent. But she couldn't speak, couldn't move.

The woman's touch was cold. The fingers curled over Catherine's face felt like marble.

"You are so young to be in this position. Poor girl."

The woman smiled, kindly it seemed. For a moment, Catherine wanted to cling to her, to spill all her worries before this woman—she seemed to understand.

Then she said, "Sleep. You've had a dream. Go back to sleep."

Catherine's vision faded. She struggled again, tried to keep the woman's face in her sight, but she felt herself falling. Then, nothing.

She awoke on the floor. She had fainted and lay curled at the foot of her own bed, wrapped in her cloak. Pale morning light shone through the window. It was a cold light, full of winter.

She tried to recall last night—she had left her bed, obviously. But for what reason? If she'd wanted wine she could have called for one of her ladies.

Her ladies would be mortified to find her like this. They would think her ill, keep her to bed, and send for physicians. Catherine quickly stood, collected herself, arranged her shift and untangled her hair. She was a princess. She ought to behave like one, despite her strange dreams of women with rich blue eyes.

An ache in her belly made her pause. It was not like her to be so indecorous as to leave her bed before morning. As she smoothed the wrinkles from her dressing gown, her fingers tickled. She raised her hand, looked at it.

A few silken black fibers—long, shining, so thin they were almost invisible—clung to her skin. Hair—but how had it come here? Her own hair was like honey, Arthur's was colored amber—

She had seen a dark-haired woman with Arthur.

It was not a dream. The memory of what she had seen had not faded after all.

That day, Catherine and Arthur attended Mass together. She studied him so intently that he raised his brow at her, inquiring. She couldn't explain. He wore a high-necked doublet. She couldn't see his neck to tell if he had a wound there. Perhaps he did, perhaps not. He made no mention of what had happened last night, made no recognition that he had even seen her. Could he not remember?

Say nothing of what you have seen, and you will keep your husband. Catherine dared not speak at all. She would be called mad.

This country was cursed, overrun with rain and plague. This king was cursed, haunted by those who had died so he might have his crown, and so was his heir. Catherine could tell her parents, but what would that accomplish? She was not here for herself, but for the alliance between their kingdoms.

She prayed while the priest chanted. His words were Latin, which was familiar and comforting. The Church was constant. In that she could take comfort. Perhaps if she confessed, told her priest what she had seen, he would have counsel. Perhaps he could say what demon this was that was taking Arthur.

A slip of paper, very small, as if it had been torn from the margin of a letter, fell out of her prayer book. She glanced quickly around—no one had seen it. Her ladies either stared ahead at the altar or bowed over their clasped hands. She was kneeling; the paper had landed on the velvet folds of her skirt. She picked it up.

Convene me horto. Henricus, written in a boy's careful hand. Meet me in the garden.

Catherine crumpled the paper and tucked it in her sleeve. She'd burn it later.

She told her ladies she wished to walk in the air, to stretch her legs after the long Mass. They accompanied her—she could not go anywhere without them—but she was able to find a place where she might sit a little way off. Henry would have to find her then.

Here she was, in this country only two months and already playing at spying.

Gravel paths wound around the lawn outside Richmond, the king's favorite palace. Never had Catherine seen grass of such jewel-like green. Even in winter, the lawn stayed green. The dampness made it thrive. Her mother-in-law Elizabeth assured her that in the summer, flowers grew in glorious tangles. Around back, boxes outside the kitchens held forests of herbs. England was fertile, the queen said knowingly.

Catherine and her ladies walked to where the path turned around a hedge. Some stone benches offered a place to rest.

"Doña Elvira, you and the ladies sit here. I wish to walk on a little. Do not worry, I will call if I need you." The concerned expression on her duenna's face was not appeased, but Catherine was resolute.

Doña Elvira sat and directed the others to do likewise.

Catherine strolled on, carefully, slowly, not rushing. Around the shrubs and out of sight from her ladies, Henry arrived, stepping out from behind the other end of the edge.

"Buenos días, hermana."

She smiled in spite of herself. "You learn my language."

Henry blushed and looked at his feet. "Only a little. Hello and thank you and the like."

"Still, *gracias*. For the little."

"I have learned something of the foreign woman. I told the guards to watch her and listen."

"We should tell your father. It is not for us to command the guards—"

"She is not from the Low Countries. Her name is Angeline. She is French, which means she is a spy," he said.

Catherine wasn't sure that one so naturally followed the other. It was too simple an explanation. The alliance between England and Spain presented far too strong an enemy for France. Of course they would send spies. But that was no spy she'd seen with Arthur.

She shook her head. "She is more than that."

"She hopes to break the alliance between England and Spain by distracting my brother. If you have no children, the succession will pass to another."

"To you and your children, yes? And perhaps a French queen for England, if they find one for you to marry?"

He pursed boyish lips. "I am Duke of York. Why would I want to be king?"

But there was a light in his eyes, intelligent, glittering. He would not shy away from being king, if, God forbid, events came to that.

He said, "There is more. I touched her hand when we danced. It was cold. Colder than stone. Colder than anything."

Catherine paced, just a little circle beside her brother-in-law. She ought to tell a priest. But he knew. So she told him.

"I have been spying as well," she said. "I went to Arthur's chamber last night. If she is his mistress—I had to see. I had to know."

"What did you see? *Is* she his mistress?"

Catherine wrung her hands. She did not have the words for this in any language. "I do not know. She was there, yes. But Arthur was senseless. It was as if she had put a spell on him."

Eagerly, Henry said, "Then she is a witch?"

Catherine's throat ached, but she would not cry. "I do not know. I do not know of such things. She said strange things to me, that I must not interfere if I wish to keep Arthur alive. She . . . she cast a spell on me, I think. I fainted, then I awoke in my chamber—"

Henry considered thoughtfully, a serious expression that looked almost amusing on the face of a boy. "So. A demon is trying to sink its claws into the throne of England through its heir. Perhaps it will possess him. Or devour him. We must kill it, of course."

"We must tell a priest!" Catherine said, pleading. "We must tell the archbishop!"

"If we did, would they believe us? I a boy and you a foreigner? They'll say we are mad, or playing at games."

She couldn't argue because she'd thought the

same. She said, "This woman made me sleep with a glance. How would we kill such a thing?" Even if they *wanted* to kill her. What if the woman was right, and if they acted against her she would find some way to kill Arthur? Perhaps they should bide their time.

"Highness? Are you there?" Doña Elvira called to her.

"I must away," Catherine said, and curtseyed to her brother-in-law. "We must think on what to do. We must not be rash."

He returned the respect with a bow. "Surely. Farewell."

She hoped he would not be rash. She feared he looked upon all this as a game.

"His Highness is not seeing visitors," the gentleman of Arthur's chamber told her. He spoke apologetically and bowed respectfully, but he would not let her through the doors to see Arthur. She wanted to scream.

"You will tell him that I was here?"

"Yes, Your Highness," the man said and bowed again.

Catherine could do nothing more than turn around and walk away, trailed by her own attending ladies.

What they must think of her. She caught the whispers among them, when they thought she couldn't hear. *Pobre Catalina.* Poor Catherine, whose husband would not see her, who spent every night alone.

That evening, she sent Doña Elvira and her ladies on an errand for wine. Once again, she crept from her chambers alone, furtive as a mouse.

I will see my husband, Catherine thought. It is my right. It should not have been so difficult for her to see him alone. But as it was the palace swarmed with courtiers.

She wanted to reach him before the woman arrived to work her spells on him.

Quietly, she slipped through Arthur's door and closed it behind her.

The bed curtains were open. Arthur, in his nightclothes, sat on the edge of the bed, hunched over. She could hear his wheezing breaths across the room.

"Your Highness," she said, curtseying.

"Catherine?" He looked up and—did he smile? Just a little? "Why are you here?"

She said, "Who is the woman who comes to you at night?"

"No one comes to me at night." He said this flatly, as if she were to blame for his loneliness.

She shook her head, fighting tears. She would keep her wits and not cry. "Three nights ago I came, and she was here. You were bleeding, Arthur. She hurt you. She's killing you!"

"That isn't true. No one has been here. And what business is it of yours if a woman has been here?"

"I am your wife. You have a duty to me."

"Catherine, I am so tired."

She knelt at his side and dared to put her hand on his knee. "Then you must grow strong. So that we may have children. Your heirs."

He touched her hand. A thrill went through her flesh, like fire. So much feeling in a simple touch! But his skin was ice cold.

"I am telling the truth," said the boy who was her

husband. "I remember nothing of any woman coming here. I come to bed every night and fall into such a deep sleep that nothing rouses me but my own coughing. I do not know of what you speak."

This woman had put a spell on them all.

"Your father is sending your household to Ludlow Castle, in Wales," she said.

He set his lips in a thin, pale line. "Then we shall go to Ludlow."

"You cannot travel so far," she said. "The journey will kill you."

"If I were really so weak my father would not send me."

"His pride blinds him!"

"You should not speak so of the king, my lady." He gave a tired sigh. What would have been an accusation of treason from fiery young Henry's lips was weary observation from Arthur's. "Now please, Catherine. Let me sleep. If I sleep well tonight, perhaps I'll be strong enough to see you tomorrow."

It was an empty promise and they both knew it. He was as pale and wasted as he had ever been. She kissed his hand with as much passion as she had ever been allowed to show. She pressed her cheek to it, let tears fall on it. She would pray every day for him. Every hour.

She stood, curtseyed, and left him alone in the chamber.

Outside, however, she waited, sitting on a chair in the corner normally reserved for pages or stewards. Doña Elvira would be scandalized to see her there.

In an hour, the woman Angeline came. She moved like smoke. Catherine had been staring ahead so intently she thought her eyes played a trick on her. A shadow flickered where there was no flame. A draft blew where no window was open.

Angeline did not approach, but all the same she appeared. She stood before the doors of Arthur's bedchamber as regal as any queen.

Catherine was still gathering the courage to stand when Angeline looked at her. Her face was alabaster, a statue draped with a gown of black velvet. She might as well have been stone, her gaze was so hard.

Finally, Catherine stood.

"*Es la novia niña,*" Angeline said.

The princess would not be cowed by a commoner. "By the laws of Church and country I am not a child, I am a woman."

"By one very important consideration, you are not." She turned a pointed smile.

Catherine blushed; her gaze fell. She was still a maid. That was certainly not *her* fault.

"I demand that you leave here," Catherine said. "Leave here, and leave my husband alone."

"Oh, child, you don't want me to do that."

"I insist. You are some witch, some demon. That much I know. You have worked a spell on him that sickens him to death—"

"Oh no, I'll not let my puppet die. I could keep your Arthur alive forever, if I wished. I hold that secret."

"You . . . you are an abomination against the Church. Against God!"

She smiled thinly. "Perhaps."

"Why?" Catherine said. "Why him? Why this?"

"He'll be a weak king. At best, an indifferent king. He won't be leading any troops to war against France. He will keep England a quiet, unimportant country."

"You do not know that. You cannot see the future. He will be a great king—"

"One need not see the future to guess such things, dear Catherine."

"You will address me as Your Highness, as is proper."

"Of course, Your Highness. You must trust me—I will not kill Arthur. If his brother were to become king—you have seen the kind of boy he is: fierce, competitive, strong. You can imagine the kind of king he will be. No one in Europe wishes for a strong king in England."

"My father King Ferdinand—"

"Not even King Ferdinand. From the first, he wanted a son-in-law he could control."

And Catherine knew it was true, all of it, the chess-like machinations of politics that had ruled her life. Her marriage to Arthur had given Spain another playing piece, that was all.

There was no room for love in any of this.

She was descended from two royal houses. Her ancestors were the oldest and most noble in all of Europe. Dignity was bred into the very sinews of her flesh. She stood tall, did not collapse, did not cry, however much the little girl inside of her was trembling.

"And what of children?" she said. "What of the children I'm meant to bear?"

"It may be possible. Or it may not."

"I do not believe you. I do not believe anything that you say."

"Yes, you do," she said. "But more importantly, you cannot stop me. You'll go to sleep, now. And you will not remember."

She wanted to fling herself at the woman, strangle her with her own hands. Tiny hands that couldn't strangle a kitten, alas.

"Catherine. Move away. I know what she is." The command came in the incongruous voice of a boy.

Prince Henry stood blocking the chamber's other doorway. He had a spear, which seemed overlarge and unwieldy in his hands. Nevertheless, he held it at the ready, feet braced, pointed at the woman. It was a mockery of battle. A child playing at hunting boar.

"What am I, boy?" the woman said in a soft, mocking voice.

This only drove Henry to greater rage. "Succubus. A demon who feeds on the souls of men. You will not have my brother, devil!"

Her smile fell, darkening her expression. "You have just enough intelligence to do harm. And more than enough ignorance."

"I'll kill you. I can kill you where you stand."

"You will not kill me. Arthur is so much mine that without me he will die."

She'd made Arthur weak and kept him fully under her power. If that tie between them was severed—

Catherine's heart pounded. She could not stop them both. They would not listen. No one ever listened to her. "Henry, you must not, she is keeping Arthur alive."

"She lies."

The woman laughed, a bitter sound. "If Arthur dies, Henry becomes heir. That reason will not stay his hand."

But Henry didn't want to be king. He'd said so . . .

Catherine caught his gaze. She saw something dark in his eyes.

Then she tried to forget that she'd seen it. "My lord, wait—"

The woman lived in shadow—was made of shadow. She started to flow back into the hidden ways by which she came, moving within the stillness of night. Catherine saw nothing but a shudder, the light of a sputtering candle. But Henry saw more, and like a great hunter he anticipated what the flinch of movement meant.

With a shout he lunged forward, driving the spear before him.

The woman flew. Catherine would swear that she flew, up and over, toward the ceiling to avoid Henry. Henry followed with his spear, jumping, swinging the spear upward. He missed. With a sigh the woman twisted away from him. Henry stumbled, thrown off balance by his wayward thrust, and Angeline stood behind him.

"You're a boy playing at being warrior," she said, carrying herself as calmly as if she had not moved.

Henry snarled an angry cry and tried again. The woman stepped aside and took hold of the back of Henry's neck. With no effort at all, she pushed him down, so that he was kneeling. He still held the spear, but she was behind him, pressing down on him, and he couldn't use it.

"I could make you as much my puppet as your brother is."

"No! You won't! I'll never be anyone's puppet!" He struggled, his whole body straining against her grip, but he couldn't move.

Catherine knelt and began to pray, Pater Noster and Ave Maria, and her lips stumbled trying to get out all the words at once.

The prayers were for her own comfort. Catherine had little faith in her own power; she didn't expect the unholy creature to hear her words and pause. She didn't consider that her own words, her own prayer, would cause Angeline to loosen her grip on Henry.

But Angeline did loosen her grip. Her body seemed to freeze for a moment. She became more solid, as if the prayer had made her substantial.

Henry didn't hesitate. He threw himself forward, away from Angeline, then spun to put the spear between them. Then, while she was still seemingly entranced, he drove it home.

The point slipped into her breast. She cried out, fell, and as she did Henry drove the wooden shaft deep into her chest.

The next moment she lay on the floor, clutching the shaft of the spear. Henry still held the end of it. He stared down at her, iconic, like England's beloved Saint George staring at his vanquished dragon.

There was no blood.

A strangeness happened—as strange as anything

else Catherine had seen since coming to England. With the scent of a crypt rising from her, the woman faded in color, then dried and crumbled like a corpse that had been rotting for a dozen years. In a moment, the body was unrecognizable. In another, only ash and dust remained.

Henry kicked a little at the mound of debris.

Catherine spoke, her voice shaking. "She said she was keeping Arthur alive. What if it's true? What if he dies? I'll be a widow in a strange country. I'll be lost." Lost, when she was meant to be a queen. Her life was slipping away.

Henry touched her arm. She nearly screamed, but her innate dignity controlled her. She only flinched.

He gazed at her with utmost gravity. "I'll take care of you. If Arthur dies, then I'll take care of you, when I am king after my father."

Arthur survived the journey to Ludlow Castle and lingered another three months. Every day he faded, though, until his soul fled. He died April 2, 1502.

So it came to pass that Henry, who had been born to be Duke of York and nothing else, a younger brother, a mere afterthought in the chronicles of history, would succeed his father as King of England.

Six years later, the old King Henry died. Prince Henry succeeded him as king, became Henry the VIII, and married Catherine of Aragon. He would take care of her, as he had promised.

He was sixteen at their wedding, a year older than Arthur had been. But so different. Like day and night, summer and winter. Henry was tall, flushed, hearty, laughed all the time, danced, hunted, jousted, argued, commanded. Their wedding night would be nothing like Catherine's first, she knew. *He is the greatest prince in all Europe,* people at court said of him. *He will make England a nation to be reckoned with.*

Catherine considered her new husband, now taller than she by a head. Part of her would always remember the boy. She could still picture him the way he stood outside Arthur's chamber, spear in his hands, fury in his eyes, ready to do battle. Ready to sacrifice his own brother. Catherine would never forget that this was a man willing to do what he believed must be done, whatever the cost.

She wanted to be happy, but England's chill air remained locked in her bones.

Harpy

by Chelsea Quinn Yarbro

There was no doubt that the woman was poor: her brass-colored hair was touched with gray and her face was fretted with fine lines, although she was no more than thirty; her clothing was made of rough, homespun linen and was far from new, its color faded from what might once have been blue to a foggy shade of gray; its skimpy folds did not conceal her advancing pregnancy. She toiled up the steep, crowded Athens street, a yoke over her shoulders balancing two large buckets filled with water that depended from either end, picking her way among vendors, slaves, goat- and shepherds, men of every age and description, and a smattering of women as hapless as she. The sun baked down on the city, making the colors on the buildings and the statues brilliant, and heating everything so that the scent of it all hung in the still air like dust motes.

When the toe of her rawhide sandal caught on a loose paving stone, the woman, light-headed from hunger, nearly went down; as she struggled with the yawing yoke to keep from falling, a stranger in black Egyptian garb but with thick-soled Persian boots on his small feet stepped out of the throng and held her up as she regained her footing. "Thank you," she muttered, prepared to pass on.

"Let me take that for you. Please," the stranger offered in excellent Athenian Greek, but with an accent the woman had never heard before. As the crowd eddied around them, she studied him, frowning, trying to discern his intentions. To her surprise, she did not find what she saw objectionable, and she realized she needed help with her load. Again she contemplated his face, trying to discern his motives: he had attractive, irregular features, an angular brow, dark, close-cropped hair, and wore a silver sigil ring on the first finger of his right hand. His manner was distinguished, with a degree of reserve that marked him as a foreigner as much as his accent and his dress.

She held tightly to the yoke on her shoulders. "No. I will manage."

The stranger gave a swift smile. "No doubt; I see you are more than capable. But why should you?"

Staring at him, she demanded, "Why shouldn't I?"

"Because you are carrying a child," he said calmly. "That is burden enough."

This time she was more firm. "You need not bother." She made an attempt to wrench herself away and was somewhat surprised when she was unable to do so, for he made no apparent effort, yet he kept her from going on. "I'm no weakling."

"Possibly not," he agreed affably. "But your unborn infant is, and it depends upon you for protection. Your pulse is strong, but it is also fast, and you are sweating, which is hard on you."

She gave an impatient cough. "I will manage," she said again, watching him with suspicion, distrusting the attention he gave her.

The stranger turned his dark eyes on hers. "I ask you to permit me to do this for the sake of your baby."

"And why should that matter to you?" she countered sharply, making no apology for her abruptness.

"Does it not concern you?" he inquired, standing so that the busy traffic of the street would flow around them. "I would have thought, from the way you are walking, that you are apprehensive about carrying the child. If I am mistaken, or if my observation is impertinent, I ask your pardon."

She stared at him. "How can you know that?" If she were not so hungry, she thought, she would not feel the need to defend herself; she could walk away from this stranger. As it was, she wanted a little time to order herself, to muster her waning stamina before continuing upward.

"Because I am something of a physician, and while I do not think coddling helps a pregnancy, I know that strenuous toil is equally compromising, particularly to someone who has miscarried in the past, which I believe you have done?" He saw her nod as he took the yoke from her shoulders and rested it across his own. "Tell me where you would like me to take this."

She sighed. "If you must, follow me," she said, resuming her climb. "But don't expect me to give you anything more than my thanks for your efforts."

"I will not," he told her, easily keeping pace with her.

"I have no money to pay for your service, and I will not be whored," she stated flatly as she reached another confluence of streets and chose the one leading off to the oblique right; she shoved past a man on a donkey and continued upward past increasingly mean dwellings. "I will not bargain about the matter."

"To your credit," said the stranger.

Three young men, their hair fashionably clipped, their beards neatly trimmed and perfumed, dressed in handsome chitons of dyed-and-painted linen, came along from the street above; they were laughing among themselves, paying little heed to their surroundings, knowing that the crowd would give way to them. One of them had an amphora in his hands, and he held it aloft as if it were a trophy.

As they went past the woman, she made a sign with her hand to ward off evil.

The black-clad stranger watched this with curiosity. "Do you dislike them so much?" he asked when the young men were safely past.

She glanced over her shoulder at him. "They're trouble. All rich young men are trouble."

The stranger nodded, and continued to climb.

A short while later she slipped into an alley, motioning him to stop. "You don't need to come any farther. I can carry the yoke from here."

"I am aware that you are able to," he said with a

kindness she had rarely known. "But, do you know, I think I will take it the rest of the way."

She shrugged. "If it suits you. I warn you, the house isn't much." The alley continued to turn to the right, growing narrower as it rose.

"That does not trouble me," he said.

"Please yourself," she said, and went on beyond the end of the alley where the street vanished into the scrubby grass and a house that was little more than a tumbledown shed stood, a rickety fence around a small portion of land inside which a scrawny nanny goat grazed on the stubble of thistles. "This is my home," she stated with an air of defiance. As she spoke, three skinny youngsters came tumbling out—two boys and a girl; all three were in stained and threadbare clothes, and only the oldest—the girl, around nine or ten—wore sandals, and they were old and tattered. "And these are my children."

"Indeed," said the stranger, setting down the water buckets and leaning the yoke on end against the fence.

She patted the younger boy—a small six-year-old with a distracted air about him—and murmured something to his tangled hair, then looked at the stranger. "He's not quite right, this one. He doesn't talk very much, and he— But the other two are fine." Her smile almost shattered as the younger boy hugged her leg.

"Has he been so from birth?" asked the stranger, no suggestion of condemnation in his manner.

"No; he took a fever when he was not quite two, and he hasn't been . . ." Her words trailed off as she swallowed hard. "Two others died of the fever—a boy and a girl. And, as you said, I have had miscarriages—three of them."

"That is unfortunate," said the stranger.

"It could have been much worse," said the woman. "They could have lived."

"I must suppose then, that you are a widow," said the stranger in the silence that followed.

"You would think so, wouldn't you? It certainly seems that way," she said with sudden heat as she squinted up toward the bright sun. "But no, I am not. I have a husband."

"And he is away?" the stranger asked.

"No. He is here in Athens," she said. "For a while." His attentive silence prompted her to go on, "He is likely to be exiled. And we with him, or be sold into slavery."

"What has he done?" The stranger looked genuinely concerned.

"Why should you want to know? It is nothing to you," she said gruffly as she tried to smooth her hair off her face.

"I am curious," the stranger admitted.

"There is nothing to be curious about. He is determined to make an example of himself, and us along with him."

"Make an example of himself?" The stranger's repetition held her attention.

"So it would seem," she said evasively.

"For what crime?" he persisted. "Surely not treason, or murder—you would be in the hands of the authorities if that were the case, so there must be other charges. What has he done?"

"Corrupted youth," she said bluntly. "That's the

charge: that he has corrupted youth. As if those young men who follow him could be corrupted more than they already are."

"How has he done that? What youth has he corrupted?"

"They accuse him of corrupting the sons of important men. My husband says he is their teacher, and it is true that a group of them follow him as if he were. It seems his teaching has corrupted them, or so many powerful men have sworn, and declared that their sons have been tainted by what my husband has taught." She reached down and picked up the younger boy, who began to tug loose the knot of hair at the back of her neck, which she endured patiently. "I know the fathers of the young men who follow my husband are opposed to him."

"What does he teach that is so intolerable—here in Athens—that he must be stopped?"

She looked at the stranger. "I don't know. He teaches them, not his family. His sons do not read or write." She was about to turn away, but abruptly continued. "Women are the beautiful evil, as we know, and when our beauty is gone, only the evil is left, or so my husband has told me on several occasions. He says I will betray him if he reveals anything to me, so he tells me little but that I am worse than a shrew for urging him to abandon his companions and undertake to provide for his family."

"His students do not pay him?" The stranger sounded puzzled. "Teachers are usually paid for their knowledge."

"No; he will not permit them to pay him." She sighed.

"But how do they expect him to survive?" the stranger wondered aloud.

"Oh, they take him to their banquets and other entertainments, so he doesn't starve. A few of them fawn on him as if he were their older lover—and he may well be, for all I know. His ideas are exciting to them, and he . . . he is encouraged to talk, to impart his wisdom, as they call it, and he does it willingly enough. They see he is clothed, although he doesn't ask it, and prefers older garments to new ones; it is a matter of principle with him, or so he tells me. The young men attend him and strive to guard him against those who . . ." She could not go on.

"They provide nothing for you?"

She gently disengaged her son's hands from her hair. "I doubt they know much about us. My husband subscribes to the custom of saying little about his wife, although he does insist that I complain too much."

"Which you have every reason to do, if the case is as you say it is," the stranger told her.

"I do not dissemble," she said sharply. "And I do not lie."

"Judging by appearances, you have good cause to be distressed."

"I will be much more when he is condemned, as will his children," she said. "This may be hard, but what is ahead of us will be far worse, I fear."

"Will none of his students take these children into their household?" It was not an uncommon arrangement, and he was somewhat surprised she had made no mention of it.

"I doubt most of his students know much about

us, or our situation." She put her boy down, tousling his hair as she did.

"Because he says nothing?" the stranger suggested.

She nodded. "And his silence contributes to his troubles, and ours."

"Then he is truly in some danger," said the stranger.

"Yes. Oh, yes. When he first became the object of suspicions, it sickened me. Now—" She pinched the bridge of her nose. "If our children weren't in want, I wouldn't object to what he does, not any longer. He is a man who has purpose and understanding. He has chosen his way, and I would not deny him anything that aided him if our children were well-fed and properly clothed. But you see how it is. My husband has forgotten us, and we are left to flounder. He does what he must, and I honor him for that, but I can't ignore the plight of these three."

"Doesn't he see what has become of you and your children when he visits you— He does visit you, does he not?"

The woman directed her gaze past the stranger's shoulder. "He visits occasionally, when he has no other obligations. When he is here, he cares only for a compliant bedmate and I do not refuse him that. I do what a wife must, but I am no longer happy about it. He has made himself a figure of importance, not to mention infamy, among the great ones of the city. He is well-fed, he has a soft bed to sleep in, his clothes are clean, and that suffices him. If he would only see that the house was repaired and I had cloth enough to make proper chitons for the boys, and a peplos for Thalia; she is getting to an age when she must be more attentive in her dress. If he would only think of finding a husband for her."

Thalia frowned at her mother. "I don't need anything yet—not new clothes or a husband."

"But you do," said her mother. "If your father cares nothing for your welfare, so be it; but you deserve better than he has given you." Her bitterness startled her daughter, and she modified her tone. "But I can't be so lax, or so preoccupied as he is. What would become of you if I didn't look after you?" This was clearly an old dispute among them, and no one bothered to continue the ritual of argument. The woman turned to the stranger. "So you see how it is."

"Yes, I do," he said, and apparently changed the subject. "Have any of you eaten today""

"There was a little cheese for the morning," said the woman evasively.

"Which it would seem you did not eat. I suppose you gave what you had to your children?" He held up his hand before she could summon up some sort of denial. "Is there anything more in the house?"

"A little flour, and we will have a bit of milk from our goat," she admitted, amazed that she should reveal so much to him. "With that and a handful of nuts, I can make flat cakes for us all."

"Hardly sufficient nourishment, particularly for your unborn child," said the stranger. He studied the three children, then said to their mother, "Would some meat and a string of onions be useful to you?"

Her sarcastic laughter sounded unusually loud. "And oil, and melons, and garlic, and cabbages, and cheese."

"Certainly," said the stranger at once. "All of that, and more besides. But have you vessels in which to cook? Do you have wood for your fire?"

"What business is it of yours?" she demanded, then fell silent.

What business, indeed? he asked himself inwardly, and decided it was as much curiosity as compassion. "I am willing to make it my business," he said aloud, "if you will permit me to." He inclined his head. "You may call it a whim, if you need an explanation."

"Such whims can be costly." She pinched the bridge of her nose again. "I do not want to be beholden to you; I have no way to redeem my obligation but with the lives of my children."

"You have no reason to fear me," he told her as Thalia tugged at her mother's garments.

"Mama, I'm hungry," she said just above a whisper.

"We're all hungry, girl," said the woman.

"If you will not object, I will fetch foodstuffs for you, and a proper pot to cook them in, and new bread." The stranger could see the disbelief in the woman's face. "I am not mocking you; believe this."

"I do as best I can," she said.

"No doubt," he agreed. "But with a little help, you will do much better."

She glared at him. "If you seek to discredit my husband—"

"I should think he has done that all by himself," said the stranger in the black Egyptian clothes and Persian boots.

Now she bristled. "He is a fine teacher, my husband, for all he is unwilling to provide for us. He is an eminent man, a hero, trying for greatness, to teach so that his teaching will be remembered. He may not treat us any better than most poor men treat their wives, but he has much to offer, and would be held in high esteem if only he didn't insist on clashing with the authorities." She squared her shoulders. "He has knowledge and imparts it well, and it is to his credit that he will not be intimidated, little as I may like what that means to us. He may have been unwise in his choice of students, and he has become a thorn in the side of the state, but his teaching deserves to be heard."

"All you say may be true, and to the extent that he is a good teacher, he deserves praise, but he exacts too high a price from you and your children for his teaching if you are hungry and he is not," said the stranger, fully aware that he had not heard the husband's side of it, but keenly sensitive to the deprivations the man's wife and children were enduring on his account; he sensed her thoughts flickering like fish in shadowed water, and he wondered what they held.

She folded her arms. "I do not want to see him harmed, but I can do nothing about that, so I will do everything I can to see that our children suffer no more for his folly." She cocked her head. "My father was a rope maker—he did quite well for himself, supplying ropes to quarrymen and the builders of temples. He arranged this marriage for me because he thought it would advance me, to be married to a man of learning. If he were still alive, he would be appalled at how I live."

The stranger nodded, and glanced toward the complex of temples on an adjacent hilltop. "Rope makers have much to do in Athens."

"Yes, they do," she said, making no apology for the pride in her voice. "He kept us fed and we lived in a sturdy house. All my sisters had dowries—not large but enough for—" She stopped, as if fearing she had said too much. "My father helped us, before he died, and my husband thanked him for it."

"A pity that did not continue."

She shrugged. "Wives must share the lot of their husbands. At least I am not confined to the house as many women are."

"No, that fate has not befallen you," said the stranger, going on more crisply. "If you will ready your hearth, I will return shortly with food for you, and a pot, as I told you. If you can rest for a short while, it will do you good."

"Rest?" She laughed. "I will make ready for your return." She squinted at the goat. "I'll milk her; that will give the children something more to drink than water."

"I will be back," he reiterated, seeing the doubt in her eyes.

"Well and good," she said, dismissing him.

The stranger took a step back, watching the three children dejectedly follow their mother into the house; he considered what he had seen and heard, then he turned and made his way back down the hill to the agora, the central marketplace where farmers offered their produce for sale and vendors of all sorts hawked their wares, while at the far end, livestock of all descriptions were bartered for. Taking stock of what was displayed, he bought a butchered lamb; a sackful of onions and peppers; a bundle of grape leaves; a spray of mint and another of basil; two strings of onions and one of garlic, a bottle of oil, a large, pale green melon, a round of cheese, three flat breads, an iron cleaver with a wooden handle, a skin of wine; a large iron pot, and a bundle of cut firewood. To this he added a bolt of green linen and one of soft Colchis wool. These he loaded onto a low sledge, which he purchased from a vendor at the front of the marketplace, and, after covering it all with a sheet of rough linen and tying it all down with heavy twine, he set about returning to the woman's house, making his dragging of the sledge appear more difficult that it was so as not to draw attention to his remarkable strength. As he progressed up the slope, he was trying to decide how to approach her about more assistance. He was fairly sure she would reject anything so obvious as outright gifts or offers of patronage, but perhaps something could be done with her older boy. He was still mulling over the possibilities as he approached her house, where he noticed two soldiers were now flanking the flimsy gate, spears in hand. He slowed his approach, trying to discern what was happening.

One of the soldiers noticed him and pointed at him with his spear. "You. Stop."

The stranger did as he was ordered. "There is trouble here?"

"And well you know it," said the soldier gruffly as he swung around to confront the foreigner in black Egyptian clothes.

"Why should I?" The stranger made sure his question had no element of challenge in it, only curiosity.

"You are bringing this woman—" the soldier began.

"I am bringing her food for her children," said the stranger, maintaining a respectful manner.

"For what reason?" The soldier put up his spear.

"They are hungry, and she is pregnant," said the stranger.

"There are many such women in Athens," said the soldier. "Why bring food to this one, whose husband is an enemy of the people?"

"I am not bringing food to her husband; I am bringing it to her and her children." He patted the covered sledge.

"For his sake, no doubt," said the soldier.

"No; I am unacquainted with the husband," the stranger said calmly. "I happened upon this woman by chance. I knew nothing whatsoever of her husband until she told me."

"It is only chance that her husband is condemned," said the soldier sarcastically, and nudged his comrade in the arm. "He is here by happenstance."

"I am," said the stranger.

"Very good," said the soldier, laughing. "A creditable liar."

"If I lie, then you may accuse me openly. You will find," the stranger went on, cutting off what the soldier was about to say, "that I am here from Egypt, although I am not an Egyptian; I lived there for some time." He did not mention that the time he had spent in Egypt was reckoned in centuries. "I arrived three days ago on the *Wings of Horus*, a merchant ship bringing cloth and dates and papyrus to the markets of Athens. Erastos of Argos, who dispatches ships for the Eclipse Traders at Piraeus will speak for me, if you require that I be identified by someone other than myself. My manservant, an Egyptian named Aumtehoutep, is at the house of Philetides Timonestheos, and will confirm what I tell you. I am trained as a physician and I am partner in a trading company."

"Why would a physician engage in trade?" asked the soldier.

"Because any good physician seeks to better his art. There are substances, herbs, and other healing items that are procured in distant lands," said the stranger politely but with an air of authority. "Being part of a trading company makes it easier to obtain those things that a physician may require."

"And you are?" the soldier asked, beginning to sound annoyed. "You must have a name."

"Djerman Ragosh-ski," he answered promptly, combining one of his Egyptian names with the patronymic of his very distant childhood. "I am a partner in the Eclipse Traders, as I told you."

"Not an Egyptian surname; and certainly not a Greek one," said the soldier, considering. "I will ask my officer if you might give this *gift*"—he made the word sarcastic—"to the woman for her children."

"Why is he here at all?" Ragosh-ski asked, making his inquiry one of curiosity, not challenge.

"Her husband's fate has been decided, and hers will be in the morning; it is likely that slavery will be her lot, and the lot of her children. There are plans she must make and arrangements to accommodate the plans. She must hold herself in readiness." The soldier nudged his companion. "The girl should bring a good price: she's young but she's promising."

"True enough," said the second soldier, sounding bored. "They'll have to sell her even if they execute the others."

"The boys, too, I would guess," said the first. "Pity that younger one isn't . . . right."

"There's bound to be a use for him somewhere." The second spat and leaned more heavily on his spear. "I don't like this kind of duty."

"The officer can't come alone," said the first soldier. "What if the woman and her children had friends with them?"

"They have this friend," said Ragosh-ski.

"But you aren't here to fight, and you're foreign, so that wouldn't be prudent," said the first soldier. "Others might be ready and able to defend them."

"And two of us might not be enough to hold them off," said the second soldier with a shrug. He regarded Ragosh-ski for a long moment, then said, "You don't strike me as dangerous."

Ragosh-ski bowed slightly. "Not just at present," he said with a chuckle.

The soldiers joined him, and might have said something more, but their officer came surging out of the house, the woman behind him, shouting insults and imprecations at him; he paid no attention. He donned his horse-hair crested helmet and signaled his men to follow him, shouting over his shoulder, "We will return in two days, and you will have to be ready or face the consequences."

The woman screamed, "My husband will be newly dead then. I must have time to mourn him with our children. There are offerings we must make."

"Mourn him in your servitude; the gods will accept your plight on his behalf. In any case, I suppose his students will probably buy you and your children," the officer yelled back at her, hardly breaking stride as he went away from her house, the two soldiers trailing behind him.

"You'd best not be here tomorrow, Ragosh-ski," advised the soldier who had questioned him. "It could work against your interests."

"It might," said Ragosh-ski, noticing the older boy staring out at him through a knothole in the wall of the shack.

"Well, I have warned you," the soldier declared as he reached the first turn in the street.

Ragosh-ski watched the three depart, his expression severe. He realized that a decision would have to be reached quickly. Once the soldiers were out of sight, he opened the ramshackle gate and went into the house, tugging the sledge with him. "I know this is not a good time, but you will want what I bring," he said as much to announce himself as to point out the fruits of his errand.

The woman looked up, staring at him. "I didn't realize you'd returned," she said, sounding dazed. She stared at him, as if not trusting her eyes. "You brought—"

The daughter lunged out of the alcove where she had retreated. "Food! He brought food!" She slapped the covering on the sledge. "I can smell it!"

Her mother took her by the shoulder. "Calm down, Thalia."

The girl did her best to contain herself, stepping back from the sledge and saying only, "I'm hungry."

"We're all hungry," said the woman, sounding utterly weary. She glanced at Ragosh-ski. "So you brought what you said you would bring?"

"Have a look for yourself," Ragosh-ski offered, bending to untie the twine that held the load in place.

There was a long silence as the woman peeled back the covering and stared at the food and the pot. "You have been . . . most kind." The words sounded harsh and unfamiliar as she spoke them. She bent down and touched the two bolts of cloth. "Most kind."

"If this suits your purposes, then I am content," said Ragosh-ski, stepping back so that the woman could begin to unload the sledge.

"This food will be useless by this time tomorrow, when the soldiers come again. They won't allow us to take food with us." She sighed. "But we will have an ample last meal together. Perhaps I can cut new garments for us, as well; we will look less like beggars."

"You need not be beggars," said Ragosh-ski.

"No; we can be slaves," said the woman without emotion.

"Not slaves either," he said.

She rounded on him. "You saw the soldiers—it must be one or the other."

"Then I hope you will make the most of your evening to consider what I offer." Ragosh-ski paused, making sure he had her full attention. "The authorities may watch Piraeus to keep you from leaving, but they will not—they cannot—be at Megara, and I can arrange for you to travel with a merchants' train of ox carts bound for there at dawn. From that place, I can arrange for you to go overland to the Gulf of Corinth, or by sea to one of the islands, as suits you. You can make your way in the world according to your desires. Depending on your skills, there will be work for you in any place."

"So you would expect me to work?" The woman did not quite laugh this time.

"No; *you* would expect to work. You have made it clear that you do not trust any aid too freely given." He looked at the children. "If you have work you would like to do, tell me so that I may find a situation for you. You would be together; your children would not be sold and you could deliver your baby in safety."

The woman looked toward her children. "I don't want to lose them."

Ragosh-ski smiled. "Yes; hard enough to lose your husband. Tomorrow the soldiers return. But they will not guard you through the night, will they?"

"Why should they?" The woman laid out the food on a narrow plank table and pressed her lips together. "Where would they expect me to go— Where would I take these children?" She shook her head. "They know where they will find us tomorrow."

"The sea laps many shores," said Ragosh-ski.

The woman laughed harshly. "And what ship would take us? Megara is all very well, but what then? And for that matter, what merchant would carry us in an oxcart? Women are known to be unlucky on ships, and I haven't money to pay for passage, and women on the road are targets for mischief." She picked up the garlic and sniffed it. "I might as well try to walk to Thessalonika, or swim to Rhodes."

"Arrangements can be made," said Ragosh-ski.

"For what?" She raised her head and glared at him. "For removing us and then selling us to foreigners, far away, where the customs and news of Athens have no meaning?"

"No. For passage so that you may have the safety of distance from Athens, and some protection from those willing to provide it," said Ragosh-ski.

"And you would know such men?" The woman laughed bitterly.

"Yes," he responded simply. "I would."

The woman looked away. "You tempt me, foreigner."

"You may call me Ragosh-ski," he offered. "That way I will be a bit less foreign."

"Such a cumbersome name— It only serves to enhance your foreignness." She looked again toward her children huddled in the corner, then shrugged, making up her mind. "Come. Unload the rest of the sledge. Put the cloth in the covered box in the corner. Thalia, use the wood to build up a proper fire so I can put this all to cooking." Taking up the new cleaver, she tested it against her thumb and nodded. "Well-honed."

"So the seller claimed," said Ragosh-ski.

She brought it down on the melon, watching the taut skin open and the soft interior with its load of seeds spill out. "Do you think there is a place it would be safe for me to go? A place where we could remain?"

"I do," said Ragosh-ski. "At Chalcedon, widows are permitted to continue the work of their husbands, until the oldest son is of age to inherit."

The woman scoffed. "What manner of teacher would I be?"

"If your husband is unknown to the people of Chalcedon, then nothing constrains you, and you may select what suits you best," said Ragosh-ski. "You will have documents to show that this is your right. You may also have documents to say your place of business was destroyed and you could not afford to rebuild. So long as you have money enough, there will be no questions asked."

"And where am I to get money? If I had money, there would have been no call for you to purchase all this." She reached for the skin of wine, unstopped it, and squeezed the blood-colored liquid into her mouth. Glaring at him defiantly, she said, "Would you want any of this?"

"No, but I thank you for your offer. I do not drink wine."

She stared at him. "Perhaps something else""

"Perhaps," he agreed. "But later."

She took an old, wooden cup from the end of the table, tipped it over, then filled it with wine, then handed the cup to her daughter. "Share this with your brothers, mind."

Thalia smiled as she took a careful sip, smacking her lips before handing the cup to her nearest brother. She wiped her mouth with the back of her hand and stared longingly at the halved melon. "Mama?"

"Take it outside and get the seeds out for the goat, and then you may have some. Remember it must be shared." The woman stoppered the wineskin again and looked at Ragosh-ski. "Tell me why you are prepared to do so much for me. And never mind saying it is a whim."

Ragosh-ski answered her slowly, thoughtfully. "Most of the people in Athens, as in all the rest of the world, are . . . as if they are sleepwalking. They live but they are not wholly alive, not vital, not immersed in living. Those who are are like beacons."

"You can't think I am one such," said the woman, shaking her head in disbelief. "How could I be?"

"It has nothing to do with situation," said Ragosh-ski, thinking back to his many decades at the Temple of Imhotep. "It has to do with the truth within."

"Now you sound like my husband," she said, and picked up the yellow and green peppers, sliced them in half, and pulled the seeds from within them, setting the seeds on a narrow shelf to dry out of habit.

"Then he must know your value," said Ragosh-ski.

"He calls me a shrew, and worse," she answered, vigorously chopping the peppers.

"In that, he is mistaken," said Ragosh-ski.

She stopped her work. "I thank you for saying so," she muttered, cautious of his praise.

"If you depart tomorrow, you will not have to answer for his actions any longer." He nodded to her.

"I would want him to know, if I decide to leave." She resumed hacking the peppers, making them into ever-smaller bits of vegetable.

"I will carry word to him, if you like," said Ragosh-ski.

She scraped the peppers into the large cooking pot, then set to work on the onions; their pungent odor quickly filled the little hut. "Better you than the soldiers, I suppose," she said thoughtfully. "At least you can tell him we are safe."

"Then you will go?" Ragosh-ski asked.

"I don't know. But tell him we are with friends, or anything you like, so long as it is not the truth." She used the edge of her hand to shove the onions into the pot.

"Not the truth?" He could not follow her intention.

"He has said he will accept whatever is meted out to him," she said, her eyes still fixed on the middle distance. "And I am certain he said it sincerely. But what if his followers persuade him to bargain? What might become of us then?" She bent to pick up the butchered lamb, slinging it onto the table and preparing to remove the meat. "Tell him whatever story you think will most serve our purpose—the children's and mine."

Ragosh-ski ducked his head. "If that is your wish."

"It is what must be done, for all our sakes," she said, and stopped working long enough to stare at him. "No matter what I decide, I am grateful to you for this, Ragosh-ski."

For a long moment, Ragosh-ski said nothing. Then, "What is your husband's name? For whom shall I ask at the prison?"

"He is called Socrates. I am Xantippe." She slapped down a wedge of lamb and began to cut it into smaller chunks.

"I will attend to it," said Ragosh-ski.

"You will return before dawn?" Xantippe asked as her children came rushing back inside, each clutching a section of melon; the two boys were yelling.

"Certainly before dawn," said Ragosh-ski.

Xantippe reached to restrain her children. "I will have a decision by then," she promised. "I will hope that sleep brings wisdom."

Ragosh-ski nodded as he went to the door. "Then I will wish you sweet dreams."

Honored Be Her Name

by John Gregory Betancourt and Darrell Schweitzer

You could have knocked me over with a feather.

You could have taken me for some kind of gaping, slack-jawed, adolescent apprentice completely at a loss for anything to say when confronted with the Great Man. Maybe that had even been the case when my father had gotten me the position and, at the age of seventeen, I had accompanied Sir Henry McPherson to Egypt on an expedition of discovery that would have made him the greatest uncoverer of legendary antiquity since Heinrich Schliemann. But the expedition had come to naught. Sir Henry had, inexplicably, on the eve of his triumph, disappeared into the night—murdered, it was more or less assumed, by Arabs.

And that was twenty-five years ago. Queen Victoria was still on the throne in those days. I had stayed on, doing my own steady but modest work in Egyptology, and I no more expected to see Sir Henry on a quiet street in Alexandria than I expected to shake hands with Ramses II.

But see him I did. And he saw me. When Sir Henry held out his hand, I took it. His grip was firm and dry.

Now all those intervening years seemed as nothing. I was a stuttering kid once more. But he spoke directly enough.

"I think it is destiny that we meet again like this, David."

Almost as astonishing as his mere presence was his appearance. Of course, it is difficult to judge with someone so much your senior, but to my eyes he looked exactly as he had when I'd last seen him in 1899. I did a quick mental calculation. He'd have to be in his eighties by now.

"Yes, I need to explain," he said, almost as if he could read my mind. "Let us find some private place. I have a story to tell."

We took a table at a Greek café, outdoors, but well under the porch and into the shadows. It was almost completely dark. The daytime pedestrian traffic had pretty well thinned out, though there were nighttime strollers. Alexandria is not what the world pictures when it thinks of Egypt. The architecture is mostly modern and European. We could have just as well been sitting in a piazza in Italy as anywhere in Africa, but for when the Muslim population was called to evening prayer.

Sir Henry ordered drinks. The Greek waiter nearly spilled them. He glared at Sir Henry with obvious disapproval, tempered by the fact that we were English and there wasn't a damned thing he could do about our being there.

I drank. Sir Henry talked.

* * *

"It was on a street like this [Sir Henry began], here in 'Lex, that I had an encounter which proved to be fully as astonishing as mine with you right now must seem. It was the stuff of romance, like something out of Rider Haggard: a chance collision with a mysterious, veiled woman, a clue leading to the discovery of the most amazing archaeological relic of them all, and even further mystery, which has shrouded the secret until now. . . . Smashing stuff, David, as I am sure you would have phrased it in those days.

"On the evening I 'disappeared,' I had come up from the dig site to Alexandria for a small conference of colleagues. On that particular evening I was pretty much lost in my thoughts, in my own little world of anticipation and theory—not a good idea, even in 'Lex. There may not be quite so many cutpurses and cutthroats here as in the back alleys of Cairo, but you still do need to keep your head about you, English or not.

"But I wasn't paying attention. My gaze wandered and I literally crashed into the woman, who was draped and veiled in the usual Muslim fashion, but not, it was curious to note, apparently accompanied by protective menfolk. She had a black bag with her. Several small objects and packages spilled out.

"I apologized profusely and crouched down to help gather up her things.

"She must not have been quite listening to what I was saying, because she addressed me in French. *'Pardonez-vous, monsieur,'* she said, in a low voice and a little husky. *'Est-ce que vous êtes Français?'*

"My conversational French is fairly good because

I have to use it at conferences, and we could have continued conversing in that language, but suddenly our eyes met—and her gaze was, what can I say? Mesmerizing, perhaps. More extraordinary still was that she next spoke to me in oddly accented, not quite classical Greek: *'It is destiny that we have met, thus. Our goddess wills it.'*

"She gathered up her things and then ran off, but not far, pausing at the end of the street, around the corner of a house, where I could still see her.

"It was only after a moment that I realized that she had pressed something into my hand. It was a stone scarab. In the course of my work I have handled thousands of such things. I fancy that I can tell a tourist's fake from the real merely by hefting it, and I must admit this felt like the real thing. I could also tell there was an inscription cut into the smooth bottom. I struck a match and quickly read: KLEOPATRA.

"Now this was the moment of decision, or destiny, or the working of the gods. Call it what you will. *Of course* I was a damned fool to run after her, and I didn't even have the excuse that I was a young and inexperienced damned fool. Like a character in some cheap novel, I felt instinct overwhelming all reason, dismissing all thoughts of back alleys and cutpurses and worse. I suppose it assuages my pride to say that I was bewitched, that I couldn't help myself, that maybe the stone scarab I held was as cursed as the ruby eye of a Hindoo idol."

Sir Henry paused. It was completely dark now, and dark where we sat. Inside the café, around a lamp, I could see several Greeks conferring, every once in a while turning in our direction with a scowl or look of alarm. One of them made a gesture, quite familiar throughout the Mediterranean world, to ward off the evil eye.

"You don't seriously mean that?" I had to say at last. "Witchcraft, in this day and age?"

"There are things that are ageless, David. Truly ageless. That is what I learned in the course of my adventure . . . an adventure which is still, even as we speak, continuing."

"So I followed her [Sir Henry continued his tale], and I cannot even say where. Explain it any way you want. We turned into streets I had never known existed in modern Alexandria. I became disoriented. I knew the sea was . . . over *there* somewhere, but I was less and less sure where *there* was.

"The veiled woman walked just a little ahead of me now. I know we drew some astonished looks at first from passersby, at the spectacle of an otherwise unaccompanied, apparently native woman being followed so closely by a European. Some people looked away, or even muttered and made signs with their fingers. Perhaps they thought she was a woman of ill-repute, and I was her companion of the evening.

"In any case, it did not matter. I was now in a part of the city I had never known existed, almost as if I had been transported back in time to the Middle Ages. There were no gas lamps, no signs that the French or the English had ever set foot here. The architecture was, indeed, very much like the close and winding byways of Cairo, complete with darkened archways choking the streets, beggars settling down for the night in corners, surrounded by animals. From somewhere there came the sound of singing, a wailing Arabic song accompanied by a soft drum.

"Reckless as I might have been, mad or bewitched as I might have been, I still drew comfort from the weight of my revolver in my right coat pocket.

"I slipped the scarab into my left pocket.

"We came upon a two-storey, whitewashed building with black double doors facing the street. From somewhere inside, I heard chanting. It wasn't the right hour of Muslim prayers, I knew, and in any case, the chanting did not sound like such, nor was it in Arabic.

"The doors were not locked. My veiled guide pushed them open and ushered me into a large atrium. I glanced around with interest. Smooth, red-and-black marble columns rose twenty feet high, supporting a domed ceiling painted with stars in half-familiar constellations. Little clay oil lamps of the ancient type flickered in various alcoves, providing some light. I had been all over 'Lex, all over Egypt for that matter; and I had never seen anything quite like this, except as ruins which one reconstructed in the imagination into a similar appearance. The place fairly oozed antiquity, like something out of pharaonic times.

"The veiled woman turned to me and said again in her strange Greek, 'Wait here and I will announce you.'

"She passed through another door, and I heard a man's voice, again speaking Greek, say something that sounded like, *'Ah, faithful Charmion, you have returned.'* She said something in reply as she closed the door, but I could not make it out.

"While I waited, alone in the atrium, I poked around into the various shelves and nooks in the walls and was astonished at some of the artifacts I found—ancient things from the very earliest Egyptian dynasties, things the British Museum would pay well to possess. They did not seem to be reproductions, either. But a great deal more: little statuettes of gods, tomb figurines, *ushabtis;* and, in particular, a large and well-worn alabaster bust of a woman with her hair tied back in a bun, a band around her head in the manner of Hellenistic royalty. It was of an obviously much later date, from Ptolemaic times, perhaps the second or first centuries before Christ.

"Next to the bust lay a silver bowl and a sacrificial dagger. I picked the dagger up. *Beautiful.* I pride myself on my expertise, as you know. This was not a fake. Something like this could only come from an undiscovered, unlooted tomb of the greatest importance—and that was when my head began to clear from whatever witchcraft had befuddled me.

"I might well be in a den of thieves, tomb-robbers whose purpose was nothing magical or romantic or particularly mysterious, just a sordid attempt to sell stolen antiquities. I did not immediately fear for my safety, but I was still glad I had my revolver.

"Someone was coming. I put the dagger down quickly.

" 'The illustrious McPherson, welcome to my home,' someone said, not in English, not in French, or even Arabic, but in that strange, half-classical

Greek. I could barely recognize my name, so rendered.

"Standing in the doorway was a man of indeterminate age, older than myself, I was sure, but by no means decrepit. He was dressed in loose clothing, a robe of some sort, not in the Arab fashion, but more—it came to me now; my mind was clearing—in the manner of the ancients. I realized, all at once, that his speech and many of the artifacts in the room were of the same time. He was speaking *Ptolemaic* Greek, which I had never actually heard spoken before. I could make out what he was saying, but it was as far removed from classical Greek as contemporary English is from that of Chaucer.

" 'Charmion has chosen well—'

" 'Chosen what, exactly? Now see here—'

"But when his gaze locked on mine, he had that same bewitching, numbing effect as had Charmion. He seemed very, very old. I felt as if, staring into his eyes, I was gazing down into a bottomless pit, to the very depths of eternity.

" 'This way, please.'

"I was directed through the door, into a spacious banqueting room and directed to recline on a couch, *as the ancients did,* while a meal was served. Again, my mind was a muddle, racing in many directions at once. I wanted to ask, but did not, how he knew my name, since I had not actually introduced myself properly to 'Charmion'—if that were really *her* name—so she could not have told it to him, unless she read minds.

"I later came to understood that *immortals,* beings who have survived two, three, or even four thousand years, might as well be able to read minds, because we are not even as children to them, all our thoughts are as familiar and obvious to them as are a dog or cat's limited repertoire of tricks to a pet owner.

"But I am getting ahead of myself.

"A sumptuous meal was served by—I do not exaggerate—noiseless, barefoot servants in plain tunics. We had been joined by perhaps a dozen others, the master of the house, who said his name was Isidoros; Charmion; another woman, like Charmion neither young nor old but ageless; and by several more . . . Greeks, all of them reclining as we did, conversing but a little in the same antique dialect.

"I don't think anyone else was eating very much, though a few went through the motions of sipping the wine.

"It was all like something in a lurid novel.

" 'Think of this as a scene out of a romance,' said Isidoros. 'Imagine what Mister Haggard could do with this material.'

" 'You read Rider Haggard?'

"He laughed. It was terrifying. Somehow, he seemed much less human when he did. 'I don't have to. He needs to come to me for inspiration. I require nothing of him.'

"It was then, perhaps because there was some fiendish drug in the wine or food, or because I was bewitched by mysterious rays emanating from the magical scarab in my pocket, or because his eyes transfixed me as would an asp's stare, I realized that I could not rise and rush for the door, or even pull out my revolver and shoot my way clear, as any sensible person might—much less a proper hero out of a romance—that I could only sit there and listen while my host explained everything, while he regaled me with a tale so fantastic, so romantic, that no one could ever set it down properly, and my attempts to summarize must remain woefully inadequate.

"The scene was two thousand years ago, 30 B.C. to be precise. Marc Antony and Cleopatra—*the* Cleopatra, the famous one, the last of the Ptolemies—having suffered defeat at Actium and retreated back to Alexandria, now awaited their doom. The skies were full of strange portents. In the night, strange revelry was heard, though no one saw the revelers, as they passed out of the city and into the desert, a sure sign that the god Bacchus, to whom Antony was devoted, had abandoned him. Stagnant, helpless months passed. Octavian and the Roman army arrived at the city. Loyal armies melted away. This much is known to history and to legend, that Antony fell on his sword, and, dying, was raised up into the tomb where Cleopatra had betaken herself.

"What is not known is that she, in her despair, thinking him already dead, had availed herself of certain arts she had gained in her profound studies of all things Egyptian. The other Ptolemies had been too proud of being Greek. They had dismissed all else as barbarian rubbish, but *she* truly appreciated the ancient and unfathomable mystery which is this land. *She* called out of the darkness, from beneath her tomb, from out of the earth's depths, *something*, some vital, infinitely powerful force, and it *changed her*. She gave up her blood. She drank of its blood. *Honored be her name!* She was changed into something *else,* not a demon, not a god, but not human either. That which *lives on* to this day. I was among her worshippers, who also lived on, those who served her, and who, this night, intended to summon *her* once more out of the darkness, to drink blood and to share it.

"It was *my* blood she was after. That was the purpose of this entire charade. And to think I suspected them of trying to sell stolen antiquities. Ha! Isidoros would have found this funny. He would have laughed that hideous laugh of his. He might have said, 'Sell antiquities? No, we *are* antiquities!' but of course he did not say it, because the joke would have been as obvious to him as a cat's trick you've seen a thousand times.

"I had been fattened for the slaughter, which was the purpose of the meal. I struggled to rise. My limbs would not quite work properly. My mind was not clear. I understood, either because someone told me or because I was starting to read thoughts myself that Cleopatra's lost tomb was *right there,* under or adjoining that house, or perhaps part of it in some magical space beyond three dimensions . . . certainly its location is unknown to archaeologists. I came to understand that *she* had had no further use for Marc Antony, who was ultimately a bungler, and so she had left his corpse for the Romans to find, but *she* vanished. That final scene in Plutarch, 'Was this well done by your lady?' and so on and so on . . . that is the kind of thing that makes *her* acolytes laugh so horribly. Yes, in eternity, they have their little jokes. *Honored be her name!*

"I tell you that Cleopatra, immortal, transformed,

more than human, came to us out of the darkness that night. There was drumming and chanting, the playing of unworldly notes on some kind of flute or horn, and a great doorway opened up where I hadn't realized there even was one. It was like the stones within a tomb rolled aside, grinding slowly, with a sound like muted thunder, and then *she* came forth to drink *my* blood and share my blood with the others—hence the sacrificial knife and the bowl—but—*honored be her name!*—I was to be initiated into this blessed, damned company, forever and ever.

"I met Cleopatra that night. I encountered her face to face. The look in her eyes . . . I cannot tell you . . . all I can say is that in a last moment of rationality I lurched up from the table, pulled out my revolver, and emptied it into her. You might say I missed, I was drugged, my hand was unsteady, and I missed. But I know I did not. *Of course* the bullets did no good. They only made her laugh. Horribly."

It was late. We were alone now, in the darkness. The street was empty. I looked back into the Greek café proper. No one seemed to be there. The few candles had burned low or gone out. The city itself seemed preternaturally hushed. No dogs barking in the distance, no night birds, no laughter or song from late-night revelers.

Hushed. Silent. *Listening.*

And then Sir Henry McPherson began to laugh, and my blood chilled at the sound of it. This was not the good-natured chuckle of the kindly, fatherly man who had once been my mentor. No, this was *something* else.

"Quite a story, isn't it, David? Yes, quite a story. The ending is all rushed and a muddle. Go ahead and critique it if you will. I value your opinion, David. You were always such a clever boy."

I couldn't bring myself to say anything.

"Here," he said.

He slid a scarab across the tabletop and I, out of some compulsion I could neither understand nor control, took it.

"You want to know, David, why Cleopatra, after two thousand years in the grave and beyond the grave, in her *undead* state, as you might call it, went through all that rigmarole *for me.* Well, I assure you, she had done this sort of thing before, summoning Arabs into her darkness, Persians, Turks, even Mongols, as each of those nations ruled the world and might be manipulated through her dark influence. *Hundreds* of them. She knows that the power is gone from Greece, from Rome, and now, *fee, fi, foe, fum, I smell the blood of an Englishman*—isn't that *funny,* David? Now she knows that if she is to rule, she must do so from London.

"So she is recruiting Englishmen, David. That's what she's doing.

"But there's more. You want to attack the plausibility of my story. You dearly wish you could bring yourself to not believe a word of it. There is one point of logic you particularly wish to assail. Go ahead, my boy, ask your question. If you must."

At last, I did find the words, and managed to say, "But . . . but . . . if the bullets didn't have any effect, *how did you escape?"*

His teeth gleamed in the darkness.

"I didn't," he said.

That was when the Greek waiters, accompanied by a priest, came charging out of the back, wielding a silver cross, knives, and a wooden stake.

Ill-Met in Ilium

by Gregory Frost

Bitten—Goddess sing of how the rescuing hand
was bitten by the radiant one it had rescued.
Taken from that son of Atreus who'd nursed and encouraged
but starved her strangeness—
a half-living state fit only for
the hidden, nocturnal aspect of Apollo called Smintheus,
bringer of plagues, lover of vermin, mice and rats.
Lustful Paris mistook Helen's unnatural beauty
as anyone would have done and, unwitting,
allowed that undisclosed unsavory characteristic
to fester in his embrace. It flowered, swelled,
consumed and conquered.
Had he known this,
would Menelaus have sailed forth
to the beach before Ilium to confront
those unyielding Trojans behind their walls?
Would he have comprehended the cost of success?
The gods, even they saw not the thing that ripened

in the dark of a hold, where it claimed, one
after the other, the will of many among
Paris' crew, while the young prince, himself a moon-
calf,
knew none of it. Well-fed, she ensorcelled him.
The ship sailed home, and slowly followed the war.

It was Thersites
That hideous warrior, shamed by Odysseus
for his effrontery and foul language,
who first of all the Achaean armies fell victim
through his treasonous rage.
Wandering from the camp in the night, he
met the Specter—
she who'd called Lacedaemon home
had escaped confinement
in the citadel, its victim
turned victimizer while Apollo,
their immortal guardian, slept.
Revenge, she would have it upon both sides.
Thersites recognized her not at all, having never set
eyes
upon her till then. He drew his sword against
the shape, as it drifted nearer.
Close up, like Paris he was smitten—
he, clubfooted and double-humped,
had little experience with the fair sex,
alive or undead.

"You," she called him,
ghostly pale as a living moon. She hovered nearer.
"I sense your contention, your leashed anger toward
the leader of your band," she whispered, and

Thersites trembled at her iced touch,
and swallowed hard his own words.
This apparition then opened the brooch upon her shoulder
and let the cloth covering her breasts drop.
For all her paleness, the tips of her breasts shown
ebony in the moon's light. She, with a finger,
drew a curve above one nipple, and a black line
flowed behind it as if she'd painted upon herself.
"Drink your fill, oh, man,"
she said. And Thersites, quivering, dropped his blade
and bent his head to the wet rivulet. Feasted long.
A taste he wanted, a taste that any man
would have desired. And little would
they or he have realized that the liquor
of a plague now flowed past their lips.
So was Thersites changed
while all attention lingered elsewhere,
upon the warring Agamemnon as he abused
the prize he'd stolen from that
swift runner, Achilles.
Gods and men alike
watched the rage unfurl, the heated words
dividing them as the walls of Troy separated
their armies from the transformed goal.
"Dog-face!" Achilles named Agamemnon
and thereafter turned his back on war.
Scant secret and less shadow was necessary
for the theft of Thersites' will by
the highborn revenant, that beauteous Helen.
Then as Dawn spread rosy fingers over the sea,
the apparition evaporated with her power implanted

in the hunchback. When the time came,
he would do her bidding.

The battles raged, the daily slaughter
for one king's greed and another's honor.
Truces struck served to delay
the challenges. The Atrides' hot words
betrayed their promises, until a son of Priam
slew Odysseus' brave comrade Leucus
and the battle lust burst again.
Spears through temples, groin,
and back. Jaws unhinged and blood
erupting like a fountain's deadly art.
Idomeneus' men slew and stripped
the corpses. Days of battle, bloodied sand.
Then came Night who makes even lofty Zeus
tremble, and the Achaeans granted Ilium
the claim upon its fallen heroes, so that
the absence of the corpses come morning
did not seem to them odd at first, but of a process
of honorable retrieval, while those of the city
assumed their enemies were playing cruelly
upon their grief in stealing the dead.
Only after the second or third time
that the same warrior, killed in previous battle,
was felled in a late skirmish, did the rumors spread
of something unnatural.

And did they, behind those wide gates,
know what plague lurked in their own midst?
It is spoken how Paris burst into action at the death
of his friend Harpalion, but not that the act
took place by torchlight, as night drew a blanket

over the sandy plain; or that Paris dropped
upon the soldier Euchenor, whose prophet father
had offered him a choice—to die of plague in his
own halls or at the hands of Trojans.
The old seer had got it right twice over.
Paris drained the life from Euchenor
without the need of lance or arrow's tip.
He had been turned sometime before.

All this while Hector slept, as others did,
safe from one death, prey to another.
How quickly it did move no one can say,
although each day warriors aplenty
faced Ajax and Idomeneus,
charged the ships and beat the Argives
back. Time and again they struck,
and their ranks hardly dwindled, never
were exhausted. Thus cautiously did the revenants ensure heir own continuance.

Patroclus, disguised, fell to Hector, else the
wretched contests might not have changed.
Hector, he the stallion-breaker, died
from Achilles' spear, went down in the dust
and had to be ransomed back.

Epeus boxed for a mule and Cassandra stood
upon the battlements at dusk, most lovely daughter
of Priam, and foresaw the death of her city.
She laughed and fairly dared those princes and kings
spread out across the blood-drenched plain to
prove themselves better men. She was by then
already turned as well. She had witnessed her fate
and embraced it willingly, inviting Helen to her bed

where she bared herself for that most painful pleasure.
The two of them next approached Hector's
wailing widow, and fed upon her in her grief, these two sisters. Engaged in their lurid business,
they failed to detect innocent Aeneas, himself whisked
from Achilles' wrath by the god of earthquakes.
Aeneas saw it all, that poor innocent, and his
martial will left him.
Weak with horror he withdrew to his family,
gathered them up and crept through the shrouded city.
At fires he saw others whom he knew. The first few
rejected his pleas, his seemingly mad warnings
of doom at the hands of fanged Harpies.
Inured to fantastical notions after years of war,
of ceaseless slaughter, they laughed.
He saw that he would
never convince good friends of this and, instead,
proclaimed the city certain to fall now
that its towering hero, Hector, had been brought down, by swift Achilles. Upon those words his number
grew, and swelling,
drew the attention of Helen's undead league.
In the end, unwittingly, his followers
carried the plague to their new land.

Through a hidden exit—
the very one that Helen had used to prey upon the
wounded and the dead upon the field—the swelling cluster
escaped the city's fate. When was brave Aeneas' wife

stolen from him? Snatched certainly by those who
wrapped themselves in darkness. The moment passed
in utter silence, so that he, brave man, didn't notice.
He led his people, his children, only to discover, finally,
her absence. Then he left his followers and raced
back into the city. There he encountered her shade,
both hungry for him and gifted now with profound sight.
"You will be great," she said, "and found a new
city in a foreign land. I cannot touch you else unmake this vision."
He could not raise his blade to her,
his wife, no matter what she had become.
He retreated from the horror, his only course.
Again, upon the beach,
he and his people eluded the Achaeans. They were themselves
too busy, engaged in erecting the scheme set in motion
by Helen through her abject slave, Thersites.
He, like a grotesque gnat, had buzzed into the ear
of clever Odysseus a scheme of great daring—
and in pretend penance, he gave credit
for the idea to that skillful one.

Thus it was that Aeneas and
most of his followers alone escaped the plague
delivered by Helen and her sisters
upon Priam's city and citadel.
The corpse of that great hero,
Hector, lay twelve days in Achilles' care

without decay nor any sign of death's embrace,
so that when Priam kissed the hand of Achilles and begged
for the body, both of them thought only that Apollo,
Troy's protector, had preserved it until its return.

On this point the blind poet
ended his story, knowing full well that what followed
was too horrible to relate. He left it
to others to tell—and those, coming so much later,
received and related only spoils,
replacing what was too impossible to state
with clever tales more likely to gain acceptance.
But here is how it truly went,
and how the blood-leeching creatures blended
into history.

The next day
only those in thrall like Thersites
roamed the streets, pushed back the broad Scaean Gates,
and strode out upon the deserted plain
haunted as it was by the ghosts of so many comrades,
to where the Argives had left their "gift."
These servile citizens
of Ilium knew what to do, guided as they were
by the mind of Helen, her body
somnolent in the heat of day.
With ropes and tackle they hauled
the monstrous horse through the gates,
into the city. As if dazzled by the offering,

by its vanished creators, they left the gates unbarred.
Even ensorcelled by the blood
they had supped, these minions found it
difficult not to laugh at the wooden horse,
at the occasional sandal, the flash of breastplate,
that showed between its ribs.

Odysseus and his small army waited through
the warm afternoon, sealed in their own
stink till it was time. Then in the darkest
of the night, they would open the trap and descend,
just as Odysseus had described to them,
as Thersites had whispered it,
as most diabolical Helen had planned it.
Philoctetes, who'd arrived at the war
last of all, lay among them in the equine belly.
He shared his hydra-venomed arrows with that other
skillful archer, Odysseus, little knowing,
either of them, how these weapons—
gifts from Hercules—would save them.
The poison in those shafts, expertly shot,
exploded every fiend it touched.
The revenant horror called Hector died again thus impaled.
Where most of the horse's band fell to the guzzling monsters,
the two brave archers fought back to back,
till Agamemnon's army burst the gate to find them,
and upon Odysseus' cry, set the torch to the enemy.
They overcame Helen's horde while Apollo,
Sungod, slept in ignorance.

* * *

Afterward, Odysseus paid the price for this
as angry Apollo blotted out the day of his homecoming
for ten years. Many others, bitten by Ilium's undead
yet seemingly alive, burst into flames aboard their ships
where there were few places to hide from the golden sun.

Only Agamemnon, because he was a king, was
able to remain in the shadows once he was turned.
It was Cassandra who drained him.
She had locked herself in a cell
and pretended to be a poor victim of her father,
instead of one of the chief plague-bearers.

Agamemnon, foolish man, carried her off as a trophy,
leaving it to his wife, Clytemnestra, to discover
what he'd become. She had taken a lover, but even
he doubted her story of her husband's unnaturalness
and abandoned her to her fate.

For nights she kept him at bay.
But finally her husband fell upon the queen
and tore at her throat.
He would have drained her dry had not the god Apollo
flung his rays just then upon the undead king,
driving him underground. She lived but would not
another morning survive without cunning and resolve.

When Agamemnon awoke that next night
he found his wife at her bath. She stood
and welcomed him, her fine body so slick with oil

that he could not find purchase,
his fingers slipping as she sank back,
his hunger growing at her enticement as she drew him
down.
He did not see the spike she brought up
out of the frothy bath and plunged
through his chest. He toppled into the water,
his body melting away like a taper. After that,
Cassandra met the same swift fate, for no one there
cared for her cries or pitied her.

And Philoctetes, whose venomed points had
saved them all—he roamed ever after across
the wine-dark Aegean in search of those monsters
who had escaped the fire and death, and who spread
the plague of their kind into his world.
He, the first hunter of vampires,
came to rest gently years later in Sybaris.
He left his quiver of poisoned missiles
with the Sungod Apollo in his temple at Krimissa,
where the fiends dared not seek them,
and where they await the next archer even now.

The Temptation of Saint Anthony

by Brian Stableford

There was no moon on the night when Anthony was bitten by a vampire as he slept within the walls of the abandoned fort at Pispir; the star shadows were so deep that he got no more than the merest glimpse of the creature. His only abiding memories were tactile: skeletal thinness and rags so fragmentary and dust-encrusted that they seemed more like the tatters of an ancient shroud than clothing.

The bite was ragged too, being perhaps more tear than bite, having apparently been inflicted by blunt and decaying teeth. It never entirely healed, although it did not become infected. Although little trace of spilled blood remained, Anthony was sure that he had lost a good deal—perhaps enough to kill him. For three full days he expected to die, and even when he stopped expecting it he was not at all sure that his condition could still be reckoned life rather than a strange kind of undeath.

When the next travelers stopped at the fort to draw water from the well that had determined its site, they found its resident hermit awake and active, but somewhat delirious. They were reassured, however, when he consented to accept a little food from them, and showed no inclination to savage them like a rabid dog. They even offered to escort him to Alexandria, if he decided that it would be best to leave his refuge, but he declined the offer.

"I have sworn to remain here for twenty years," he told them. "There will be time for preaching when my own education is complete."

"There are schools in Alexandria," the caravan's leader told him, "and the greatest library in the world, despite of the neglect it has suffered."

"That is not the kind of learning I seek," he replied. "I want to know what is within myself—what the Lord might communicate to me if only I may hear him."

The travelers were not Christians, but they understood his notion of the Lord better than a Roman would have done. "This is the desert," the leader of the band told him. "Here, the voices of the djinn are louder than the voice of God. Solitude leads to madness."

"The Devil will undoubtedly tempt me," Anthony admitted. "I am ready for that." He did not tell them that the thirst was already building within him for something richer by far than water or wine, nor what effort it required to resist the urge to cut his visitors' throats and suck the wounds till he could suck no more.

He had always thought that solitude was the best

thing for a man of his sort. The fact that the company of living human beings would henceforth be an endless torment of unacknowledgeable desire only served to confirm his judgment.

The travelers went on their way on the thirty-first day after Anthony had endured the vampire's bite; after that he was alone until the evening of the fortieth day, when he woke from a doze at sunset to find a simulacrum of Christ offering him a cup.

"This is my blood," said the apparent Christ. "Drink of it, and be saved."

"I have been expecting you, Satan," Anthony replied. "I knew that you would seize upon my new weakness. Why else would you have sent the demon to suck the fluid from me?"

"This is my blood," the false Christ repeated. "It is my gift, and the way to salvation."

"You are the Devil," Anthony retorted, "and you have no gift to offer but eternal damnation." He got up and went to the well, setting Satan firmly behind him. He lowered the bucket and brought it up again. He drank but he was still thirsty, and he knew that the darker thirst would not be assuaged by water.

Anthony did not doubt that the fluid in the Devil's cup really was blood, nor that it would answer his terrible need, but he had not come to Pispir in search of satiation—quite the reverse, in fact. He did not drink water to salve his thirst, but only because he would die without it; had he been able to drink and keep his thirst he would have done so. To be able to drink and still have thirst to test him was a privilege of sorts.

When he turned around again, determined to see

things in the light of his faith, the Devil was cloven-hoofed and shaggy-legged, with horns set atop his brow. Satan did not seem comfortable in this form, for his eyes seemed pained and his gaze was roaming restlessly, but Anthony assumed that this was because honesty was a sore trial to a creature of his kind.

"You are foolish to insist on seeing me thus," the Devil complained, casting aside the cup, from which nothing spilled as it rolled over the flagstones bordering the well. "I am neither the Great God Pan, nor the Father of Lies, nor a prideful angel cast out of Heaven. I will admit to being a temptation personified, but mine is the temptation of knowledge and progress. I am one who can and will reveal secrets, if you will only consent to listen."

"I will not," Anthony told his adversary. "I am deaf to all but the word of the Lord, and knowledge of the Lord is the only wisdom I seek."

"I did not send the vampire to bite you," the Devil insisted, his agonized eyes looking upward as if to welcome the deeper blue that was consuming the sky from the east. "That is not my way of working—but if I were of a mind to create such creatures, I would shape them as seductive women, whose bite would be a glorious indulgence and a pleasure unmatchable. The wretched parasite that attacked you was one of nature's sports. If God were responsible for such monstrosities—and I cannot believe that He is—they would be evidence of His sickness or His sense of humor."

"Have you come to debate with me, then?" Anthony asked. "I do not mind in the least, for the nights are long at this time of year, and often surprisingly cold. It will be a futile occupation, though, from your own point of view. There are many souls in the world, alas, that might be won with far less trouble than mine."

"This is not a contest," the Devil said, seeming a little more at ease now that the evening star was shining brightly and the atmospheric dust in the west had taken on the color of blood. "There was no war in Heaven, and there is no war on Earth for the souls of humankind. You conceive of yourself as a battleground in which a higher self of faith of virtue, aided by a guardian angel, is ceaselessly at war with a lower self of insatiable appetite and uncontrollable passion, provoked by mischievous imps, but all of that is mere illusion. If solitude really allowed you to look into yourself more clearly, you would know that you are less divided than you imagine, and that the world is not as you imagine it to be."

"Excellent," said Anthony. "Nothing can warm a man more, in the absence of tangible heat, than the labor of cutting through sophistry. Sit down, my enemy, I beg you. Let's make ourselves as comfortable as we can, given the hardness of the ground and the aching within."

"Oh, no," the Devil said, seeming to grow larger as the night advanced, and now unfurling wings like those of a gigantic eagle. "I can do better than that, my friend, by way of distracting us from our mutual plight."

Anthony had observed that the Devil, in what he took to be the dark angel's natural form, was not well-adapted for sitting. His goatish limbs were not articulated like a human's; even squatting must be awkward for him. He had not expected compliance when he made his teasing offer, but neither had he expected to be carried away.

The Devil did not grow claws to match his wings; indeed, the wings themselves refused to coalesce into avian feathers, but continued to grow and to change, as if they were intent on attaining the pure insubstantiality of shadow. By night, it seemed, the Ape of God and the Adversary of Humankind had more freedom to formulate himself as he wished—and what he wished to be, it seemed, was a vast cloud of negation.

Anthony felt himself caught up by that cloud, but he was not grabbed or clutched, merely elevated toward the sky. The cloud was beneath him and all around him, but it was perfectly transparent—more perfectly transparent, in fact, than a pool of pure water or the unstirred desert air.

Anthony tried to resist the sensation that he could see more clearly through the cloud of absence than he had ever been able to see before, but his eyes were unusually reluctant to take aboard his conviction and he had to fight to secure the dictatorship of his faith.

He saw the walls of the fort shrink beneath him, until the ruin was a mere blur on the desert's face. Then he saw the coastline of North Africa, where the ocean was separated from the arid wilderness by a mere ribbon of fertile ground. Then he watched the curve of the horizon extend into the arc of a circle, and he saw the sun that had set a little while before rise again in the west, as the edge of the world could no longer hide it.

"You cannot trouble me with that," he told the Devil. "I know that the world is round."

The Devil no longer had eyes to reflect his anguish, nor a leathery tongue with which to form his lies, but he was not voiceless. He spoke within Anthony's head, like an echo of a thought.

"Fear not, my friend," the voice said, softer now than before. "I have brought air enough to sustain us for the whole night long—and if, by chance, you would like to slake your thirsts, I have water and blood enough to bring you to the very brink of satisfaction."

"I have drunk my fill of the Lord's good water," Anthony told him, "and human blood I will never drink, no matter how my Devil-led thirst might increase. I can suffer any affliction, knowing that my Lord loves me and that my immortal soul is safe for all eternity."

While he spoke, Anthony observed that the world was spinning on its axis and moving through space as if to describe a circle of its own around the sun. The moon and the world were engaged in a curious dance, but the sun—whose disk seemed no bigger than the moon's when seen from the land of Egypt—seemed to have become far more massive as the cloud moved toward it.

"Were you expecting a sequence of crystal spheres?" the Devil whispered from his hidden corner of Anthony's consciousness. "Were you unmoved by my promise of air because you never believed in the possibility of a void? Did you think that you could breathe the quintessential ether as you moved through the hierarchy of the planets toward the ultimate realm of the fixed stars?"

"There is but one Lord," Anthony replied, "and I am content to breathe in accordance with His providence."

"Alas, you'll have to breathe in accordance with my providence, for a little while," said the Adversary of Humankind. "There is neither air nor ether outside this nimbus. Can you see that the world is but one of the planetary family, toiling around the central sun? Do you see how small a world it is, by comparison with mighty Jupiter? Can you see that Jupiter and Saturn have major satellites as big as worlds themselves, and hosts of minor ones? Do you see how the space between Mars and Jupiter is strewn with planetoids? Can you see the halo from which comets come, beyond the orbits of worlds unseen from Earth, unnamed as yet by curious astronomers?"

Anthony, who was familiar with the story of Er as told in Plato's *Republic*, looked for the Spindle of Necessity and listened for the siren song of the music of the spheres, but he was not disappointed by their absence.

"I am riding in a cloud formed by the Master of Illusion," he said, not speaking aloud but confident that the Devil, cornered within him, could hear him perfectly well. "You cannot frighten me with empty space and lonely worlds. If the earth is indeed a solitary wanderer in an infinite void, I shall feel my kinship with its rocks and deserts more keenly than before."

"The Master of Illusion is sight constrained by

faith," the Devil told him. "I am an iconoclast, committed to breaking the idols that filter the evidence of your earthbound eyes. I do not seek to frighten you but to awaken you. Do you see the stars, now that we are moving through their realm? Can you see that they are not fixed at all, but moving in their own paces about the chaos at the heart of the Milky Way? Do you see the nebulae that lie without the sidereal system? Can you discern the stars that comprise them—systems like the Milky Way, more numerous by far than the stars they each contain?"

"It is a pretty conceit," Anthony admitted. "Evidence, I trust, of your sense of humor rather than your sickness of mind."

"It is the truth," said the voice within him.

"If it were real," Anthony retorted, "it would not be equal to the millionth part of the greater truth, which is faith in the Lord and His covenant with humankind." He knew, however, that while the Devil was lurking inside him, borrowing the voice of his own thoughts, he had no means of concealing the force of his realization that perhaps this was the truth, and that the world really might be no more than a mediocre rock dutifully circling a mediocre star in a mediocre galaxy in a universe so vast that no power of sight could plumb its depths nor any power of mind calculate its destiny.

Curiously enough, however, the Devil did not appear to be privy to that unvoiced thought, formulated more by dread than doubt. "It was not always thus," the Devil said. "In the beginning, it was very tiny—but that was fourteen billion years ago; it is expanding still, and has a far greater span before it, until the last fugitive stars expend the last of their waning light, and darkness falls upon lifelessness forever."

"The Lord said 'Let there be light,'" Anthony reminded the Adversary. "He did not say 'Let there be light forever'—but what does it matter, since our souls are safe in his care?"

"*Our* souls?" countered the Devil.

"Human souls," Anthony corrected himself. "Those human souls, at least, which contrive to stay out of your dark clutches."

The cloud seemed to come to a halt then, in an abyss of space that suddenly seemed vertiginous in every direction, where whole systems of stars were reduced to mere points of tentative light. "This is not so awesome," whispered the Devil, "compared with the emptiness inside an atom, where matter dissolves into animate mathematical entity and uncertainty refuses the definition of solidity. I wish I could show you that, but a human mind's eye is incapable of such imagination. Trust me when I tell you that there is void within as well as without, and that substance is rarer than you could ever comprehend."

"There is no void where the Lord is," Anthony replied, "and the Lord is everywhere—except, I must suppose, in the depths of your rebellious heart, from which He has been rudely cast out."

As he spoke, though, the hermit became more sharply aware of his thirst for blood, the curse that the Devil had inflicted upon him in order to increase his vulnerability to unreason.

Anthony struggled to keep his next thought unvoiced, but in the end he decided that he had no need to hide from the Devil while he was still committed to the Lord. "I am a vampire now," he said, without waiting for any reply to his previous observation. "But I am no more a sinner than I was before. I thirst, but I trust in the Lord to deliver me from evil. I will not drink of human blood, no matter how intense my thirst becomes. If my life is to be a trial by ordeal, then I shall be vindicated."

"And if you should live forever, unable to die?" the Devil murmured. "What then, my friend? What if your thirst should become as infinite as the abyss of space, never ceasing to increase?"

"Eventually," Anthony reminded him, "the last star will expend the last of its light, and darkness will fall forever. I shall be safe in the bosom of the Lord."

The cloud condensed around him then and moved through him, as if it were turning him inside out or drawing him into a fourth dimension undiscernible by human eyes—but then the dark abyss of intergalactic space was replaced by the familiar gloom of night on Earth. Anthony found himself on the edge of a cliff not far from his fort, kneeling on the bare rock and looking out over the desert dunes.

Anthony bowed his head and was about to thank the Lord for his deliverance, when he caught sight of a moon shadow from the corner of his eye. It appeared to be the shadow of a human being, but Anthony knew better than to trust the appearance.

He turned to look at the Devil, who now wore the appearance of an Alexandrian philosopher—an Epicurean, Anthony supposed, rather than a neo-Platonist.

"What now?" the hermit said, glad to be able to

speak the words aloud, although his tongue felt thick and the inside of his mouth was parched. "Have you no one else to tempt and torment? I have seen your emptiness, and yet am full. I will no more drink of horror and despair than of human blood. I must suppose that I am a vampire now, but I still have my faith. I shall never be a minion of the Prince of Demons."

"This is not a contest," the Devil said, again. "I have nothing to gain or lose by tempting you. I do not need and do not want your soul, your heart, or your affection."

"And yet, you seem to have a thirst of some sort," Anthony observed. "Perhaps you are a vampire too, avid for human blood despite your best intentions."

"There is a thirst," the Devil admitted, "and it might be mine. Have you ever met the Sphinx, my friend, in your lonely fort? Has she ever asked you her riddle? Her true riddle, I mean, not the one contrived by Sophocles."

"I have never met a sphinx," Anthony said, rising to his feet and brushing the dust from the hem of his ragged coat. "But if I ever did, I would know you in that guise, and I would answer you then as I answer you now: I trust in the Lord, and Jesus Christ is my savior. I fear no possible consequence of that declaration."

"And yet there are heretics already within the Christian company," the Devil said. "There is division, disharmony, and distrust even among those who worship the One God and accept the same savior. If you could see the future . . . but I dare say that you would see it as selectively as you see the present, filtered by the lens of faith. They will call you saint if you preach in Alexandria and write letters to the emperor Constantine when you are done here. You will be the stuff of legend, and I shall not be entirely blameless in that, should I fail in my endeavor—but the vampire's bite is your secret and mine, and will remain so. History always has its secrets, and a world like yours has more than its share, since it uses writing so sparingly."

Anthony could look into the Devil's eyes again now, and could see that they were as restless as they had been before, although their pain seemed to have been dulled. He saw the Devil lick his lips, as if to moisten them against the dry and bitter wind that blew from the dunes.

"The scriptures are a gift from the Lord," Anthony said, although he knew that no defense was necessary. "The commandments are preserved there, as they need to be now that the Ark of the Covenant is lost."

"Writing is an awkward instrument," the Devil remarked. "Without measurement and calculation, linear reasoning and syntactical complexity, science is impossible. But the learning of letters and numbers requires specialist teachers, and the custodians of culture inevitably become jealous of the privilege they control, establishing themselves as arbiters of faith. Their empire is fragile, though; once a man is taught to read, he is better equipped to think . . . and to doubt."

Anthony's eyes were scanning the eastern horizon, searching for the twilight that would precede the dawn, but there was no sign of it. There must still be several hours of night remaining. He licked his own lips, thirsty now for more than blood.

"I want to show you the answer to the Sphinx's riddle," the Devil said, softly. "The riddle of life and death, of growth and aging, of competition and selection. I cannot force you to read its significance, but I shall write it in your eyes regardless."

"I am weary," Anthony admitted, "but you cannot defeat me. My thirst may be a torment, but it keeps me alert to your wiles."

"Look," said the Father of Lies, pointing out into the shadowed desert, where the dunes had begun to stir and shift.

Anthony knew that moonlight could play tricks in the desert night. The haze that blurred the air by day seemed to disappear by night, but the fugitive light was deceptive nevertheless.

It seemed to him that the fine sand eddied into life, and that its motes, at first dissociated, began to cleave together into imitations of complex organic forms: leaves and tubers, worms and mites, slugs and crabs, trees and snakes. He saw all these creatures growing from tiny seeds and eggs into complex forms that produced more seeds and eggs, each generation dying off as the next emerged. He saw that in order to grow, the creatures fed upon one another, not randomly but in measured and defined ways. Even the sedentary plants, whose only necessary nourishment was wind and sunlight, accepted the substance of the decaying dead into their own flesh, so that nothing that might be incorporate in flesh was lost or wasted, but always recycled and transfigured. He saw that the feeding was always competitive, and that there was also competition to delay the moment when the living became food, so that no succeeding generation was exactly the same as the one that had gone before.

Everything was changing, and would continue to change. Creation was continuous, and would never be complete.

Anthony saw, then, that the human species was a product of this process of ceaseless change, and deduced that the human species was no more immune to further change than any other. He understood that human beings were merely a part of a much larger pattern: a temporary artifact of the irresistible organic flux, a momentary fancy of the interminable restlessness of the molecules of life, which were forever in the process of consumption and excretion, hurrying from form to form with only the merest pauses for sleep, death, thought, and faith. The answer to the Sphinx's riddle, the hermit determined, was that life had its own energy, its own circulation, and its own busy complexity. It did not need a sculptor—and he sensed that any sculptor who ever tried to tame its innate exuberance would surely fail.

"What is this to me?" Anthony said to the Devil. "I came to the desert to escape tumult, not to conjure it up in my dreams. It is in loneliness that one finds the Lord, and becomes close to the Lord. Life's transactions are not uninteresting to me, nor are they irrelevant, but my first concern is the immortal soul, which rests immune from all of this confusion."

"And yet, my friend," the Devil said, "you thirst

for water and you thirst for blood. Your flesh has no immunity to need, and your mind can have no immunity to the thirst induced by that need."

The disguised Father of Lies took a dagger from the folds of his clothing, rolled up his sleeve, and cut his forearm from the crook of the elbow to the junction of his palm. "Come and drink," he said, as the blood welled out and began to rain down on the rocky escarpment. "Drink of my blood, and be content."

"I will not," Anthony replied. "Not now, or ever. You cannot terrify me, demon that you are, for I am armored by my faith in the Lord, and in Jesus Christ my savior. You cannot tempt me, demon that you are, for I am armored by the certainty of my salvation, and the inviolability of my immortal soul. Water I shall drink as the need arises, but blood I never shall; I shall bear my thirst to the grave, no matter how long it might take to arrive there."

The Devil lifted his arm and licked his own blood, seeming to take considerable comfort therefrom. Then he turned and looked behind him.

Anthony had not seen the four human figures that were creeping through the night until the Devil looked directly at them, but that did not mean that they had not been there all along, moving forward surreptitiously, as men who are abroad at night are wont to do.

"Ah!" the Devil said, as if he were not surprised to find them there, even though he had not suspected their presence until some tiny sound caused him to turn around. "Here are some who won't refuse a drop of blood, though I dare say they haven't thirsted quite as long as you, my friend." He held out his arm, inviting the four to approach.

They did so, warily. They, at least, were surprised. They were not used to such offerings—or, indeed, to any offerings at all.

Anthony stared at the shadowed figures as they came closer, illuminated by a moon that was less than half full but whose light served nevertheless to augment the feeble glimmer of the distant stars. The newcomers were so thin as to seem like walking skeletons, their clothing reduced to mere ribbons—but their eyes were large and bright and greedy, and their thin lips were pursed in anticipation.

The Devil offered his arm freely. The cut was long enough to allow them all to drink simultaneously, two on each side; if the Devil had as much blood in him as a common man, they might have taken a stomach full apiece and still left a residue behind. But that was not what happened.

The four vampires leaped upon their prey like a pack of jackals, clawing and snapping at him and at one another. Maddened by the combination of their thirst and their proximity to the means of slaking it, they lashed out in every direction, each of them seemingly more intent on keeping his companions away from the prize than to claim it for himself.

They bit and sucked, lapped and swallowed, but for every drop they claimed a dozen were spilled on the rocky ledge. The Devil went down beneath their assault, bitten on both his legs as well as his arms, and about his face and throat as well. He sustained a dozen new wounds within a minute, a hundred within five.

All of them bled with what seemed to Anthony to be unnatural copiousness—as if the vampires' saliva had some agent within it that prevented the blood from clotting.

In his hometown of Coma and in Alexandria too—within the shadow of the library wall—Anthony had seen starving dogs fighting over a bone, but this was different. Even starving dogs retained some vestige of respect for one another, snarling and howling at the expense of inflicting deadly bites. The four vampires knew no such restraint. They did not howl and they did not snarl, but they clawed and they bit. They gouged at one another's eyes and aimed deadly blows at one another's throats. Their intentions were rarely fulfilled, in the immediate sense, but as time went by, and the Devil's blood leaked away unharvested, the destruction they sought to wreak could hardly be avoided.

They were close to the edge of the cliff. One went sprawling over the edge, and then another. That left two—at which point the conflict became far less chaotic, more sharply focused.

The two vampires fought with all their might, and the Devil's precious blood continued to ebb away.

Anthony watched, dumbfounded.

Eventually, one vampire went down for the last time—not dead, but broken in his limbs and stunned into unconsciousness. The survivor, who was by no means uninjured, immediately set about trying to lick the last few rivulets of blood from the Devil's wounds, and to lap up the few fugitive pools that the rock had cupped. It was, it seemed to Anthony, a rather meager meal.

When the vampire had finished, he sat back warily, supporting himself with his scarred and twisted hands, and he looked up at Anthony. His eyes were bright and wild, but not devoid of intelligence.

"You can't allow yourself to be paralyzed by fear, my friend," the vampire said. "You're one of us now."

"Are you the one who bit me?" Anthony asked.

"What does that matter?" the vampire retorted, licking his lips avidly in search of one last drop of sustenance. "It's done. You should come with us—we're heading for Alexandria."

"Us?" Anthony echoed. "I think you will be alone from now on—and deservedly so, given that you treat your friends so vilely."

"They'll recover," the vampire said. "They'll be thirsty, but their bones will knit and their scratches will heal. They'll bear me no ill will. They know that there's strength in numbers, even if the contest that results when we find a lone victim can have only one winner. In Alexandria, it will be different. Cities were made for our kind. If you stay out here, though, alone, living men will catch you eventually. Then they'll behead you and burn your body. There's no way back from that. You'd best come with us. You have a great deal to learn."

"You have the Devil's blood in you now," Anthony told the creature. "It might make you stronger, I suppose, but it's poison nevertheless."

"If that were true," the vampire replied, "it would make little enough difference to me, who was damned a long time ago, but I know the blood of a philosopher when I taste it. An Epicurean, I believe—the least intoxicating of all."

"He wore the guise of an Epicurean," Anthony admitted, "but he was the Devil. He had been a cloud of transparent darkness only an hour or so before."

"The desert's full of djinn," the vampire told him. "There's no blood in them, but they can play tricks with your head. Thirst makes it easier. If he gets up again, he'll be one of us, but they don't always get up. I was lucky; so were you. Him too, though he won't feel it when he wakes up." The creature inclined his head briefly in the direction of his erstwhile companion and adversary, who was still unconscious.

"You cannot hurt me, monster," Anthony said.

"I certainly could," the monster replied. "But I've nothing to gain by it, and the thirst will punish you enough, if you insist in your stubbornness. You're welcome to come with us if you wish. If not, do as you will."

"I shall pray to the Lord for my salvation," Anthony said, defiantly. "I shall bear my thirst proudly, grateful to be tried and not found wanting. I shall guard my immortal soul until I die, and then confide it to the loving care of my savior and my Lord. The Devil could not tempt me, nor shall you."

The vampire came to his feet, wincing at the pain in his limbs and spine. He leaned over the Devil's body, then knelt down beside it. "He might come back, I suppose," was the monster's offhand judgment, "but I doubt it. Too much damage done. They say that nothing short of beheading and burning will make certain, but that's just superstitious dread. Don't worry about inviting me back to the fort—I'll camp out down there in the shadow of the cliff till nightfall comes again. Are you sure you won't come with us to Alexandria? They'll start hunting for us eventually, of course, and we'll have to move on, but there's plenty of blood to be had in the meantime. The city is our natural environment."

Anthony gathered himself together and came to stand opposite the vampire, looking down at the body of the man who had consented to be murdered. Anthony had to agree that it was impossible to believe that the corpse would ever be reanimated—but the Devil was a master of deception. He turned around abruptly and walked away, in the direction of the fort. He suspected that the vampire was staring at the back of his head, but he did not look back.

"The flesh is a distraction," the hermit said to himself, formulating the words clearly although he did not pronounce them aloud. "Its mortification is an irrelevance. The spirit is capable of rising above such trivial matters. Prayer will sustain me, no matter how long I am forced to endure this torment. As God wills, I shall do, even if I live to be a hundred."

According to history, he lived to be a hundred and five, but he knew what a liar history can be when legend-mongers get involved in it, and he had lost count long before he died. Once he was officially declared a saint, Anthony was able to ascend to Heaven and look back upon the earth, so he was able to watch with interest when his old Adversary the Devil tried his luck again in Heidelberg thirteen hundred years later, with a slightly different result.

After that, the cities of the world began to grow in earnest, and vampires to multiply. Anthony estimated that it might soon be time to call a halt to the whole sorry mess, perhaps to try again somewhere else in the vast and various universe, but he was not privy to the Lord's intentions.

"Personally," Saint Leocadia said to him one day, as they watched the outbreak and rapid progress of World War Three, "I'm glad to be out of it. I don't miss a single thing—except, I suppose . . ." She trailed off, as the saints always tended to do at that point in the conversation.

Anthony was too polite to finish the sentence for her, although he knew perfectly well what she meant. He certainly didn't miss the terrible thirst for blood that the Devil's minion had cruelly inflicted upon him, nor any of the thousand other shocks that flesh was heir to, pleasant or unpleasant, but every so often, he missed the little intellectual shocks that had stimulated his mind while his faith was yet to find its final justification.

The saint knew now that he had been right all along to trust in his savior and the grace of God, and that he would be right in everything he believed for all eternity. There was a certain undeniable satisfaction in the irresistibility of that confirmation—but he also understood, now, what the Devil had meant when he had insisted that it *wasn't a contest*. The Devil really hadn't had the slightest interest in winning his soul and really had been trying to explain the answer to the Sphinx's riddle.

By virtue of that realization, every now and again—if only a little—Saint Anthony couldn't help missing temptation.

BOHEMIAN RHAPSODY

by Ian Watson

After the rain of the past few days, the sky over Prague was eggshell blue. A cool breeze tickled at Tycho Brahe. Autumn was on the way. So as to avoid sneezing, he cupped the warmth of his hand over his false nose of silver and gold as he headed uphill from the Sign of the Golden Griffin toward the sprawl of the castle dominated by the cathedral. If he sneezed a few times, people might imagine that the plague was returning. A good thing if it did—the court would quit Prague, and so could he!

A warm nose made him think of a living body burning on a bonfire in Rome. Bruno's body, back in February—burned for claiming that our world circled the sun, and that many inhabited worlds existed. Of course the Copernican notion of a central sun was nonsense, but to be burned for *thinking*. And now those damned stupid malicious Capuchin monks were accusing Tycho of malice and black magic.

Supposedly the monks' prayers, emanating from

their residence near the palace, had been interfering with Tycho's alchemical witchcraft, keeping him from turning base metal into gold. Allegedy, as the emperor's astrological adviser, Tycho had persuaded Rudolph to turn the monks out.

"Gold, indeed!" Tycho snarled to himself in Danish, which no passerby would understand.

Gold, if only. The treasury could dearly use some gold. That's what the scientific wizards in the Powder Tower were trying to accomplish. Tycho himself was only interested in the alchemy of medicine, which protected him from plague. The monks were very far from the mark. They had the minds of monkeys as well as the appearance.

Who could *advise* a mentally unstable melancholic such as Rudolph had become? The sheer waste of Tycho's time, being hauled to the capital from his observatory at Castle Benatky with its indoor plumbing and so many other conveniences and graces, to be crammed into the Golden Griffin along with his family and assistants. Oh, Tycho could draw up astrological charts perfectly well regarding decisions of state, but would the emperor actually make any decisions based on advice? State documents continued to languish unsigned for far too long. Rudolph's zodiacal sign was the Crab, and he was behaving just like a crab withdrawn into its shell. No, that was how a tortoise behaved. Anyway, Rudolph was *in* his shell.

This was becoming a serious problem which potentially imperiled Tycho—not merely in the matter of his domestic finances, but also as regards to his safety. *Bruno had burned in Rome.* The great patron Rudolph could protect the assorted alchemists and magicians and lapidaries and artists and philosophers who crowded Prague—if not always pay them! The Emperor was a moderate Catholic; he needed to be moderate, given his occult and exotic tastes. But if he lost control there might be popish persecution, supposing one took a bleak view—that would please the Spanish Habsburgs. Or there might be Protestant persecution, supposing one took an alternative bleak view—that would please many Germans. Rudolph's titular Holy Roman Empire was becoming ever more unhinged as, alas, was Rudolph. At least Tycho had been able to leave young Kepler some useful calculations to work with.

Clutching in his free hand astrological charts bound with purple ribbon, barrel-chested, red-bearded, balding Tycho strode onward, his stiff white lace ruff like a splendid halo which had slipped down to circumscribe his neck, his dark velvet cloak revealing a blue doublet in the Spanish mode, threaded with gold. The costs of being a courtier!

As he was heading across the bustling main courtyard adjacent to the cathedral, he was hailed by a dirty individual who might recently have been rolling in the ashes of a dead bonfire. Smudges darkened the man's cheeks and his eyebrows seemed singed.

Tycho recognized Bartholomew Guarinoni. Most people knew that Guarinoni was in rivalry with his fellow Italian Octavian Rovereto to become Rudolph's favorite physician, an unlikely ambition when Mathias Borbonius was the most sought-after doctor in Prague. Could Rovereto have discharged a blunderbuss loaded with filth at his colleague? The cause was bound to be a laboratory explosion.

Guarinoni's eyes were gleaming, not only in contrast to the dirt surrounding them.

"Noble sir," he said in German, "I may see His Majesty this afternoon at last!"

About money, of course. What else? Especially if the Italian had just wrecked his workplace in the tower.

"In that case I advise you to change your clothes and wash your face."

Tycho had access to Rudolph—*obligatory* access, often twice a day. The emperor needed constant astrological guidance about his campaign against the Turks on the Hungarian front. What a tedious bore it was to appease the emperor's credulity, especially when free will obviously modified the influence of the stars. But at least Tycho could cope excellently. The emperor valued the Dane's objectivity at a court where everyone else was maneuvering for this or for that, whereas Tycho himself only yearned to get back to his observatory.

Oh, yes, he could more than cope with Rudolph's caprices and anxieties; and being so highly valued was admittedly pleasurable. Tycho preened himself somewhat in front of the Italian, who had little hope of an audience. Except—

"*How* may you see him, signor?"

"At the tournament in the Vladislav Hall."

Its staircase especially designed for horsemen to ascend, for indoor tourneys.

"Why should His Majesty attend that, when he attends little else?"

The besmirched Italian wagged a finger.

"Because Albrecht the Dwarf will ride the emperor's giraffe, and that will be a rare sight! Allow me, allow me, to escort you to the zoo to witness preparations. I shall count it an honor."

Indeed, it *would* be an honor for Guarinoni to be seen in the prolonged company of someone who had the emperor's ear. Tongues would wag. However, Tycho's curiosity was piqued. Momentarily he glanced at the sun, gauging its position. Time enough remained before he needed to meet with Rudolph.

The Italian brushed himself off to little effect, and the two men set out for the royal garden beyond the Brusnice stream, regarded with interest by passersby.

The rhinoceros was looking very rusty. How much had it cost, and what use had it ever been, except for amazement? In the watery climate of Prague, the animal's great plates of ferrous armor had lost all the sheen and polish gained from African sand and sun. As the beast ambled around its yard, its armored parts shed rust like dandruff. Still, what a remarkable creature, another of the marvels that Rudolph collected. Supposing the rhinoceros died of internal rot, could those plates be scraped clean and polished or oiled and fitted on a big war horse?

If the rhinoceros did die, thank God its fate wasn't astrologically linked to the fate of the emperor in the way that Rudolph's pet lion's was. Chained in the entrance hall of the palace as a jovial challenge to visitors, the lion enjoyed better protection from the weather, as well as good bloody meat and a daily bucket of milk.

Tycho and the Italian strolled past the rhino yard to the little paddock where two grooms had restrained the giraffe. Two other grooms stood on step-ladders strapping the specially constructed saddle to the animal. The seat of the saddle rose high at the rear so that the rider wouldn't promptly slide down the animal's steeply sloping dappled back. The destined rider, in protectively padded garb, shouted, "Tighter!" Little Albrecht mightn't weigh much but he wasn't about to take any chances. (He was no relation to the great Dürer who had first captured the look of a rhinoceros with such accuracy almost a century earlier in a drawing that Rudolph adored—just as, indeed, the Dutchman Bosch had perfectly depicted a giraffe.) Noticing spectators, Albrecht waddled toward them and bowed low, no great effort for a dwarf. Albrecht eyed the Italian askance as if Guarinoni, clown-faced due to soot, was competing with the dwarf as a buffoon.

Ridden by Albrecht, the giraffe would likely cause much comedy, probably commencing with its indoor ascent of the staircase up to the Vladislav Hall—the giraffe would need to bow its horned head.

Someone had been clever! Rudolph mightn't put in an appearance for any ordinary tournament in the hall, but the prospect of his giraffe taking part might well entice him from his melancholy seclusion.

"Whose idea was this?" Tycho asked the dwarf.

Someone fairly important, who wanted a chance to speak to Rudolph . . .

Albrecht shrugged, but Tycho did not feel like dispensing any silver to find out.

"Have you practiced riding the giraffe much?"

"Oh yes. At first she capered about, and I slipped off but I clung upside-down to her neck and she tired of carrying my weight. She won't bite, although you need to watch out for the hooves. Don't stand behind her." The dwarf indicated a wooden contraption resembling a gateway at the end of the paddock. "She learned to lower her head and pass through there to get lettuces."

"Well," Tycho said to Guarinoni, "this is all very interesting, but I must meet His Majesty. I assume you do have a change of clothes in your tower."

The Italian hesitated in the most peculiar way—almost as though he did not wish to shed his alchemy-stained garments and wash himself, or at least not yet.

"Are you hoping to demonstrate devotion to your science, signor? When what you demonstrate is a failure, grime not gold."

Suddenly the Italian began to talk rapidly in ever more broken German.

"One of my colleagues," by which he probably meant *competitor*, "is hinting at erotic ecstasy available at the new Sign of the Jade Dragon. He went there for a take-out meal following a similar mishap as mine—"

Doubtless the Italian hoped to delay Tycho yet further in his company! Well, he succeeded.

"Erotic ecstasy? Jade Dragon? What do you mean by a 'take-out' meal?"

Tycho listened to Guarinoni carefully for several minutes, until really he could delay no more.

In the arcaded courtyard of the royal palace hustle and bustle presaged the tourney. Preferring to avoid Rudolph's chained pet lion, Tycho ascended the staircase intended for riders into Vladislav Hall itself, its ceiling a beauty of reticulated vaulting.

Two-thirds of the way along the floor stood a quintain for tilting. The imperial marshall was thrusting at the target—a shield painted with a Turk's head—to ensure that the counterweight bag of sand swung around smoothly enough to clobber a lanceman who didn't follow through smartly although he would also need to halt his horse quickly to avoid colliding with the barrier of mattresses protecting the far wall.

Onward to the antechamber, to be saluted and admitted. Rudolph liked items from his treasury and art gallery to be on display in this part of the palace for a few months at a time. Tycho barely glanced at the large globe and the gilded engraved brass armillary sphere, or at *Venus and Adonis* on the wall, or the *Head Composed of Vegetables.*

Thence to the Green Room, where the waiting chamberlain stood with his back to *Tantalus on His Wheel.*

"His Imperial Highness is expecting you—"

And finally to the royal bedchamber, its windows draped to exclude daylight, many candles lit. Hardly the best conditions for admiring *Pan and Venus* or *The Rape of Helen* or a lyre embossed with a mustached face or a statue of Daphne in gilded silver, coral, and semiprecious stones. In a richly carved chair Rudolph slouched, attired in a fur robe, his delicate lace ruff collar resembling an explosion of pearls from a milky pool.

He looked distinctly autumnal, his pear of a nose

overripe on that long, sloping face, his abundant mustaches overdue for harvest, his mulberry eyes lugubrious.

"Brahe, have you news of my assassination?"

"Sire, the fact that your noble father was assassinated at the same age as you are now conveys no inevitability for a repetition of the same fate—nor do the stars."

"I know I am dead and damned," declared Rudolph. "I'm a man possessed by a devil."

"In what sense exactly?"

Rudolph tapped his nose.

"A false nose of metals is part of your face, Brahe, ever since you lost your fleshly nose in a duel long ago. I know that in my very soul there is a foreign part—and in my body too! A part that comes from elsewhere evil! A part that I must suffocate and keep confined in darkness, otherwise . . ."

". . . otherwise, Brahe, I tell you, I would yearn . . .

". . . to sup your blood to nourish me!" Rudolph pulled himself up hectically while Tycho took a wary step backward. "Do you understand me? It is far better that my own blood should be spilled in an assassination!" Then, in the candlelight, Rudolph seemed to blush with shame at his outburst.

The Holy Roman Emperor added more quietly, "I cannot appear in public, in daylight."

"Not even to see your jester ride your giraffe in the tourney?" And then, perhaps, to see the ambassador from Muscovy too?

Rudolph shivered and pulled his cloak tightly around himself.

"Borbonius did promise something of the sort. He imagines this will infuse my spirits with hilarity. How wrong he is."

Oh, so the frolic was a bright idea of Borbonius'—medicine for the mind, where physic could not prevail. That was preferable to this being some other ambitious courtier's idea.

"Some teeth sink too deeply into the soul," muttered Rudolph.

Tycho decided to interpret this literally rather than metaphorically and symbolically as Rudolph surely intended.

"What has bitten you, and when?"

Hauntedly, Rudolph whispered, "Our enemy the Turk—in the form of a bat with scimitars on its wings—from Transylvania weeks ago. Borbonius says I do not have rabies or I would be dead."

Hmm. Rudolph's mind was possessed by symbols and emblems, yet could there be any truth in this? The emperor's Hungarian opponents in Transylvania were allies of the Ottomans in Constantinople. A bat biting Rudolph could be a metaphor for some strange visitor who had deranged the credulous emperor's senses . . . and maybe his body too? Oh to be able to shine a bright light into Rudolph's labyrinthine darkness!

Brahe recalled what Guarinoni had told him regarding the Sign of the Jade Dragon and that rumour of the *illuminatory* ecstasy obtainable there.

Could it be that Guarinoni had exploded his own equipment deliberately, so as to appeal to the Chinese proprietress of that establishment? If so, Guarinoni had chosen an unsuitable time of day . . . On the subject of suitable and unsuitable times, the horoscope for events in Transylvania certainly needed discussing! And if anything could ever be decided, and if Rudolph could be cured of his mad malaise, and if the Catholics and Protestants in Bohemia could avoid killing each other, maybe, just maybe Tycho could get back to precisely instrumented measurements of the heavens!

When Tycho finally emerged from a tedious audience requiring much soothing of Rudolph, Vladislav Hall was loud with the noise of the tourney.

Ladies and lords looked on as horsemen sat resting in their armor, most being spiky and fluted in Maximilian style, made in Nuremburg. Since the emperor might be attending, they were wearing their smartest metal suits rather than heavy tilting armor. Many breastplates were crested above the sternum with a double eagle.

The marshall accosted Tycho, and Tycho promptly shook his head.

"His Highness will remain in his bedroom."

So the marshall gave a signal.

The floor was a bit slippery for a giraffe accustomed to a paddock. However, fixed above the Turk's head, on the target of the quintain, was a lettuce, so when Albrecht leaned back and slapped the animal on her rump, she broke into an eager canter.

Albrecht righted his posture, pointing his lance at the target. Aware now of the lance as a possible rival to reach the lettuce, the giraffe lowered its neck, thrusting her head forward. Thus the dappled beast's mouth reached the lettuce before the tip of the lance could touch the Turk's head.

As a result the countweight promptly swung around and slapped the giraffe hard on her backside, just as she was about to slow. Legs splaying, she slid onward while Albrecht soared over her head. His lance impaled the mattresses and he hung there briefly, legs pumping. A moment later, lettuce and giraffe snout thwacked him right between those legs—and how he howled as he fell.

Bracing herself, the giraffe succeeded in halting as Albrecht sprawled on the floor beneath her feet, clutching his bollocks.

Howls of laughter arose as riders clashed the shielding vamplates of their upright lances against their breastplates in mock salute.

Having seen enough tomfoolery, Tycho strode off. He must visit that Chinese take-out, down by the river near the Charles Bridge. If what Guarinoni said had any validity, maybe a cure for the emperor might come from an unexpected quarter.

Here was the very house. A dragon of precious green jade, fit for the emperor's own collections, stood behind slim iron bars in a niche above the doorway. The house was only a stone's throw from Charles Bridge, crowded with carriages and pedestrians. Not for the first time Tycho thought that the bridge could look really handsome if there were statues along its sides. Statues, perhaps, of famous scientists such as Ptolemy and Pythagoras and Archimedes and Paracelsus and himself.

The door of the Jade Dragon was open, releasing odors of cookery at once unfamiliar and enticing. A front window contained a signboard painted with prices and enigmatic signs such as a beehive and a lemon and a pig. Tycho entered and beheld his first Chinese woman: almond eyes in an oval face, long black hair in strands decorated atop by a pink rose that looked to be made of silk and a long silver hairpin—which she could perhaps wield like a dagger, if need be. Standing behind a low counter, she was wearing a green dress that hugged her slim figure, and a long neckerchief of red silk. She was beautiful and looked no older than twenty-five, although Tycho suspected that people with such smooth, tight skin and flat features might appear to age at a different pace from people in Bohemia or in Denmark. Upon the counter Tycho noted a different sort of counter, consisting of beads on thin metal bars inside a framework, that looked mathematically interesting. On the rear wall hung another signboard, just as in the window.

A customer was receiving a take-out which proved to be a simple wooden box the length and breadth of one's hand, some steam rising from around the lid. A few other such boxes stood on the counter, empty except for what looked like stretched pig bladders—washed and dried ones, of course—fitted as bags gaping open to receive pourings of food, after which evidently a lid would cap the meal. The Chinese woman passed a pair of wooden sticks to the customer and he departed, beating a merry tattoo on the lid of his take-out as if he were a drummer boy.

For larger orders, a heap of simple little hessian sacks with handles awaited, into which several boxes would fit.

"Good day," Brahe said in German to the exotic woman. "I am the Imperial Star Watcher and Adviser, Tycho Brahe. May I ask your name?"

"My name is Su Nü, but you not succeed in pronouncing, so please call me Frau Sonne." Her accent was twangy.

"Su Nu," attempted Tycho.

She giggled. "No, no. Oh no."

"Frau Sonne, then. May I ask how you got here from China?"

"Along Silk Road," she said, and it seemed to Tycho that a road as smooth as silk could be no ordinary road, but might well be something occult, and definitely better than arriving in Bohemia on a broomstick.

Tycho pointed at the signboard.

"What is a beehive and a lemon and a pig?"

"Sweet and sour pork. Delicious!"

"Hmm, I may try some."

Now came the difficult part, requiring a certain diplomacy, at which Tycho had at last acquired considerable skill after various contretemps in the past.

"I understand that you offer other services here . . ."

"Items of private delicacy?"

"Earlier today, I was talking to an alchemist whose laboratory exploded."

"Another explosion? Ah, your alchemists!" Su Nü sighed with pitying compassion. "So many miss point of true alchemy, which is transformation *of person* in body and soul, not making of mere gold."

"I believe," Tycho remarked huffily, "that superior alchemists strive to create the philosopher's stone, thus making gold, so as to purify themselves spiritually in the process; and vice versa. Personally I'm mainly interested in *medical* alchemy."

Su Nü looked at him intently. "Make love, not gold! That is secret. We Chinese have known for centuries."

"Indeed?"

"In-deed! Intimate secrets of cinnabar grotto and gully of gold and inner elixir we call *nei tan*. Would you like private consultation? This evening, my lord?"

Hmm, cinnabar—the red powder efficacious in gold-making—was a mixture of philosophic mercury and philosophic sulphur . . .

"The cinnabar grotto: that's the vessel containing the cinnabar powder?"

"*Dry powder?* My lord, grotto should ooze with juices like mucus of a snail! If not, adept is inept. Cinnabar grotto is part of cunt. Your alchemists miss whole point. They make apparatus. They need skilled woman instead. Consultation, my lord?"

Tycho was not yet a lord in Bohemia. He really must petition Rudolph for citizenship and noble status so that Kirsten and the children could benefit, especially by the children thus being able to inherit and marry into noble families in their adopted homeland. However, he did not at all mind being called a lord.

"I am faithful to my wife," Tycho told Su Nü.

"Good health comes from good sex," she observed, "and woman is sexually stronger than man, so she assists him through her pleasure to become mystic master of grotto, thus of himself and of his well being."

Hmm, could this Chinese woman really help restore Rudolph's well being? Tycho needed to think for a while.

"For the moment," he said, "may I have some beehive lemon pig?"

"Certainly! On bed of white rice, which sweet sauce stains?" Everything that Su Nü said seemed to have erotic implications. Goodness knows what rice was.

Tycho nodded, and Su Nü slipped away into another room from which the odors issued. She returned very soon with a filled container, lid in place. Then she presented Tycho with two plain wooden sticks.

"Shall I demonstrate, my lord?"

She seized his fingers and placed the sticks within them in a certain way, then manipulated his hand so that the sticks opened and closed. Her touch was at once subtle yet firm.

"You bring box back clean another time, get small refund."

Tycho sat on a block of sandstone by the end of the Charles Bridge, musing while he mastered the art of eating beehive lemon pig with sticks. Rice looked like maggots but must be a grain of some kind, swollen by boiling. Very tasty stained with sauce. Surely she must use sacks of it. Had the rice slid magically along the Silk Road too?

Reaching a decision, he returned to the Jade Dragon, where, once she had finished serving another customer, Su Nü listened to him intently.

Yes, she would perform a take-out service, of herself, since obviously an emperor could not visit her humble dwelling. Traditionally, in her far-off homeland, she remarked, if an emperor was wary of assassination, a consort for him would be stripped and searched intimately then wrapped in a silk bag and borne to his bedchamber by a eunuch, to be returned home in the same manner after the union. Thus she would carry nothing with which to harm him.

"Must leave hairpin here, my lord!"

Tycho was relieved that she did not expect him to carry her in a silk sack to the castle, but instead would walk along with him.

Traditionally, it transpired, a Chinese emperor's intercourse was monitored either by a female official or by a eunuch, who would carefully record the number of thrusts made by the emperor and who, if she or un-he deemed these excessive, would halt further activity by reading a cautionary memorandum from a revered ancestor.

"We do things differently here," said Tycho, although by now he realized that Su Nü was teasing him mischievously—maybe excited by the prospect of every Chinese's woman's dream coming true, alhough with a melancholy Holy Roman Emperor, not a Chinese emperor. "An astrologer does not need to be present in the bedroom, nor a doctor either."

She became serious. "You say he thirsty for blood?"

"So he implies. But he resists the compulsion, and this takes all his energy away from matters of state. Frau Sonne, you may be in a little danger if you're in bed with him."

Suddenly Su Nü performed a very wild dance—accompanied by "Ha! Ha! Ha!"—and that long tight dress of hers proved to be slit from thigh to ankle, allowing her legs to kick. Her feet flashed out, then her hands; then silently she mimed riding a horse, then she stood on one leg.

"What is that dance called?" asked Tycho.

"Kung fu," she replied. "Self-defense and harmonious living. If I expel black bat from him, I must kill it. Hmm, chicken blood mixed with sticky rice can help defeat Chiang-Shih devil, which steals breath from people instead of blood. Therefore chicken breath mixed with rice may help defeat bloodsucker devil."

"How can you persuade a chicken to breathe on rice without eating the rice at the same time?"

"No, no, use chicken lungs, chopped."

"Oh I see, the *symbol* of chicken breath." That made sense. Particularly with Rudolph, this might be effective.

"I will know best route when his jade stalk rises and his orchid bags sway. Later too, when I smell his yogurt." What was *yogurt?* Tycho decided not to ask.

Su Nü continued standing on one leg like a crane. Tycho leaned across the counter and gazed at her embroidered slipper.

"What small feet you have."

"My golden lotuses. Walking on them strengthens muscles of hidden valley."

Another customer came in, wanting duck with long worms.

Two audiences with Rudolph in one day was not unusual for Tycho—would that it were, and that the ambassador from Muscovy could enjoy even half an audience!

By the time Tycho reached Vladislav Hall again, it was empty. Some horse turds lay on the floor, or maybe those were giraffe turds if the beast had shat after it skidded. Just as well; Tycho's mission was a discreet one.

"How is the darkness within, sire?" Tycho enquired.

"Stirring," whispered Rudolph. "Stretching its wings. I can smell your blood, Brahe."

"Maybe what you're smelling is beehive lemon pig on my breath." Tycho hoped so, at any rate.

"Brahe, the moon is filling."

Tycho was perfectly aware of this, both as an astronomer and in common with any ordinary person who bothered glancing into the sky by night. Yet *how*, in this heavily curtained bedroom where candles burned . . .

"Do you mean that you can *feel* it filling, within yourself?"

"Yes! It will fill me within, usurping what remains of my will. Soon I must drink blood, or be blessedly assassinated."

Guarinoni's information, and the resulting trips to the Jade Dragon, had come none too soon. What else could be done for Rudolph, in his delusion or—Heaven forbid!—in his realization of the cause of his problem, whether that were due to deliberate magical malice by Turks or Hungarians in Transylvania or even by his nephew Leopold or whether it were due to something which had come out of the night, the night of darkness and also of evil?

"Sire, I believe I have discovered a solution to your dark malady."

"You have found it in the stars?"

No, I found it in a Chinese take-out near Charles Bridge . . . Tycho did not voice this, yet as the thought passed through his mind it struck him how remarkable it was that Su Nü had come to Prague at such an appropriate time along that Silk Road, almost as if she were a hunter who posed as prey for carnal appetites, while also being an adept instructor seemingly wiser than any other alchemist he had met—except of course for himself.

"Yes, in tonight's stars!" Tycho fibbed. "Venus is entering the Crab."

A moon much closer to full than to half hung low over Prague, lighting the climb to the castle, dimming nearby stars. Tycho disliked the term *gibbous* for such a phase of the moon because the word seemed supernaturally menacing, as if beholding it caused people to gibber with fear.

Yet there was ample reason for trepidation. Su Nü walked with a wobble, which would be strengthening her hidden valley in preparation for onslaught by the imperial jade stalk. Yet Tycho had also seen her leap into action. Consequently he hoped that Rudolph wouldn't be injured in any way, either as regards his jade stalk or his personal esteem. Su Nü carried one of those little hessian sacks into which she had put a box of sticky rice and chicken lungs for the emperor's nourishment during their encounter.

Su Nü was in the bedchamber for almost two hours, while in the antechamber Tycho variously performed mathematics in his head and contemplated *Tantalus on His Wheel*. How could erotic activity possibly last for so long? A few times, muffled by the stout door, he heard, "Ha! Ha! Ha!" or some such sound. Maybe that was an outcry of joyful release.

At long last the door of the bedroom opened, and there stood Rudolph and Su Nü, both clad. The emperor *glowed*, might be the best way of phrasing it, mere candlelight notwithstanding. If he had been late autumn earlier, now he was summer again. His cheeks were red as apples, his nose a pear at its best, his huge moustaches were like corn, and his eyebrows resembled hairy golden caterpillars.

"Be here early tomorrow, Brahe," he called out. "Much awaits." The Emperor ushered the Chinese woman courteously from his bedchamber, then he withdrew and shut the door.

Tycho hastened towards Su Nü.

"Was there any need of . . ."—what was the name of that dance?—"any need of kung fu?"

"Not on this occasion. I must be private quickly, My Lord, to massage vigorously to expel all yogurt."

"Yes, yes, of course." Tycho knew of a suitable

closet. Seizing a candelabrum, he led Su Nü to a spiral stairway, down two turns, threw open a door to a privy room, planted the tree of candles within, then waited outside in the moonlight coming through a narrow window.

Presently Su Nü emerged, clutching her little sack. She whispered, "Expelled much black yogurt." That word *yogurt* again. "But I cloak it in *my* ejaculation." Whatever was she talking about? Women couldn't ejaculate—but maybe Chinese women could, from some organ inside themselves? She clutched her little sack tight. "I will throw in river, like abortion, weighted with stones."

Could it be that the emperor had burst a blood vessel inside himself? Yet Rudolph had looked so radiant and restored, at least compared with how he had been previously, in the depths of despair.

"Frau Sonne, I don't understand. What exactly did His Majesty expel, and how exactly?" Tycho was forever preoccupied by exactitude. His great quadrant was ten times more exact than any previous instrument for measuring celestial positions.

"Vampire essence, my lord! Evil elixir dirties channels in body. Clever acupressure for long time delays explosion from jade stalk. Thus great pleasure-tension sucks black essence together, bottling like lava under volcano. At last volcano erupts with ten times more bang than ordinary."

So that was why she took two hours, making the time by now so late . . .

"Lucky I catch him still living, before become dead and vampire. One more week, woe! Black residue may linger in emperor, make him moody sometimes, not enough change him into blood-drinker."

"He may need another treatment?"

"Not necessary."

Tycho wished to know more, but . . .

"I must go home. It seems I need an early night. First I'll escort you, Frau Sonne."

"And payment?"

"Yes, yes. I have the gold with me."

"See!" She grinned. "Make love makes gold. Best way."

It was two tedious days of horoscope casting before Tycho had a chance to revisit the Jade Dragon. So many questions to ask! Not least about what other occasions the Chinese woman had been referring to. When had those been, and where?

Drizzle was drifting. For a moment Tycho thought he may have mistaken the building, or even mistaken the cobbled street. But no. This was the place. Above the door, around the niche, were those slim iron bars, yet the dragon of jade was absent. Gone, too, from the window was the signboard promising beehive lemon pig and other delights. Within the room into which he peered: a low counter and nothing more. No counter of beads, no signboard on the wall, no sign that Su Nü had ever been there as cook and as adept in an alchemy scarcely known to him, and also, he was now sure, as a warrior against darkness, traveling a silken road that she alone perhaps, and some others like her, could perceive and use.

A letter had come from Kepler at Castle Benatky.

The problem which Tycho had set Kepler concerned the image of the sun passing through a pinhole onto a screen. The image appeared too large for the moon to be able to eclipse the sun completely, although the moon certainly did so in reality. Kepler wrote of "light rays," a whole new concept in geometrical optics, or so he claimed. And he whined about money.

Rays of light preoccupied Tycho as he strode away from the empty house of enlightenment. In competition with the actual sun, Frau Sonne was eclipsed.

Green Wallpaper

by Tanith Lee

O God! I could be bounded in a nut-shell, and count myself a king of infinite space, were it not that I have bad dreams.

—William Shakespeare, *Hamlet*

The spirit, finally, will always conquer the sword.

—Napoleon Bonaparte

Below the equator and above the Tropic of Capricorn, a speck in the widest nowhere of the Atlantic Ocean, built from the tall black debris of an ancient volcano: the island. Too far from Africa, too far to matter—and from Europe as far it seems as hell is from the earth, once one has been cast down into it. Winds that are fevers blow in this place. The humid gray heat shatters only on icy, greasy rain, which smokes as the heat resumes. Yet a colonial town goes on about its business here, and private houses scatter the heights. Hundreds, it is true, have supposedly died of the climate, of the very remoteness. And no one with a choice ever stays long. Yet the island is the possession of a great worldly power, and so tons of soil were long ago deposited and spread, and gardens and woods planted. They grow quite richly now, pasted all over the rough, badly finished plaster of the black rock. Like green wallpaper.

He has been thinking . . . or dreaming, he isn't sure, of that second woman who was his wife. Curious, really. His first wife was several years older than he, the second a lot younger. Some sort of balance in that, maybe. The first wife he had loved and she was barren, and had betrayed him over and over with other men—but in the end she clung to him, was jealous, *wanted* him—died without him. While the second *never* wanted him, pretended, was entirely faithful while they were together—as far as he knew, and he *would* have known if she were not—quickly providing him with a son. But then, when his star fell, and everything crashed about him, she ran away, taking his son with her, robbing him of his child—his future—and now she lies in bed with some nobody of an Austrian officer. *She,* his empress, who had shared his throne. Just as the first wife had been his empress before.

Yes, a balance, probably.

As in a mathematical problem.

It's all like that.

He sighs—he sighs often—and hauls himself up from the wooden chair, pushing back from the wooden table. How heavy he feels. Legs, arms. Lack of enough exercise. Lack of—everything.

He walks round the room, once, twice, picking up a few objects, two books, a quill. A small coin someone's found. Heaven knows, they need any funds they can get.

He is indulging in one of his five-day stints of seclusion. Later, very likely, he'll call one of them in, dictate a little more of his memoirs. But he finds increasingly, if he is honest, that now the desire to put the record straight is offset by the need—to do nothing.

Nothing!

He, hero, general, king, emperor, once almost master of all Europe. Oh, he could have had the world. It was running toward him as eagerly as he ran with his armies to seize it.

But then . . .

He feels he has lived a long time. His life seems to stretch back forever, in tumults of battle and pageantry, and in cosy domestic scenes, power and glory and content and grief. But not forward, of course. Never that.

His belly hurts, but it always does. Always did. Confound his body. Men have obeyed him but the machine of his body would seldom fully obey. He had had to break it to his will and now, as sometimes even in the past, it outwits and overcomes him. At last, like all the rest, seeing him fallen, it too creeps forward like a cowardly hyena, to paw and rend.

Some noise outside? What's that? Marchand, his manservant, calls softly through the door that leads into his private rooms. Apparently the English governor, Lowe, had called again, wanting to speak to him. That ginger-haired, crawling thing. Has he gone? Yes.

He says, absently but with a flicker of old firmness, See anything is wiped over, if he's been near it."

The house is very high up on the bleak tableland among the diseased and arthritic gum trees. Here the winds really blow, like trumpets. Another new tree lost its branches in the garden only three nights back. Up here, it's more difficult to cover over the gray and black with green.

Besides this house—this *place*—it comprises a cowshed, washhouse, and stable, inadequately cobbled together and ineffectually disguised as being fit for human habitation. The floors break, leaking moisture, stinking of old manure. Rats dance in cupboards, chewing the mahogany that slowly rots anyway, along with all the books, due to the damp. Every day the silver lamp in his bedroom is cleaned, briefly removing a perpetual dull film. The rest of the silver's gone, of course. He had had to part with it. But it was sold cheaply to the evil Lowe, who would allow no one else in the town to buy it. The town is always full of notices warning the townspeople that none must fraternize with the French enemy on the height. He is legally restricted to a few miles' radius that stretches about the "house." Sometimes he absconds—but no, he hasn't bothered with that for a long while. He used to ride or walk all day. When his belly prevented him from riding on the Russian campaign, among those mud- and snow-smothered steppes, he strode league after league with his men instead.

He thinks of Moscow, burning. That beautiful, domed city put to the torch only to spite him and stop him. They would have seared all Russia off the face of the earth if that had been the only way. He recalls the tsar whom he had charmed and enticed into treaty, like a silly girl into bed.

Outside the gray brightness is fading to gluey grayish blue. The sun must have set. There's only the evening now to cope with. One more victory, then. One more day tossed onto the rubbish heap of history.

Of course, when first delivered up here, he had thought frequently of some means to escape. The notion of escaping still haunts him, even now, just as it haunts the obnoxious Lowe, who himself sneaks about the area continually. Yet escape is out of the question.

He believes he is resigned to this.

Therefore, only his mind can escape into books and memories, his thoughts, his dreams.

Something moves softly.

Is it a rat, shifting along the bookshelves, or under the camp bed in the adjacent room?

Generally the rats are more bold, noisier.

The two chambers are otherwise empty. The man who lives here has moved out into the dining room, where his fellow exiles have tonight made the effort, all of them, to join him for supper.

It is full night now.

The soft rustling, fluttering, comes again. Perhaps a large moth, a bird even . . .

Something ripples, there—there—*under* the brownish nankeen that swathes the walls of the bedroom.

Or is it only a trick of the half dark? The muslin curtains are undrawn and some kind of outer glow—a lamp, the clouded stars—gives partial light but not enough.

No, after all, the nankeen covering is quite static.

Yet something *is* here.

And it does move, if only faintly discernably, and that moving being noticed more by the sense of *touch*, like a quiet breath over the rooms, a sigh, that goes *through* things—furniture, carpet, a wall.

It looks into the dining room.

Yellow candlelight, and the crowded table surrounded by people with once fine clothes and creased faces, one beautiful woman and one less so, a young boy, a noisy baby now being carried out—men in medals that commemorate triumphs.

The supper looks frugal. Earlier today, at dinner, the meat was rancid again. The governor sees to that.

What looks in looks without eyes. Invisible, and yet not *completely* so. Somehow a sort of shadow is present that's cast by nothing in the room, so the beautiful woman suddenly starts and says a creature is there, is it a lizard? Send it out, kill it—

But then the shadow *isn't* there, isn't anywhere, and only one man puts his hand to his cheek, feeling a mild moist breath smooth over it, perfectly clean, except for a little mustiness, perhaps . . .

Rustum, the servant who has just crossed an outer room, feels something slide over him—now like a weightless, silky shawl. His eyes glitter as they follow intuitively what they can't see. Tonight, should he sleep against his master's door, as he has so often in the past? No. It will be no use. The elder people from whom Rustum descends, they have names for such things and know neither a door, nor a man, not even a sword, can keep the demons out. No precaution or act will work.

"Fah! This wine is putrid!" exclaims one of the younger men angrilly. He adds. "Sire, we should slaughter that villainous little fiend Lowe."

"The English would love that, their representitive, my jailer, murdered," says the one addressed as sire. "What do you think they'd do? They're faithless." He's no longer an emperor, but still he must be called "sire," although such a title, he has said, means nothing, and never did.

The two women are stiffly arguing in an undertone. Someone shushes them.

The ex-emperor wants his coffee. Then he will want to play chess or cards. Then read them a Greek play or a French play by Racine, talk to them about bygone days. Always it is like this. He keeps them up half or all the night, wears them out, drains them, exhausts them, casts them aside. Even when he dictates the accounts of his life and battles, he can go on and on, pacing the rooms, paying out his acute and finely tuned phrases, for the classical education of his youth has informed his syntax, just as much as once it did his genius in war, despite the accent, which he's never lost. *He* then can continue in this recital ten hours or more, but his secretaries collapse, fall asleep, faint even. Then he calls in another. Wears *them* out, drains *them*. The ex-emperor is a sort of vampire. He's never known, and would be enraged and would disbelieve, if told. He has seldom—ever?—been able to empathize. For he is the center of the world. From the beginning, until the end. They—all other things—bit players, useful, magnetizing, inadequate.

An invisible shadow now hangs up on the ceiling like a cobweb. It still looks down, attentively watching. Some ebb of its formless form unravels, trails negligently along the floor. And a single rat, sidling from the mahogany sideboard into a space under the planking, slinks aside to avoid all contact.

He's dreaming . . . or thinking . . . the fires of burning Russian villages or the campfires burning in Paris across the Seine, that night at the beginning of the last act of downfall—the city full by then of his foes, and his young empress already fled—

Fires. Genius, the fire from heaven—not every brain is equipped to receive it.

He smells a delicious perfume. He knows it—less the unguents with which she would lave herself, and which she would rub into the curly reddish darkness of her hair—than her own *personal* sweet odor. Oh, yes. He had written to her once—*I am hurrying toward you—do not wash.* She was one of those rare women who never had an impure smell, not even her breath when first she spoke in the morning—sweet, always sweet, the loveliness only heightened when she refrained from the bath.

Marie-Josèphe. Joséphine.

He opens his eyes and through the dim dark of the small bedchamber, *sees* her standing there by the fireplace. She's dressed in a white gown. It isn't one of the scandalous gowns that she and some of her cronies used to wear at Malmaison when he was well away, the kind that, when sprayed with water, became transparent; this was the garment of an empress. And on her head, the royal golden wreath he himself had crowned her with. She had worn her diadem for him that night after the coronation, he and she alone.

Joséphine.

"Here I am," she says. She is the age she was when first they met, her early thirties. Pearls glimmer in her ears. Her skin is juicy, ravishing. Beautiful woman. The only woman he had ever truly loved—almost that.

"You haven't missed me at all," she says.

"Always."

"Never, once I grew old."

"Ah, Joséphine. But now . . . you're young again."

"All this while I've waited for you. I saw you at Malmaison once, you sat there alone, mourning for me. Don't you want to be with me now?"

"More than I can say." He sighs. "To lie in your arms. To rest against you."

"Then why won't you come to me?"

Some element penetrates, hard as a bullet. The old wound in his Achilles tendon—such a blatant emblem—stings. He raises himself on his elbow and feels too the throb of the anguish in his gut and knows he's wide awake after all.

"What are you?"

"I am Joséphine! Remember the house, and the red geraniums pouring over from their pots, the flowers I brought all the way from Martinique. And the Temple of Love, in the gardens—"

He tries, properly, to push up from the bed, and

finds it difficult. His head spins, a common ailment in this fever-drenched pest hole the English have sent him to, to make sure he dies.

When finally he gets his feet onto the worn carpet, he turns again and she's gone.

Yes, it's fever. That's all it is. A brief delirium. But it was so like her, wanting him to kill himself and hurry to meet her—he must assume that was what the hallucinatory Joséphine had required. She always wanted him away at first, so she could have her fun with all the others. And then, when he fell in love with his Polish girl, *then* Joséphine had wanted to be there with him. And now, in some place beyond the world that could not exist, impatient, she asked: *Why aren't you here?*

He shakes his head. Outside stars are blazing in a brief opening of the cloud. He remembers remarking once, "Say what you will of the absence of a creator, but who made all *those?*"

When the candle's alight, he gets up and goes to inspect the area where the apparition stood. On the floor there seems to be the faintest dusting of white powder—the sort she had used on her face and shoulders—but no, it isn't anything . . . loose plaster, no doubt.

Panting, his unhealthy fatness that has little to do with diet making him sweat, he climbs back onto the bed. A stab of infernal agony drives through his belly like a claw. So bad now. He supposes it can only get worse. Tomorrow, to soothe it, he will spend several hours in a scalding bath.

But even now he can fall asleep at will, like an

animal. He falls asleep and dreams of Joséphine among her self-imported geraniums. His little son, that the other one gave him, the traitorous Austrian woman, runs by her side.

Something floats over him, a cloud that in sleep he does not see. Then the nankeen ripples behind the bed. In the morning, Rustum and Marchand both, coming in, will notice this brownish wall cover has become a little green in tone. Naturally, in this climate, there's mildew outdoors and in, lichen even, everywhere.

All of his companions here argue continuously among themselves, and some of them come to him raving or whining with complaints. At certain times they have only communicated with each other by means of written notes.

What is all this inanity? His canvas had been the world—now he's trapped in a nutshell, with these persons who seem unable to understand that his eternal suffering does not need to be augmented by their pettiness. Oh, let them all go, for God's sake. If there were a God.

He thinks of the other two islands, the rugged, forested country of his early childhood, and the island of his first exile, this one mantled with stone pines, fig trees, shapely crags, walking among whose vineyards he had lamented, *This place is very small.*

Something must have been listening. If not a God, then some other imbecile tyrant. If Elba was small, what is *this* tiny dot?

And his mother had been permitted to come to

him on Elba, and brought him all her carefully saved money, enabling him to finance a voyage back toward the coast of France.

He thinks of the loyal guard they had let him keep on Elba, shouting for him, and the army he had raised there besides. He thinks of the march back to Paris, and all the troops sent out to impede him, thousands upon thousands of men, and how he had gone out alone before his little force, stood there with cloak thrown back, weaponless, and bellowed: "If you would kill your emperor—here he is." Which brought those thousands rushing to his side like liberated happy dogs: "Life to the emperor! Life and glory!"

He reads a play by Sophocles.

He recalls the coronation, setting the laurel wreath on his own head—he who has been crowned by gold and iron.

The day goes. Eleven o'clock. He can resort to bed.

When he wakes about three in the morning, Josephine is there, lying beside him.

He looks into her chestnut eyes.

"Go away," he says quietly. "I'll be a ghost soon enough. But I don't want you yet. And this bed isn't wide enough for us both."

As she fades, he remembers how her little hound, Fortunate—fortunate indeed it *had* been, the brute, that he'd never killed it—would constantly get between them, biting him, jealous.

There is no sugar for the breakfast coffee again. He stands looking at the portrait of his Austrian wife and their son, and at his silver alarm clock that had belonged to a mighty Prussian king.

He can hear the two Corsican servants arguing now, in an outer room.

The ship should arrive tomorrow with more books.

At the afternoon dinner he eats in the English soldiers' barracks. They always welcome him with respect and great politeness, even though he has little English. Soldiers are all the same, once their mettle is proven. And they know the miracles he's wrought and value him for them. He was a worthy foe. Worthy. The English prince should never have treated him in this way. He'd thrown himself on English mercy—and received none.

He thinks, sitting there in the drab dripping heat, of the ship *Bellerophon* (harsh name—Bearer of Darts) and how he had won her officers over, and they had seemed to promise him a safe retirement in England.

It's never occurred to him, and doesn't now, that after he had sworn to wipe England's status and future off the face of the world, it was unlikely England *would* harbor him.

He hears the old revolutionary anthem in his head, the "Marseillaise," despite the fact he himself had banned the singing of it. It spoke too much, he had said, of violence and the wrong issues.

Something moves the curtains. A slight breeze. For a moment he sees his own cannon, under his orders, mowing down French citizens in the streets—the rabble—but that, so long ago. Before he became their father, their protector.

His eyes focus on the curtains to blot out memory. How inventive. The curtains seem to have taken on the shape of his young Austrian empress. She had been quite succulent—one could forget the slight pockmarks on her face. She's nicely dressed. Satin shoes. Little buckles.

His eyes are tired and playing tricks, for the figure in the curtain looks solid, pink and ivory, smiling in her playful, spiteful, catlike way.

This damned malaise. Perhaps he can ride off the fever. Even inside the narrow twelve-mile limit of the cordon that legally restricts him.

Yet when they bring out his horse, he sends it back. It looks as feverish and tired, as forlorn and crestfallen, as he. And he notes it's been bitten by a rat.

The exiled party at the makeshift house on the tableland is now much smaller. They are always leaving him, these loyal adjuncts of his—their health gives way, they're urgently needed elsewhere. And they, of course, can choose. The one sane, reliable physician, O'Meara, has left too, some while ago. The other, inevitably, is useless.

It isn't so much that he has become used to the dreams that seem to arrive even when he is awake, it's that he doesn't dislike them. For that reason too, probably, he who talks and writes about every aspect of his all-consuming life and self doesn't record them. Exactly as he always refuses to hear, or to tell, a bawdy tale. They must be secret too, then, as relations with a chosen woman. And possibly tinged with something he himself is partially ashamed of. Maybe only his own weakness. He's old, in his fifties, fat and in pain, sluggish. Bored. He is entitled to a few private dreams.

All of them have come to him now, his women—Joséphine and Austrian Thérèse and Maria, his exquisite, dovelike Polish mistress—generous and thoughtful as always, since she even brought with her the illusion of a ballroom sparkled with champagne and candlefire. There have been a handful of others . . . girls from here and there, blondes, brunettes.

He has turned them all off. It goes without saying. Joséphine with the frankness of familiar habit. Thérèse perhaps unkindly—but then even in the dreams she refused to bring his son to see him. Maria with a tenderness fitted to her patient, undemanding simplicity. The rest only needed a snap of his fingers—sizzle! Gone . . . They always return anyway.

Only this afternoon, walking into his study, the floor carpeted by new books recently read cover to cover and then cast away, Maria is standing in the bedroom doorway.

"What shall I do about you?" he asks her. "You have a good husband now. Why steal away to see an old fat fellow who has lost everything and is exiled to a rock?"

"But I miss you," she says gently. "Can't I come to visit you?"

A thought strikes him uncomfortably. "Are you sick, Marie? Tell me you're not dead, like the Empress Joséphine."

She blushes as if he had made a sudden—wanted amorous—advance. "No, no, my dearest lord. I'm well."

"And your boy?" With her too there had been a son, but too late. All too late.

"He's well, dear wise one."

She loves him. It's clear in her lambent eyes. Poor child.

"I think I hear our son calling you, Marie," he playfully says, and she turns her lovely head and indeed seems to hear someone call, and then she turns entirely and entirely vanishes.

And then he's sorry. Before, strictly, he pulls himself up.

He slumps at the wooden table. He is being courted by ghosts both living and dead. A harmless pastime? Or just a persistent fever?

Take medicine then.

Get better.

For there's still a chance his world may change, his chains struck off, his eagle wings able to open once more to flight—

No, old fool. Be still. That's over and done. Even should the poison-tongued English relent, and witless France come to her senses, what could he do now, shut in this sack of blubber and worn bones? *Here's my true prison—my own flesh.*

He walks to the mirror and surveys himself. *Once I resembled, closely, the Roman Emperor Augustus. Who now is this scarecrow?*

In the mirror too, over his shoulder, he sees Maria lying naked but for an enticing, modest shawl, on his narrow bed.

He shuts his eyes, undoes them. She's gone. His old enemy Talleyrand sits there instead, swinging his courtly white-stockinged leg, clicking his gold braid, leering and laughing at him.

A flash like cannon shot passes through his blood. He almost runs at Talleyrand, clever, traitorous Talleyrand, to wring his chicken neck.

But he doesn't. For *this* Talleyrand isn't real.

Later there is a storm. And in the flame of the lightning, he sees one by one his family members about the two rooms, his mother, Laetizia, in a chair; his brothers that he made kings, and the one brother, Lucien, he made nothing, posed on silent duty like wet birds; his feckless sisters in their gowns worth thousands of francs, his stepdaughter in her diamonds . . . His worst enemy, Bernadotte, parades by the bookshelves, and Fouché poses, shouting didactically until the lightning punches a hole right through him, and he shatters like a glass.

O'Meara, the physician who left, might have been spoken to about all this. But there's no one now.

Again he thinks of escape—will these futile thoughts never leave him? How could he do it, unless he were invisible? He smiles drearily. Death will provide the escape route then.

To Marchand, who arrives in the aftermath of the tempest to say another of the newly planted trees has lost a limb, and then peers anxiously at him, he says, "Yes, the pain's bad tonight. But there we have it. Only *Napoleon* can overthrow Napoleon."

"Sire—"

"Ssh. Light the candles. The wind blew them out. The dark's a strange place to inhabit. When I shut my eyes, every mistake I have made marches before me. Whole battalions pass."

"Your noble life, sire, was—"

"A ballad, Marchand. A saga. The hero always dies."

Something . . .

. . . there it goes . . .

Rippling like a sea wave behind the wallpaper. If

anyone troubled, if they noticed, they would take one of his candles from its eagle sconce and go and stare very hard at the badly damp-stained nankeen on the bedroom walls.

It had a Chinese pattern once, now faded to marks like those large insects might construct.

It is very green, nearly the color of the ex-emperor's old coat. Half close one's eyes and the impression is of a jungle growing over the material of the nankeen and the plaster. When it moves—seems to move—the idea is very strong of a forest shivering at the passage of a muscular wind, or of some large, predatory creature.

He lies tossing about under the wall. He's dreaming of circumnavigating the Alps in a torrent of an army, of the iron crown of Lombardy, of a sullen fortress in a desert that would not yield, sitting alone on his horse in the waste of sand while his legions marched away—only he having the courage to gaze at what he was unable to defeat.

The current doctor believes this once omnipowerful man is a liar, who pretends, for politically manipulative reasons, to pains in his belly and teeth. The doctor treats all symptoms with bitter and useless things dissolved in water. But unlike damp, clean water too is scarce here. The governor—always he—has made sure of that.

But this sick, tossing man can always sleep, deeply.

Something . . .

. . . flows out of the green on the wall.

Now it's beside the bed, positioned there, still rippling faintly, an image like that of a breeze over a lake. One couldn't say it *stood* on the floor. It simply *is*.

Formless and translucent and much less green than the stain it's brought out on the wall. There's a light herbal smell, rather like scythed grass, or wet trampled ferns.

Presumably the preliminary contacts, although inconclusive and so unfulfilled, have strengthened it, for it was invisible before, and limited in revelation to that sense of a thick cool breath or a piece of silk or an obscure shadow. Even where he has seen it directly, they haven't yet touched.

It's also fed, lightly, on all the others in the house. This had made them extra fractious, draining them, affecting their well-being. Just as he has done, if it comes to that. But remember, hundreds have died here of those fevers and ailments that haunt the island. The apparition is itself a sort of fever that preys on human things, or on animal ones when nothing else is available. Its existence began as the plants grew upon the barren rock. It was brought close to the present victim when he had his garden made, just out there against the house, and when he tended and watered it so assiduously. Ever since, *this* has looked in at his windows, slid in at his walls. Had it needed to be invited? Then he *has* invited it. His need, his *hunger* calls out to its own. Hundreds have died through both of them, because of the ex-emperor on his inadequate camp bed, and because of the demon that quivers beside him.

Like attracts like. Vampire lures vampire. It isn't always essential to draw them in with voluble welcome across a threshold. Recognition is one of the most potent introductions.

A lizard runs abruptly down the farthest wall. It squeezes through a crack in the planking beneath the carpet, and has escaped. But the shimmering greenness has taken of the lizard no notice whatsoever. It bends lower toward the fallen emperor, *drinking* his dreams, feeding superficially and deliberately, for the best dish is now, without doubt, already being prepared.

The life of a happy man, this man had said, is a silver sky, spoiled only by a few black stars. An unhappy man's life is like the ordinary sky all men see by night—black, with only the spreads of silver stars to mark his separated moments of joy.

The strangest thing . . . opening his eyes he sees the sky of dawn beyond the window. It's shining clear and brilliantly silver just before the rising of the sun—and a handful of little black clouds litter it, scarcely visible, like dim black stars.

Then a figure moves between him and the window.

"Good morning, sire," says the young man who sits on the end of his bed. The young man's mouth quirks with an ironic smile, amused, but it's not a face for humor especially, more priestly and stern, although very handsome, the thick, dark hair not yellowishly powdered today, but hanging silkenly to his collar, his blue-black eyes intent and steady as those of a trained gunner—not suprising, for he had been such a gunner.

For a few seconds the ex-emperor does not know

him. Or rather mistakes him first for several others in turn—friends of his youth, his brothers—even an enemy he can't name. Recognition, then, doesn't always provide the instant introduction.

Yet they are eye to eye.

I to I.

The young man is his younger self.

He speaks quite tenderly. "You didn't want any of the others I showed you, did you? You want only *you.* And so, he is here."

Every one of the few left here know now the man who was their emperor is sick—to death. Even Governor Lowe is sure, and rushes to the house, and desires very imperiously and repeatedly to see the captive, for how else can the staunch and suspicious governor be certain the prisoner hasn't escaped? The governor becomes quite certain, in fact, and takes to his heels when the prisoner bellows at him, unseen, from behind his locked door.

"So," he says to the apparition on the end of the bed. But it isn't an apparition. More convincing than any perfume, he can smell its youthful and healthy body, and the freshness of the clean linen he had always insisted on, once he could. "So, you can haunt me at daybreak too, then."

"I'll always haunt you. I am you."

"No. No, you are *not.* You called me *sire.*"

"Courtesy. Until you grew used to what you saw."

He's silent. The other, the younger him, turns and points out of the window. The sun is coming up, the silver sky giving way to gold.

"From the east," says the other. "The sun, beloved of the bee and the eagle, and the Lion of Leo, our birth sign. Think of the East. Do you remember?"

He sighs. He sighs so much. "Yes."

"Egypt, the gateway. That campaign which, if wholly successful, would have split England from her Eastern empire. Then on to the lands of fable—Arabia, Persia, India. Your goal, our goal. The same road that was taken by the mighty Alexander of the Greeks. He almost conquered and ruled all the known world. As we did, almost, our much larger world. Is this not true?"

"Perhaps," he says. "But there was too much to do. The farther I went, the more I had achieved, the more complex and petty the ramifications. Surrounded by fools and foes . . . No, I'm my own worst foe. And if you are myself, you phantom, then maybe you *are* that worst foe, externalized."

But the man sitting on the end of the bed shakes his head so the shiny feathers of his young hair fly.

"Think of it this way," says the younger man. "As you grew in knowledge, expertise, and power, as your genius was burnished and jeweled by experience, time trampled you and you aged. Me you left behind—a genius also—but untaught by that experience, *unleavened.*"

"If you were left behind, it wasn't ever my choice. All men age. I before my hour, I believe. I've lived life more than most certainly, lived enough life perhaps for two men. What am I? Fifty-one years. Then in truth I must be one hundred and two. Small wonder I should look and feel it."

His stomach gripes, agonizingly as always now.

His other self watches with a curious apparent mixture of concern and impatience. "It was all that fasting and famishing in our youth," he murmurs, as the face of the older man gradually clears. "That will upset all the mechanisms of a body. The fat on you comes from that, too. We were poor and starved for years. Then we ate. Such things never work out."

"Yes, yes, I'm fat enough. Soon I'll be bone thin."

"So you resign yourself—*our*self—to death."

"I can do no other. I always scorned to take my own life unless all hope was gone. I traveled through Russia with a black bag of poison around my neck, ready. Now life and hope depart together."

Outside the door a soft scratch, and Marchand clears his throat.

Where the younger self is, a smoky flicker appears in the air. He has vanished, yet even as the door opens, the ex-emperor hears his own young voice whisper at his ear, "Tonight, put out the chessboard. I'll play a game with you."

Marchand, troubled, for he thinks he's heard his master not only talking to himself, but muttering answers, advances into the room with a little hot water and the accessories kept for shaving.

And his master looks very ill this morning, Marchand thinks. The yellowish tone of his skin seems heightened by the horrible glowing mossy shade of the wallpaper, and the heartless brilliance of the morning sky.

That evening after supper, he doesn't want to dictate or debate any reminiscences. Nor to read aloud the play by Racine he had placed nearby. He smooths the play regretfully. Its soul-searching drama calls to him even as he moves away.

In the bedroom he stands in his red slippers. Night covers the imprisoning island, flecked, in only a very few areas, by silver stars.

Instead of getting into bed, he goes back into the outer room where he has arranged the chessboard with its array of fierce figures.

How childish to put this out, expecting a phantom to join him. Then, oddly, with the same little ironic quirk of a smile his own other self earlier displayed, he sets a glass of the thin wine on either side the table, and lugs the other chair into position.

Something laughs, up in the ceiling.

He knows the laugh. His own.

Turning, he's just in time to see the green mist that blooms against the dirty brown wallpaper, and how it lightly opens, like a curtain, and out of it, and down, as if descending a brief stair, unerringly runs the short and slender form that long ago was his.

Dreadfully—it startles and shames him—the ex-emperor's eyes expand with tears.

He blinks them back.

But the eyes of his other self are wet also.

The other self holds out its hand.

Frowning now, he clasps it. The hand is warm—strong, calloused as he—anyone—would expect, from swords and guns and reins—and as real.

They sit down. Both raise their glass at the same instant, and both drink. Both view the board carefully.

"Tonight," says his other self, almost flirting, "I shall be Russia."

"Then what am I?"

"Napoleon," says the other self. "What else *need* you be? Life to you, Emperor! *Play to win.*"

Yes, it *is* a flirt, this thing. I am you it says, then courts him. Despite its words of being left behind without his learning, perhaps his experience is already being drunk down by it out of the air.

They play.

The pieces slide and click across the squares. Hours melt like candlewax from the clock.

Neither can win. How could they? They employ the same strategies. Ah yes, it *has* learned.

"You see after all," admits the young man, nearly shy but not unwilling. "Now I've gained your mature cunning."

"And I've lost all my edge."

"Here it is, your edge. It is *me.*"

How young or old precisely is the other? The ex-emperor considers him judicially. He doesn't need the other to say to him, as soon he does, "Do you remember Toulon?" it merely confirms the idea his younger self is approximately twenty-three or twenty-four.

"After Toulon, the beginning of your ascent to power," says the ex-emperor rather drily.

"While yours collapses and ends."

"All things end."

"Not all. Of course, not all."

He considers this. Then looking at the board, suddenly he sees the younger man has left him an opening—perhaps left it purposely—or not. He makes his move and wins the hours-long game.

"So you've taken Russia," gravely announces the

young man. "Soon you can claim the East as well. Not only a united Europe, but a united earth. An end then to *all* war. The wings of the eagle will cover everything and keep it safe."

"Hush, it's lost, that great game. Soon I'll be dead."

The other says disdainfully, "You're not dying. You will live on. True, in vicious pain, in cruel frustration and unhappiness, losing gradually not only yourself, but every faculty you still command—no longer able to ride, then no longer able to walk, no longer able to *think*—a fat old grasshopper all withered up in this prison cell atop the tiniest islet in the world. Do you believe by now you shouldn't already be dead? The English jailer has tried enough, and always, to starve and wound and break and so kill you. In spite of your weakness and despair and the rat that gnaws in your guts, you have the constitution of a lion. Yes, you'll live. Another five, ten, fifteen years. On and on into increasing debility and old age—without teeth or sight or sense—until, as you say, finally you die and crumble to dust. But it's far away. A long and arduous road to reach your grave."

He smiles, bitterly. "If I'm to live, I have no choice. I'd trusted this misery was almost over."

"It can be," says the other, flippant. And abruptly standing up—he's gone.

"Come back, you rogue—you devil—" he catches himself calling it to return. And sighs again.

There is the smell in the room of newly cut greenery, and he recalls the oily scent of broken geraniums by the Temple of Love at Malmaison.

But Joséphine won't visit him again. It was true, he hadn't wanted her, or any of his women. Nor his enemies. His son he had wanted. He'd thought possibly this haunt or demon, whatever it was, might have presented his son to him. If only once. But also now it's too late for that. It knows it has fascinated him entirely in this one shape.

Even though he thinks this he doesn't believe in the demon, which is perhaps why he isn't afraid of it. Naturally he has played the chess game against himself, and drunk both thimbles of vinegary wine.

He lies down on the bed. Sleeps. Dreamless, now.

"Do you remember Toulon? Mondovi, Mantua, Alexandria, Austerlitz?"

Yes, he remembers.

The demon returns, returns. They relive the campaigns, the chess pieces becoming whole armies. Once more he dashes forward into battle, skilled, braver than lions, risking all and taking all. Careless, too, sometimes, determined, as if, stripped of weapons, still he would bite his way through the enemy ranks—

The demon isn't real.

It is a fever dream.

They talk of Corsica, his birthplace. He sees it appear before him—a mirage—the tree-covered heights, the polished shores—

"You didn't want your women, not even your mother—not even your son—oh, be honest. It's this you want. Your past. And me. You want me that is yourself and your youth, when you grew upward into the light of victory."

The demon is correct.

He watches it—himself—narrowly. And so makes more mistakes at the chess—*loses* at Toulon, *loses* at *Austerlitz*— "Once you allowed me to win," he tells the demon. "Our first game."

But the demon checkmates him without answering, leans across the wooden table and, casting its own convincing shadow, clasps his hand, warmly, strongly, once more.

"I can tell you how to win."

He sits back then and the creature lets him go. It speaks softly in his own inventive, fluent French, accented always with Italian.

"You must tell them you're dying."

"I do so. I am."

"That's good. But I've watched you. You must say it with more conviction. Make out your will."

"A wise thought. I shall, God help me."

The spasm in his belly rears and racks him and he doubles over in a cold thick sweat, retching once or twice. The demon waits politely for some while, until the agony withdraws.

"Yes. It will be easy," the sick man grates.

The demon replies, "Easier than you know. You have only to give me yourself, and then I shall be yours."

He straightens. Wipes his face. Through the door he glimpses the unnerving wallpaper.

"You want my soul," he suggests.

"*Souls!* You don't believe in them. This is a bargain of the flesh. I have all your youth, and now all of your wisdom. What you would want therefore is to be me. And I—" the whisper falls like drops of water in his ears, "what I want is the renewal of my self, through the vitality of your remarkable blood."

The older man lets out a long, hoarse laugh.

"My blood's rotten. I have the canker in my guts, like my father before me."

"Nothing of the sort. Your blood is of the best. Why else should I want it? I've supped all these years off the vital fluid of worthless men, or off the gore of rats and reptiles. But you—you tempted me. The blood of a hero and a genius."

The old man watches his adversary now. The old man's eyes, though bloodshot, and the whites a little discolored, are still dark. They seem to see at last very well what the thing is that appears to be himself, and that has learned to speak in his voice. How peculiar, the mouth—his own—avid now as his had never been, no, even in the throes of great rage or passion, and the young eyes themselves glittering like those of a rabid fox.

"You'll drink my blood then."

"I don't drink." Disdainful. "I *absorb.*" The human phrase somehow disturbingly apt, even on that fox tongue. "Some are simple to drain. Not you. Without you allow it, I can do little." Avid. He sees it is avid, and it permits him to see, through every non-corporeal atom, the avidity made concrete by its seeming physicality. As a man lets a woman see his lust, knowing it will move her, when she is attracted.

Yet, *Without you allow it . . .*

After all a threshold, over which this fiend must be specifically invited.

"I say again," says the old man, gray from the

bout of pain, but ever steady eyed, "if you have my blood, I'll die."

"No. You will become what you see before you, your former self. The world will lie at your feet again. When you're strong enough to seize it."

He lowers his eyes. The vampire can probably see him thinking. It would seem, however, not *what* he thinks. For he knows it lies, of course. The exchange will result in strength for it, and an end for himself.

In the window, a hint of morning.

"How long," asks the old man, "will the process take?"

"Not long."

He rises, clumsily. The pain has left an afterglow of scalded horror. He's tired. It takes too much, this long road.

"I shall make my will," he says again to the thing across the table. "Come back when it's done. Then you can have what you want. Understand me, I don't believe in your bargain. But I've done enough. They took my means of a swift death from me, along with all my power and possessions. You then shall replace the little black knot of poison I carried for such a while. You shall be my suicide. As before, only torture and death stand waiting for me. No Roman could do more, or less, than I. Come back when I've seen to my will."

He watches it gleam suddenly through all the solid and human flesh and life it's put on to woo him. Will that disguise adhere, if wanted? But it fades anyway, smiling its fox smile. In its excitement, it has forgotten a moment *only* to resemble him.

* * *

Fighting exhaustion and pain he makes the will, filling the testament with lies, recriminations, accusations, and tricks. This takes days. He dispenses fortunes that maybe will never be honorably extended to the beneficiaries. These riches include hidden stashes of francs, gold, quicksilver, his hair, and his silver lamp, which he leaves to his mother in Rome. Unshaven, he lies spent on the bed. One of the remaining companions comes sometimes and reads newspapers to him. He gives his gold snuffbox to the untrusted doctor, with a demand for a prompt postmortem autopsy. It seems the ex-emperor actively wishes his body cut open, disemboweled—as if to be sure it can never reengage itself.

At close, regular intervals, the stomach spasms convulse him. Between them he dreams, and tells those in the room Joséphine was with him, but wouldn't embrace him. She had instead assured him that soon they would no longer be parted.

Not long, then. Not long before death sucks him down. Behind the bed, a backdrop, that wallpaper must always have been so green, and with the strange marks on it, which must be a pattern, surely.

"What a vast time . . . you've made me wait," the sick man says.

"And you, what a time I have waited for *you*." There it is, bending over him, himself, the other, twenty-three, twenty-four. The other murmurs, "Are you prepared?"

"One last—tell me, how is it I must *allow* you this? Couldn't you have taken my blood otherwise?"

"I've said. With others. Weaklings. Not you—a

worthy adversary. I've tasted your ichor in superficial sips, from your dreams, memories . . ."

"From my thoughts?"

"Not those. Your kind of strength shuts doors. Only your longings—and even there I misjudged, didn't I, until I knew you better. But now I shall feast on you. Are you afraid?"

"No. I always had a curious nature. Mathematics, the sciences intrigue me. This too has a sort of mathematic, so I believe."

The thing that wears his shape bends closer and closer. The sick man, scenting skin, linen starch, hair, sensing its warmth, again notes how well it has made itself to please him. In further proof, his own young hair brushes the sick man's face. And at this instant he feels the essence of his blood begin to drift away from his veins and heart and brain, unhurtful and terrible, into the substance of the demon. He sees the creature too, lit with a kind of bloom, like a plant well watered, and how its eyes—his *own* eyes—bulge and fixate. It gives a strangled moan. Delight? Satisfaction? Then he hears it shriek, far off as a gull above the tableland. Yet the words are clear. "It burns! Your blood—it burns!"

The sick man, not quite so sick as he's pretended, puts up his arms as if to clasp a beloved son, and seizes the vampire by the waist. He finds he is still strong enough to surprise himself—to surprise both his selves. He hauls it down on top of him. It thrashes, but already something's amiss with it and with its timeless procedure.

He gives it no space either to draw back or to

recover. He sinks his own sore teeth into its throat, mauling and biting, snapping through until he can taste the blood of *it*—green as sap, boiling and slippery, not unpleasant, like herbs or medicine, or geranium leaves in a salad—

The vampire is thrashing and screaming on the bed. Something has occurred. As the emperor, swallowing one ultimate mouthful of green wine, rolls aside, letting the creature go, he beholds how the vampire has been altered.

It's bloated, and changed both shape and color. It is no longer that film which floated from behind the wall, nor is it any longer in the form of the young and handsome man who had operated the guns at Toulon. Now, flopping over onto its back, it is a swollen man-fish dragged, engorged with fever and internal venoms, from some awful sea, sallow and fat-bellied and broken, the sunken face old before its time, the dark eyes bloodshot and the whites liverishly yellow.

Yes. Still the vampire is himself, but now his aged recent *ruined* self. Nevertheless, still fleshy, and if not warm to the touch, more clammy, yet able to *be* touched, and handled.

His blood. His *ichor.*

He had seen men in the desert as they marched, days without water, forcing gallons between their lips at some oasis and then foaming at the mouth, vomiting, dying. The vampire had waited so long for his blood, only *sipping.* Then taking it fast and in such quantity, greedy, *thirsty*—too much. *It burns!*

It kills.

The creature, poisoned by the power of light that lingers still in every hero, even those who make mistakes and grow old. Only Napoleon can conquer Napoleon.

The emperor stands by the bed, shaking back the lush silken hair that hangs to his collar.

In every muscle, artery, and bone, he feels the shining sap of the vampire bounding and coursing in a wonderful mad ride, metamorphosing him back through time, making him young again, perhaps forever. What from him has poisoned the fiend has, from the fiend, done the hero only perfect good.

Center of the universe—how could he ever properly have credited he could die? He was immortal.

But the palpitating lump of apparently human wreckage on the bed rasps from its rattled throat, "You knew—you knew—" petulant as a child.

He replies. There is space for it, now. "Not certainly. But it was worth the risk. I built my life on such risks. And on charming my adversaries. Then. But now . . ." He pauses, wonderingly. "I am a private citizen of the world. No island can contain me, only the earth herself—" The young man stands there, his head lifted. Everything beckons to him. Will his life be like his former life? Or quite different? God knew. "My God," he says, turning to the window, "look at the stars!" And *vanishes* into thin air.

The bargain, although it has not transpired as intended, is fulfilled, it seems.

Moments later, one of the ex-emperor's attendants rushes into the room, having heard weird distant cries he had, at first, taken for those of a night bird.

As he runs forward, the dying remnant on the bed leaps upright and grips him so tightly, astonishingly, that the attendant can't even shout for assistance. But the doctor, hearing wild thuds, presently intrudes and pries the man from the invalid's uncannily strong grasp.

The ex-emperor collapses back on the bed. Behind him the wallpaper stays an intransigently faded green.

He survives only another day, while rain smashes against the cowshed house and greenish mist streams through every one of the wet, noisesome rooms. Sometimes he seems to crave drink, but can swallow nothing. That evening another tree is uprooted by the wind.

Late the following day, as the sun sets wearily into the Atlantic, they find the heart of the ex-emperor has also gone down into the dark.

Bribed by the gold snuffbox, and surrounded by witnesses, the doctor cuts deeply into the body cavity of the corpse, exposing and removing certain organs. If anything has lived in this body, undeniably it can no longer do so.

The verdict as to the cause of death is variable and inconclusive. It will remain a topic of debate for at least two centuries.

Long after the body, buried on the fever-blighted island of St. Helena, is disinterred and rehoused, with some ceremony, inside a tomb of sable and crystal, in the heart of France.

Napoleon, they say with sad irony, is once more in Paris.

Is he?

SEPULCHRES OF THE UNDEAD

by Keith Taylor

One of their last clans must have been the first priests and rulers of old Egypt—the evidence seems clear enough in the animal and half-animal gods the Egyptians worshipped and the demons and the evil magic they feared.

—Jack Williamson, *Darker Than You Think*

I

Terror lay across the two lands of Egypt, upper and lower, fear so awful that most endured it by refusing to know it. Menkhaf the soldier was not so lucky. Circumstances had stripped him of happy ignorance. A monster had killed the kindly uncle who had raised him and his brother from orphaned boys, and Menkhaf knew what sort of monster. Because of that he crouched on the dusty Dahshur plateau beside a large but simple tomb, a mastaba, with a silver-headed spear in his hand, waiting in ambush.

The plateau looked barren and cold in the moonlight, a place between life and death. If his two companions told the truth, it had become just that. All three of them wore leather kilts and collars of stiffer, thicker leather around their throats, while a mixture of oil and crushed garlic coated their bodies. Menkhaf's own rank sweat reeked more than the garlic. With fear gripping his bowels, he felt as though he very badly wanted to use a latrine—and Menkhaf had fought both Libyan raiders and lions.

He made no sound. His companions had warned him repeatedly about that. Unlike Menkhaf, they wore masks in the likeness of the sun-falcon. By the bargain he had sworn, he was not to see their faces until this night's work was done. They carried curious nets of pliant silver mesh and knives of the same metal were sheathed at their girdles. Although young and fit enough, they had not the look of soldiers. Their hands were smooth. They talked like learned men. Priests, was Menkhaf's guess.

Dazzling in the moonlight rose the pyramid of King Snefru, cased in pure white limestone, and farther away, though still in plain sight, the so-called bent pyramid. Snefru had built that one also. Menkhaf had given them little thought until now, though no Egyptian king had raised such imposing tombs before. King Khufu, of course, appeared set on outdoing his father.

Why, of all places, should they lie in wait for a vampire here?

Menkhaf's nearer companion gripped his shoulder and pointed to that part of the sky just beneath the moon. A dark flitting speck showed there. It drew swiftly closer, flitting and veering. Only a bat, Menkhaf thought, and what was noteworthy about that, except its nearness? Suddenly his sense of perspective shifted. He was not looking at a small bat very close to him. It had not come closer than a spear's cast yet, and it was enormously large.

Menkhaf clamped his jaw and remembered his uncle. Rage came to his aid, driving away the fear. He gripped the silver-headed spear in both hands. The huge bat descended. Gusts from its wings blew dust across the mastaba's gritty surface. Even little pebbles went flying. Some of the dust settled on Menkhaf's oiled hide where he crouched at the base of the mastaba. Blinking, he peered up. Although he had lost sight of the monster as it settled atop the tomb, he knew where it was, and that he had come to destroy it. Enough for a soldier to know.

With a desperate battle roar he sprang out of the sand and up the side of the mastaba. The men in falcon masks followed him closely, but he reached the top first. The gigantic bat sprawled awkwardly on the flat stone slab. As he rushed upon it, the head turned to glare at him, and its mouth opened, full of broad triangular teeth. Its wing span measured four times Menkhaf's height, and the body rivaled a spotted hyena's.

The little eyes blazed red as it saw the spear. Swiftly, incredibly, its shape began to alter, the wings dwindling, but Menkhaf was upon it before the transformation could go farther. Bellowing again, he rammed his silver spear into its body, thrusting for the heart. He felt the soft, heavy resistance of muscles and organs, even though they had told him the vampire had no corporeal substance when it traveled from its tomb. Menkhaf wasted no thought on the contradiction; he had the thing impaled on his spear like some immense moth, but he had missed the heart, the seat of thought and soul. He drove the spear deeper.

Then the hawk-masked men were beside him. They whirled their silver nets. The vampire began to dissolve in a pale mist that merged with the moonlight, but the supple mesh of one net wrapped around it, then the second, and the men drew them inexorably tighter. The vampire thrashed, writhed, shrieked in a way that hurt Menkhaf's ears, but he twisted the spear about and finally touched the pulsing organ he sought.

The vampire convulsed. Before Menkhaf's eyes it began subliming in black fumes. In a moment any coherent shape was gone. The thing itself was gone. The silver nets lay flaccid and empty. Nothing stained Menkhaf's spearhead.

"What?" he croaked. "Where is it? Did it escape?"

"No, friend," one of the hawk-masked men assured him. "It did not escape. The touch of silver is one thing they cannot escape. It perished. Its physical body is down in this tomb, but it's just a corpse now, nothing more. The spirit form is destroyed. She will not return."

"She?" Menkhaf echoed.

"Yes. Before she died she was a woman."

"Man or woman, you are certain she was the fiend that drained my uncle dry?" Menkhaf asked, and when the priests answered him with simultaneous definite nods, he growled, "Too good for her, then. Now it is over."

The priests stood rigidly still. Their silence spoke loudly. Menkhaf looked suspiciously from one to the other.

"What?" he demanded.

"It is not over," the second of them said. "There are more of these demons, and now that you have slain one you have made them all your foes. They will seek you out, believe me. It will not be over until the last one returns to dead dry flesh."

Menkhaf had never been too fond of priests. He said past the bile in his throat, "You did not tell me that before. I don't know that I believe it now."

"You believed us when we swore to lead you to the vampire that drained your uncle, and we have kept that promise fully." The second priest's voice grew sardonic. "We would have told you who the vampire was, also, if you had troubled to ask. You had better know now."

"She was Hetepheres," the first priest said curtly.

"Hetepheres? King Khufu's mother? The late queen?"

"The thoroughly late queen, now," came the dry answer. "Yes. You will see that you cannot just walk away from this matter dusting your hands and saying, 'It is over.' For now, though, we must leave this place. It would not be well to be caught here."

Menkhaf believed that, at least. Minutes later there was nothing under the moon but the bare surface of the tomb, and sand whispering in the breeze as it shifted above the buried vampire. And the pyramids raised at the command of King Snefru, enigmatic, unprecedented, holding a secret no tomb painting or inscription would ever record.

II

Khufu, son of Snefru, looked arrogantly down upon the building site of his own pyramid from the topmost height it had yet reached; half what its finished altitude would be. That was still high. About four-fifths of the building stone required had gone into that lower half. The rest, of course, narrowed ever more sharply as the monstrous tomb rose higher.

The sights far below Khufu seemed to satisfy him: the temple complex, the wharf and canal by which granite and fine limestone came to his site, the workers dragging stone-laden sledges under the strict direction of foremen, looking no bigger than beetles from his vantage, and the narrow ramps rising up the sides of the pyramid. It was when his dark eyes moved to survey the flat surface around him, where numbered core stones were being levered carefully into place, that Khufu's face showed misgiving.

He reached a decision. "Halt the labor, kinsman," he ordered with a snap of his fingers. "This will not do."

Prince Hemiunu, the king's nephew, vizier, and grand architect, gave the order immediately. He had expected this from Khufu. Considerably though it irked him, his bland official features stayed inscrutable. He had become practiced in hiding his personal feelings over the years.

"Not do, Great One?"

"By no means! I have reconsidered! The burial chamber will be proof against mortal thieves, no doubt, and my temple will guard it forever, but what if an earthquake should come? The chamber would collapse! My sarcophagus would be crushed! You must design a new burial chamber, higher, with less rock above it and greater safety."

"At your command, Great One. It can be done."

"How will you do it?"

Hemiunu had his answer ready. He had planned and discussed the problem with his subordinate builder, Zezi. They had been compelled to revise plans for the immense artificial mountain twice already. First they had constructed a descending passage to a chamber cut from the rock beneath the pyramid. Daunted—though no one said it—by the thought of the gigantic weight of rock that would lie atop him in his sarcophagus, Khufu had called for a burial chamber within the pyramid itself. Therefore a new, rising passage had been cut through blocks already laid, an inconvenient business, then run level to a second burial chamber.

Now Khufu had become dissatisfied with that too.

"Great One, these few freshly laid courses of stone blocks obstruct us. We shall cut a new passage through them. Then a new ascending gallery, such as I sketch here—" He illustrated what he meant on one of the stone blocks exposed to the daylight. "—will lead to the higher burial chamber we shall construct."

And I hope that one will satisfy you at last.

"Beware, kinsman, no swift or careless building." Khufu gave his nephew a menacing glare. He had to look up to do it. They were markedly unlike, despite their relation. The Godking of the Two Lands, Bringer of the Yearly Flood, holder of many other titles, showed quick, impatient vitality in all his speech and movement. His broad face, jutting nose, and narrow eyes were not handsome, but they showed a nature with which one might not trifle safely.

The vizier, larger and younger, big-bellied, big-shouldered, with heavy limbs, owned considerable useful muscle under his sheath of fat. The round, fleshy face was a skilled courtier's. He had proved himself no mean administrator either.

"My uncle!" Hemiunu protested. "I have planned for this possibility and others. All care shall be taken, I make my oath! The weight above your chamber shall be relieved by a series of hollow compartments, each roofed by a thick slab to maintain strength. If your greatness will honor me by dining with me this evening, I will be pleased to display the plans."

Khufu accepted. His nephew had thought he would. More than finicky obsession lay behind the king's concern for the design of his tomb. With his heritage, Khufu had other reasons than religion to know that he would survive death. Hemiunu looked slowly around him at the royal tomb he had charge of building—the mightiest structure ever raised by mortal hands, to house an immortal vampire and protect him, invulnerable, after his body died and was embalmed. Just that, no more. No other purpose.

And no one outside the royal clan knew it.

The vizier gazed out and down at the swarming

workers, swiftly taking advantage of the unexpected order to lay down tools. He thought with dry amusement that no matter who else might suffer from the royal vampire's predations, they were quite safe. The importance of their labor aside, their rations included generous amounts of garlic.

"Have you heard, kinsman, that my mother's tomb was defiled of late?" the king said abruptly. "Robbers tried to break into it. The side was damaged, but they failed to find ingress. How dared they? I shall find them."

The king meant that he would hunt them by night in his own way. Thinking of it, Hemiunu required some effort to maintain his stolid manner. A half-breed, he did not have the complete vampire's power of leaving his body in any form he desired—a bat, a mist, a black dog, or a snake—but he did possess the ability to lay highly effective curses, and he could foresee the future to a certain degree.

"May it be so, Great One," he murmured.

"My own queens shall rest in lesser pyramids near mine," Khufu snarled. "My mother's sarcophagus shall be moved to a new, secret resting place for safety. See to it, O Hemiunu."

The vizier bowed and assured the king of his efficient obedience.

III

Vampires did not hunt in the noonday. For that reason, the Brotherhood of Ra, the hidden conspiracy against the night-winged ones, chose noon to bring

Menkhaf to its conclave. He was ushered in blindfolded, his arms tied securely by a band of leather.

Because the place was cool and smelled of slowly burning lamp oil, he assumed it was underground. He also smelled dust, and apart from the arbitrary bite of the strap around his arms, he could feel flat laid stone under his feet. All around him men were breathing, now and then scratching, shifting their weight, though they kept a disciplined silence otherwise. Once someone coughed. Then a voice spoke from directly in front of him. Toneless and measured, it had evidently been disguised.

"Menkhaf, commander of a hundred, you have slain a vampire. Few can boast that! Be assured that she was indeed the murderess of your uncle. You have avenged him."

Menkhaf said, "Was she truly Hetepheres, the king's own mother?"

"She was. Do not resent it. Before our brotherhood led you to the demon, with the means to destroy her in your hands, you swore you cared nothing for consequences if you could only repay your kinsman's murder. We took you at your word. Was it the truth, or mere light talk?"

"The truth!" Menkhaf answered hotly, not liking the blindfold. "Now unhood me. I talk to no one pinioned and blindfolded."

"Not until you have heard us," a second, sardonic voice answered. It had the thin sere quality of age. "You may be glad of the blindfold then, and wish you had been deaf, besides. A clan of vampires threatens all Egypt. Soldier, do you truly know what a vampire is?"

"A ghost that nourishes itself on the blood of the living," Menkhaf answered impatiently.

"Not quite that, and more than that. Vampires begin as living men and women, but of a monstrous, accursed breed. It was ancient before the first brick of Memphis was laid. The trait comes to them in their blood, a dark and evil inheritance flowing like a river, down out of a past we know not. They are born so. While they live, they have great gifts of magic, and their spirit doubles can leave their bodies in the hours of night to work harm in any form that pleases them."

"I saw that, let me tell you!"

"And having seen, we now expect you to believe. Only a true vampire, a complete vampire, is strong enough to survive death and return from the sepulchre! There are half-breeds and quarter-breeds aplenty about. They may become murderers, magicians, or priests; some turn against and conquer their wicked heritage. O Menkhaf, I myself am a quarter-breed. This it were best that you know at once."

Menkhaf shivered.

"There are only three ways known that they can be killed forever when outside their bodies. By being caught in sunlight, with silver, and by finding their physical bodies and destroying their hearts. A wooden stake steeped in garlic will serve, or a silver dagger—but silver is an import, the royal clan controls it, and silver weapons are a means we rarely use. They are conspicuous. To be found with one means death."

The first voice, the younger, heavier voice, resumed. "While a vampire still enjoys the fleshly life of the body, there are other, simpler ways. Cutting out the heart and burning it. Decapitation. These you will learn."

Menkhaf said slowly, "What, my master, did you mean that the royal clan controls the import of silver?"

"Fool! The true, full vampires today are the royal clan. You destroyed Hetepheres. We had already disposed of King Snefru, her lord. That is the reason he worked so greatly in his day to perfect the vast pyramid tomb. For safety! That is why Khufu today raises a greater pyramid than any of his father's. It obsesses him; vampires too can become mad. We have carefully laid plans to deal with him in good time, which you need not know."

"You must see now, though," the other, aged voice resumed, "in what danger the Two Lands are. This breed of monster would rule and rule, having all Egypt's peasants to work on their tombs in mass conscriptions, building the vile ones impregnable refuges from which they may prey on the living, while their heirs rule in the body and join them after death, swelling their numbers, increasing the misery of Egypt, and affronting the gods forever."

The word *forever* had never chilled Menkhaf's heart as it did then.

"Now we call on you to swear our fatal oath and join us. We have long plotted in secret, and from the time we began to plot, we knew that we are certainly dead men. We conspire against the royal clan, who are believed divine by commoners. But for all that, we can win. The true vampires are few as yet. They were the secret conspiracy once, their filthy seed scattered, until they drew together again and bred. Khufu and his named heir Kawab are two, Radjedef a third, with others—not too many to destroy. We have too few redoubtable warriors in the Brotherhood. We need you. You, assuredly, now need us."

Menkhaf understood. If he refused, they could do nothing but kill him. Besides, what were his choices, even without that inducement? Leave Egypt—his children and grandchildren, if he survived to have any—to be the prey of vampires, forever?

He swore their oath. It was one from which only death could free a man. An oath which, as the aged voice had said, none but a dead man would take in the first place.

IV

The vizier Hemiunu, large, strong, and corpulent, sat on a balcony in company with King Khufu and the chief court magician, Djedi, an old man who looked little and light as a cricket beside the vizier. Both were part vampires, and well aware that Khufu did not trust them on that account. Khufu trusted nobody. He never forgot that no matter what honors and power he gave to his minions, their human side and their human ties might triumph. Hemiunu's wife Nibi-nefer believed with all her heart that their children would be of the true breed, as she called it, and able to survive death. She believed equally, though, that she would do so herself, which Hemiunu thought doubtful. Neither of them carried enough of the vampire heritage, and she less than he. Not that he said as much to her. Saying to Nibi-nefer what would be anathema to her dainty ears was always unwise.

Those dainty ears heard nearly everything, though, even at a distance, and carried it to Khufu. That was Nibi-nefer's gift, no trifle in a court riddled with spying and backbiting. Therefore she also was present.

"Has my mother's coffin been reburied?" the king demanded.

Hemiunu answered unctuously. "Yes, Great One. Secretly, in a deep shaft-grave. None shall disturb it there, and the offerings at her mortuary temple shall continue forever."

"Who committed such a vile crime?" Nibi-nefer asked, her little teeth glinting. "I would have them impaled, then restored to life by you, excellent Djedi, to die in manifold other ways."

She spoke with derisive malice. She knew very well that Khufu had once requested, to amuse him, that Djedi show his powers by restoring a prisoner to life—Khufu's intention being to have the man beheaded then and there. Djedi had pleaded, with all his decades of wit and tact, to be excused, and made his demonstration on a goose instead. Which, although just as wonderful, to Nibi-nefer seemed a sign of weakness.

"Tomb robbers?" Hemiunu suggested.

"Or the Brotherhood of Ra." A scowl convoluted the thousand wrinkles of Djedi's face.

"That accursed Brotherhood!" Khufu said vehemently. "I should have done more than close the temples. I should have wiped out the priests. I may yet."

His narrow eyes glittered. He sat brooding. In his

own palace apartments, among intimates, he laid aside ceremonial headdress and wig. The peculiar slanting shape of his skull showed with striking obviousness above his serpentine eyes. It was one mark of the vampire breed, though not infallible. Hemiunu's own cranium was broad and rounded, his wife's small, neat, and feline, short from the crown to the chin.

"And the escape shafts in the great pyramid? How do they progress?"

"Straight and true. One is aligned upon Sirius, one on Orion. The tale for the workers is that they exist to guide the king's ka to the stars."

Khufu nodded in brusque approval. "I will inspect it as each course rises. You may now begin the design of a pyramid for my heir Kawab, who will reign after me. It must be raised close to mine."

Others had discussed the reign and fate of Kawab that same night, and the results of their deliberations were soon carried to Menkhaf. The soldier had been posted to guard duty in the palace. A man of action but no fool, he had immediately seen the hand of the Brotherhood of Ra in that turn of events. Many of them were priests and officials who had turned against King Khufu, or their conspiracy could never function, and some must be wizards also.

He wondered darkly about the real nature of the conspiracy. Was it really as they had told him? Or were they merely seeking to overthrow Khufu's dynasty and replace it with another? They would be glad to spread monstrous lies about Khufu and his parents in that case. Yes, but Menkhaf had encountered a vampire coming back to a royal tomb, and seen it trapped and killed with silver weapons, had taken a major part in the killing himself. That it had been Hetepheres he did not doubt . . . and such speculation led nowhere but in empty circles. He was committed now. He had pledged it with oaths a god would scarce dare break.

Two days afterward, a fellow palace guard approached him, clasped his hand with a peculiar grip, and then led him to a concealed chamber. A man in a plain white robe gave them their next command through a veil.

"This night you must act together and slay Prince Kawab."

"The king's heir?" Menkhaf said, astounded. "How can we even come near him?"

"He will be with a woman. One of his father's own harem women, so naturally he will be clandestine. You must behead him, then cut out his heart, and bring it with you to this room."

"That was not required with Hetepheres!"

"The accursed queen was dead, and could travel only in spirit form. Nothing can kill them then but silver or sunlight. When they still have life in the flesh, the ways I have described will do. That you are green to the Brotherhood I know, but I had thought you grasped as much."

"There'll be much blood," Menkhaf said stubbornly, in case his new masters had missed the obvious—or simply did not care if their assassins were captured.

"Eye of the Sun! You must do the deed naked. There will be water nearby to wash you clean. Be quick and silent and all will go well."

Menkhaf thought of a dozen more questions. In the end he asked none of them. His comrade, walking with him in a known part of the palace again, said quietly, "The woman will not scream. She is part of the plan, one of us. All we need do is silence . . . the man."

Menkhaf thought, *If that proves to be untrue I will not be captured alive. The weapon that slays Kawab can do me a last service too.*

That evening he and his fellow assassin moved through the palace shadows toward a lovely pleasure kiosk in the gardens, beside an ornamental lake. A lamp gleamed through fretted copper screens. Neither of them whispered a word during their approach, for the vampire breed had uncannily sharp ears, even in their fleshly housing.

Menkhaf and his companion discarded their clothes, even their sandals. Holding heavy bronze blades and small round shields fashioned from hardwood and bound with leather, they crept nearer. Certain sounds emanated from the kiosk on the perfumed air. Prince Kawab was indeed there, it appeared, and certainly with a woman.

The assassins rushed in. Prince Kawab reacted as swiftly as a leopard. He sought to detach himself from the woman gasping and squealing beneath him, but she clung to him with all the strength of her arms and legs. Rising upward, he thrust her violently away, so that she crashed into an ornamental screen. It toppled over.

Looking like any naked young noble surprised on the wrong couch, the prince opened his mouth to yell. Menkhaf swung his round shield, caving in the prince's throat. A normal man would have collapsed to the floor with a death gurgle coming from his ruined larynx. Kawab seized a heavy sword from a nearby stand and attacked the two intruders. He had not come unprepared to his illicit tryst.

Menkhaf and his companion caught the prince's strokes on their shields, first one and then the other, waiting for their chance. With blood on his mouth and his face blackened, the prince had no aspect of the human about him now. His straining attempts to cry out from his ruined throat were ghastly to see.

Setting his teeth, Menkhaf rammed his blade deep between the prince's ribs and twisted. Then he warded off a terrible stroke with his shield, which split straight across as Prince Kawab's weapon also broke. Menkhaf's companion hacked into the prince's neck, and an instant later Menkhaf's blade grated unpleasantly upon it within slashed, bleeding flesh.

Kawab's head came off with a little more twisting and chopping. Blood sprayed wildly, splashing his killers, the couch, and the royal concubine. She had neither moved nor screamed, just as Menkhaf's companion had told him. Nor did she look away while they bent and cut out Kawab's heart.

Horribly, the decapitated corpse fought them with both hands, while the head glared and mouthed silent curses for a while. Menkhaf rose with the red heart in his hand as the corpse gave its last twitches. His skin crawled with horror.

His companion was looking at the woman. "Cousin, Nemaathep—"

"I make you free and I bless you," she said calmly. "Now!"

He killed her with one quick stroke.

Menkhaf's horror increased. He would not have believed that could happen, not on this night, but it did, and yet there was no time to remonstrate. Fleeing outside, they ducked in the lake to sluice the vampire's blood from their skins, and then recovered their clothes. It was some time before they were sure no pursuit had begun, and a longer time before Menkhaf could find anything to say. Then it was only the bald, obvious, "You called her cousin."

"She was," the man said wearily. "She was also with child, by Khufu or his whelp, what does it matter? And since she carried the vampire taint herself—half vampire; I am a quarter—she could well have borne such a monster. She preferred to die."

Tears ran down his face, thick among the lake water.

Menkhaf said slowly, "There are no words."

"There are not." His companion added some, nevertheless, in a savage tone. "I hope I die in this cause before too long."

V

Hemiunu and Djedi sat together under an awning by the pyramid site, dust and noise and sweat powerful in the hot air. The vizier's big broad face, smooth as a pomegranate, made a ludicrous contrast with the magician's little wrinkled visage. Djedi carried a scroll of spells to be incorporated into the upper part of the pyramid. He had also cast some effective ones against being overheard.

"I have lived long and seen purges of the court

and bureaucracy, but none like this," Djedi said somberly. "The murder of his heir has enraged the king out of reason. He craves blood, and more blood. Even you and I are in danger."

"Huh! If you think you and I are shitting rocks," Hemiunu said crudely, "take good note of Prince Radjedef. Many suspect that he slew Kawab to become the new heir, his sire included, O most efficacious wizard."

"Even if the king suspects him, he will not execute him, no matter what Radjedef may be fearing. There are too few of the full breed as yet."

"Yes. And none of them doubt any longer that the Brotherhood of Ra is real, and a menace. Not after Kawab's death and the concubine Nemaathep's. They ought to have been certain of it before. I have been telling them so, and presenting evidence, for long enough."

The vizier of all men was in a position to know for certain. He and Djedi led the Brotherhood of Ra. By slaying Prince Kawab, or having him slain, they had reduced the number of full-breed vampires by one; two, perhaps, counting the child in unlucky Nemaathep's womb, and they had made the royal clan suspicious of each other. The action had its disadvantages, though, and Djedi mentioned one.

"Slaying the prince may yet prove a mistake. The opportunity was there, yes, but taking it may have been too hasty, too ill-considered. How much suspicion has fallen on you?"

"No more than on every other high official. I am closely watched by spies, my sweet wife included. My voyage upstream to inspect the realm was canceled by the king himself. He says, with many words of praise, that he will not risk my life. He means that he will not let me out of his sight. And you, Djedi? Have you cast auguries as to my future?"

"Thrice. Each time the result was the same."

Hemiunu heard the old man's tone, and studied him long with his heavy-lidded gaze.

"Not auspicious, eh?"

"I am sorry. Far from it. You will be denounced. One of your subordinates will bring the charges, and Nibi-nefer will support him to save her own skin and, to be just, the lives of your children."

Hemiunu's laugh was bitter. "The ass! Does she think that will save her, or them? You are sure this will be?"

"Alas, I am sure, Hemiunu."

"Well, I have foreseen that strong possibility without magic, but now we are sure. I shall at least not wait for the king's torturers to question me."

"If you take poison, it will be as though you confessed the truth to Khufu."

"And doom my family no less. Not to mention my closest associates and the Brotherhood itself. Yes, old friend, I know. Well, from the time I joined I knew I was a dead man. Meseems I have a way of turning this to useful account. Suspicion of me should certainly vanish if I myself am assassinated by the Brotherhood."

Tears had not wet Djedi's ancient eyes in so long that the ducts had shriveled. Yet the urge came now. He rested a hand on Hemiunu's heavy shoulder.

"It is a cleaner way to die."

"By Horus and Set, but that's true!" Hemiunu

agreed with the bleakest of smiles. "It will confuse the accursed ones, and I hope make them afraid. Kawab, then the vizier—why, who is safe, and who can avoid the avenger's blade? Better yet, it will lead them to look in wrong directions. Nothing must overturn our plans for Khufu himself."

"Nothing will," Djedi promised. "Nothing. By the time of his death all the embalmers will be suborned, and it will be I who presides over his mummification. I will remove his heart along with the other organs and replace it with the heart of a pig. The secret will be kept forever once his body is wrapped, plastered, and coffined. Khufu may lie at rest in his magnificent pyramid. Never through all of time will he leave it seeking blood. Not once his heart has burned on a fire of herbs and ebony."

"I hold you to it."

Laid and carried out with care, the plan would succeed. With Ra's favor, the same could be done to at least a couple of Khufu's successors until the pure vampire breed was extinct, their monstrous heritage diluted and spread among the swarms of normal human beings. After that, hopefully, it would never be gathered together again. The custom of pyramid building should fade away too, the true reason for it forgotten in the dust of centuries, and that was a thing worth dying for.

Hemiunu did not set his affairs in order. He forbore even to make a fresh will. He gave no sign that he expected his own murder, or any other event out of the common. Hemiunu had never been that kind of fool, even before years of directing the Brotherhood of Ra had sharpened his wits relentlessly.

In a secret conclave, wearing his hawk mask as head of the Brotherhood, he commanded the slaying of Hemiunu, the demon King Khufu's demon vizier. There was irony in that. Then he did what was necessary to make the assassins' task easy.

At the arranged time he sat alone, unguarded. Under his hand lay some of the multitudinous reports and orders that were his responsibility and soon would be someone else's. He wrote on with a steady hand.

He sensed rather than heard the competently soft footstep behind him, the stir of air pushed in front of an approaching person.

Hemiunu never turned his head.

About the Authors

JOHN GREGORY BETANCOURT is the author of over thirty published novels. He is presently engaged in extending Roger Zelazny's celebrated Amber series. Among his other novels are *The Blind Archer, Johnny Zed,* and *Rememory*. His short fiction has been published widely. He has edited anthologies. He was one of the founding editor-publishers of the revived *Weird Tales* magazine, left for a while, and has now returned as publisher and coeditor. He is also founder and owner of Wildside Press, which publishes numerous magazines and has over two thousand books in print. Despite this he finds time to have a family, own a home, and, occasionally, exhale.

P. D. CACEK, a winner of both the World Fantasy Award and the Bram Stoker Award, has her own history with vampires (*Night Prayers* and *Night Players*), angry Native American gods (*The Wind Caller*), ghosts (*Sympathy for the Dead),* and erotica (*Eros Inter-*

ruptus). Some of her shorter fiction may be found in *Weird Tales, Weird Trails, Hotter Blood 13: Inferno,* and *Night Visions 12.* She has also edited one anthology, *Bell, Book, and Beyond,* and does editorial and production work for various publishers. She is dangerous to be around because she bakes very good cookies which cause editors to gain weight.

GREGORY FROST says he decided to write "Ill-Met in Ilium" after hearing Robert Fagles recite from his translations of the *Iliad*, the *Odyssey*, and the *Aeneid.* He's been a finalist for the World Fantasy, Hugo, and Nebula awards among others. His latest book is the short story collection *Atack of the Jazz Giants*, which *Publishers Weekly* called "one of the best fantasy collections of the year."

RON GOULART responded to the request for blurb material: "I seem to be in a vampire mode these days. Glad you caught me before sunrise. My latest novel came out last summer—*Groucho Marx, King of the Jungle.* Like all of the other five books in the St. Martin's series, it takes place in the Hollywood of the late 1930s and early 1940s. My latest nonfiction is a trade paperback reprint of *The Adventurous Decade,* a history of newspaper adventure strips—*Dick Tracy, Terry & the Pirates, Flash Gordon,* etc.—of the 1930s. The character Hix, as I think I've mentioned, has appeared in such novels of mine as *Skyrocket Steele,* about the strange events surrounding the making of a movie serial in Hollywood in 1941 (and now available again as an e-book) and many short stories. One of them, *The Werewolf of Hollywood,* I adapted some years back for a George Romero TV show entitled *Monsters*. Because of the budget, however, it didn't take place in 1930s Hollywood and Hix got dropped."

SARAH A. HOYT has published over three dozen short stories in venues ranging from anthologies to magazines such as *Asimov's, Analog, Amazing,* and *Weird Tales*. Her Shakespearean fantasy trilogy earned critical acclaim and the first book was a Mythopoeic Award finalist. Her shape-shifter fantasy novel *Draw One in the Dark* will be released in November. Her mystery novel *Death of a Musketeer*, written as Sarah D'Almeida, will also be released in November. Sarah is not now nor has she ever been a communist or a vampire.

TANITH LEE is the world-famous author of *The Birthgrave,* the Flat Earth Series, and far too many other books to list. At this time of writing (2006), she said, "I'm working on Volume 3 of the Lionwolf Trilogy: *No Flame But Mine*. This year I'll be writing a third book in the young adult 'Piratica' series, the second book, *Piratica* 2, was recently published. This year will also see publication of my nvella 'Strindberg's Ghost Sonata' (in *The Ghost Quartet* from the Science Fiction Book Club of America) and short stores in *Realms of Fantasy, Weird Tales,* and *Asimov's* magazine. A contemporary novel, *L'Amber,* will also finally be released. Though this is not fantasy or science fiction, it's easily much more popular. A second, unrelated but also bizarre contemporary novel, *Greyglass,* should follow."

MIKE RESNICK is the author of more than 50 science fiction novels, 175 stories, 12 collections, 2 screenplays, and the editor of more than 40 anthologies. He has won five Hugo Awards and has won other major awards in the United States, France, Spain, Croatia, Poland, and Japan. Two of his popular Teddy Roosevelt stories have been nominated for Hugos.

BRIAN STABLEFORD's recent novels include *The Wayward Muse, The Stones of Camelot* and *Streaking*. He has translated Paul Féval's *Salem Street*, one of the pioneering Black Coat series of crime novels, and followed it up with another in the series, *The Invisible Weapon*. He recently published a 400,000-word reference book, *Science Fact and Science Fiction: An Encyclopedia*, which is his hundredth book.

KEITH TAYLOR is a leading Australian author of historical fantasy, whose work has been appearing since the 1970s. He has written much material set in ancient or early medieval Britain, such as the Bard series (four volumes), but has more recently turned his attention to ancient Egypt. His stories of Kamose the sinister priest of Anubis have been a popular feature in *Weird Tales* for several years now.

HARRY TURTLEDOVE is an escaped Byzantine historian who writes alternate history, other science fiction, fantasy (much of it historically based), and historical fiction. He is a Hugo and Sidewise winner and a Nebula finalist. His short fiction has appeared in most of the major magazines and many anthologies.

He is married to historian and writer Laura Frankos; two of their three daughters are history majors in college. "Environment or genetics?" he asks.

CARRIE VAUGHN is the author of many short stories and the novels *Kitty and the Midnight Hour* and *Kitty Goes to Washington*. She has a masters in English literature and the Tudor dynasty is one of her favorite periods in history. She lives in Boulder, Colorado, and doesn't ski. Visit her Web site at www.carrievaughn.com.

British-born IAN WATSON has been a full-time writer since 1976 after previously teaching literature in Tanzania and Japan, then science fiction and futurology at an art school in Birmingham, England. As a result of nine months spent eyeball to eyeball with Stanley Kubrick in 1990, Ian has screen credit for screen story for *A.I. Artificial Intelligence*, directed by Steven Spielberg after Kubrick's death. Ian's newest story collection—his tenth—is *The Butterflies of Memories*. Currently he's completing a collection of crazy stories in collaboration with his Italian surrealist chum Robert Quaglia. His Web site with funny photos is at www.ianwatson.info.

CHELSEA QUINN YARBRO has been selling fiction since 1968. She recently completed book sale number seventy-nine, and counting. She received the 2003 Grand Master award from the World Horror Association, the second woman to receive it. The International Horror Guild named her a Living Legend for 2005, the first woman ever to receive that honor. Besides that she is world-famous for the Saint-Germain books, which are certainly the most successful vampire series of all time. The twentieth Saint-Germain novel, *Borne in Blood,* will be published in 2007. She has written a great deal of other fiction too, which is listed on her web site: www.ChelseaQuinnYarboro.net

ABOUT THE EDITOR

Darrell Schweitzer has been coeditor of *Weird Tales* magazine since 1987 and before that did editorial work for *Isaac Asimov's Science Fiction Magazine* and *Amazing Stories.* With George Scithers he coedited two anthologies, *Tales from the Spaceport Bar* and *Another Round at the Spaceport Bar.* He was also somewhat mysteriously responsible for the recent Wildside Press "facsimile" of the April 1933 *Weird Trails: The Magazine of Supernatural Cowboy Stories,* which is either a "concept" anthology (with many of the same contributors as the volume you are holding in your hands) disguised as a reprint of a nonexistent pulp magazine or a security leak from another dimension. As a fiction writer he is the author of three novels, *The White Isle, The Shattered Goddess,* and *The Mask of the Sorcerer* and about three hundred published short stories. He has written books about H. P. Lovecraft and Lord Dunsany. He has been nominated for the World Fantasy Award four times. Despite all this he has a deep and abiding fear that he is actually best known for his limericks.

C.S. Friedman

The Best in Science Fiction

THIS ALIEN SHORE 0-88677-799-2
A *New York Times* Notable Book of the Year
"Breathlessly plotted, emotionally savvy. A potent metaphor for the toleration of diversity"
—The New York Times

THE MADNESS SEASON 0-88677-444-6
"Exceptionally imaginative and compelling"
—Publishers Weekly

IN CONQUEST BORN 0-7564-0043-0
"Space opera in the best sense: high stakes adventure with a strong focus on ideas, and characters an intelligent reader can care about."*—Newsday*

THE WILDING 0-7564-0164-X
The long-awaited follow-up to *In Conquest Born.*

To Order Call: 1-800-788-6262

DAW 17

C.S. Friedman

The Coldfire Trilogy

"A feast for those who like their fantasies dark, and as emotionally heady as a rich red wine." —*Locus*

Centuries after being stranded on the planet Erna, humans have achieved an uneasy stalemate with the fae, a terrifying natural force with the power to prey upon people's minds. Damien Vryce, the warrior priest, and Gerald Tarrant, the undead sorcerer must join together in an uneasy alliance confront a power that threatens the very essence of the human spirit, in a battle which could cost them not only their lives, but the soul of all mankind.

BLACK SUN RISING	0-88677-527-2
WHEN TRUE NIGHT FALLS	0-88677-615-5
CROWN OF SHADOWS	0-88677-717-8

To Order Call: 1-800-788-6262

DAW 18